THE CROSSROADS OF LOVE

Beautiful Penelope Creed had known Piers Luttrell from childhood. They had early pledged their love to each other, eagerly awaiting the day they could turn it into a lifelong reality.

But now there was another man in her life. A dashing figure of a London dandy, the witty, worldly, handsome Sir Richard Wyndham, a man who made his own rules of life and love, a man who was everything Piers was not.

How could she choose between them? How could she even compare these two who shared nothing in common? Nothing, that is, but her heart . . .

THE CORINTHIAN

A vibrant and thrilling romance set amid the flowering excitement of Regency England.

Georgette Heyer

The Corinthian

BANTAM BOOKS
TORONTO · NEW YORK · LONDON · SYDNEY · AUCKLAND

*This low-priced Bantam Book
has been completely reset in a type face
designed for easy reading, and was printed
from new plates. It contains the complete
text of the original hard-cover edition.*
NOT ONE WORD HAS BEEN OMITTED.

THE CORINTHIAN

*A Bantam Book / published by arrangement with
E. P. Dutton Inc.*

PRINTING HISTORY

First published in the U.S.A. 1941 under the title Beau Wyndham

*E. P. Dutton edition published January 1966
2nd printing . . . . . May 1966*

Bantam edition / August 1967
2nd printing . October 1967 5th printing . . . . . June 1969
3rd printing . . . March 1968 6th printing . . . . . July 1970
4th printing . . . August 1968 7th printing . . October 1971
*New Bantam edition / April 1974
9th printing . . . . . May 1974
10th printing . . . . April 1975
11th printing . . . . . July 1984*

ISBN 0-553-23308-4

*Bantam Books are published by Bantam Books, Inc. Its trade-
mark, consisting of the words "Bantam Books" and the por-
trayal of a rooster, is Registered in U.S. Patent and Trademark
Office and in other countries. Marca Registrada. Bantam
Books, Inc., 666 Fifth Avenue, New York, New York 10103.*

PRINTED IN THE UNITED STATES OF AMERICA

O   20   19   18   17   16   15   14   13   12   11

The
Corinthian

·₷ *Chapter I* ₴·

THE company, ushered by a disapproving butler into the
yellow saloon of Sir Richard Wyndham's house in St James
Square, comprised two ladies and one reluctant gentleman.
The gentleman, who was not much above thirty years of
age, but sadly inclined to fat, seemed to feel the butler's
disapproval, for upon that dignified individual's informing
the elder of the two ladies that Sir Richard was not at
home, he cast a deprecating glance at him, not in the least
the glance of a peer of the realm upon a menial, but an
age-old look of one helpless man to another, and said in
a pleading tone: 'Well, then, don't you think, Lady Wyndham——? Louisa, hadn't we better——? I mean, no use
going in, my love, is there?'

Neither his wife nor his mother-in-law paid any attention to this craven speech. 'If my brother is gone out, we
will await his return,' said Louisa briskly.

'Your poor Papa was always out when one wanted him,'
complained Lady Wyndham. 'It is very affecting to me to
see Richard growing every day more like him.'

Her fading accents were so lachrymose that it seemed
probable that she would dissolve into tears upon her son's
doorstep. George, Lord Trevor, was uneasily aware of a
handkerchief, clutched in one thin, gloved hand, and put
forward no further objection to entering the house in the
wake of the two ladies.

Declining all offers of refreshment, Lady Trevor escorted her parent into the Yellow Saloon, settled her comfortably upon a satin sofa, and announced her intention of
remaining in St James's Square all day, if need be. George,
with a very clear idea, born of sympathy, of what would
be his brother-in-law's emotions upon returning to his residence to find a family deputation in possession of it, said
unhappily: 'You know, I don't think we should, really I
don't! I don't like it above half. I wish you would drop this
notion you've taken into your heads.'

1

His wife, who was engaged in stripping off her lavender-kid gloves, threw him a look of indulgent contempt. 'My dear George, if *you* are afraid of Richard, let me assure you that *I* am not.'

'Afraid of him! No, indeed! But I wish you will consider that a man of nine-and-twenty won't relish having his affairs meddled with. Besides, he will very likely wonder what the deuce it has to do with me, and I'm sure I can't tell him! I wish I had not come.'

Louisa ignored this remark, considering it unworthy of being replied to, which indeed it was, since she ruled her lord with a rod of iron. She was a handsome woman, with a great deal of decision in her face, and a leavening gleam of humour. She was dressed, not perhaps in the height of fashion, which decreed that summer gauzes must reveal every charm of a lady's body, but with great elegance and propriety. Since she had a very good figure, the prevailing mode for high-waisted dresses, with low-cut bodices, and tiny puff-sleeves, became her very well: much better, in fact, than skin-tight pantaloons, and a long-tailed coat became her husband.

Fashion was not kind to George. He looked his best in buck-skin breeches and top-boots, but he was unfortunately addicted to dandyism, and pained his friends and relatives by adopting every extravagance of dress, spending as much time over the arrangement of his cravat as Mr Brummell himself, and squeezing his girth into tight stays which had a way of creaking whenever he moved unwarily.

The third member of the party, reclining limply on the satin sofa, was a lady with quite as much determination as her daughter, and a far more subtle way of getting her wishes attended to. A widow of ten years' standing, Lady Wyndham enjoyed the frailest health. The merest hint of opposition was too much for the delicate state of her nerves; and anyone, observing her handkerchief, her vinaigrette, and the hartshorn which she usually kept by her, would have had to be stupid indeed to have failed to appreciate their sinister message. In youth, she had been a beauty; in middle age, everything about her seemed to have faded: hair, cheeks, eyes, and even her voice, which was plaintive, and so gentle that it was a wonder it ever made itself heard. Like her daughter, Lady Wyndham had excellent taste in dress, and since she was fortunate enough to possess a very ample jointure she was able to indulge her liking for the most expensive fal-lals of fashion without in any way curtailing her other expenses. This did not prevent her from thinking herself very badly off, but she was able to enjoy many laments over her straitened circumstances without feeling the least real pinch of poverty, and to win the sympathy of her acquaintances by dwelling sadly on the injustice of her late husband's will, which had placed his only son in the sole possession of his immense fortune. The jointure, her friends deduced hazily, was the veriest pittance.

Lady Wyndham, who lived in a charming house in Clarges Street, could never enter the mansion in St James's Square without suffering a pang. It was not, as might have been supposed from the look of pain she always cast upon it, a family domicile, but had been acquired by her son only a couple of years before. During Sir Edward's lifetime, the family had lived in a much larger, and most inconvenient house in Grosvenor Square. Upon Sir Richard's announcement that he proposed to set up an establishment of his own, this had been given up, so that Lady Wyndham had been able ever since to mourn its loss without being obliged to suffer any longer its inconvenience. But however much she might like her own house in Clarges Street it was not to be supposed that she could bear with equanimity her son's inhabiting a far larger house in St James's Square; and when every other source of grievance failed her, she always came back to that, and said, as she said now, in all ill-used voice: 'I cannot conceive what he should want with a house like this!'

Louisa, who had a very good house of her own, besides an estate in Berkshire, did not in the least grudge her brother his mansion. She replied: 'It doesn't signify, Mama. Except that he must have been thinking of marriage when he bought it. Would you not say so, George?'

George was flattered at being thus appealed to, but he was an honest, painstaking person, and he could not bring himself to say that he thought Richard had had any thought of marriage in his head, either when he had bought the house, or at any other time.

Louisa was displeased. 'Well!' she said, looking resolute, 'he must be brought to think of marriage!'

Lady Wyndham lowered her smelling-salts to interpolate: 'Heaven knows I would never urge my boy to do anything distasteful, but it has been an understood thing for years that he and Melissa Brandon would seal the long friendship between our families with the Nuptial Tie!'

George goggled at her, and wished himself otherwhere.

'If he doesn't wish to marry Melissa, I'm sure I should be the last person to press her claim,' said Louisa. 'But it is high time that he married someone, and if he has no other suitable young female in his eye, Melissa it must be.'

'I do not know how to face Lord Saar,' bemoaned Lady Wyndham, raising the vinaigrette to her nose again. 'Or poor dear Emily, with three girls besides Melissa to dispose of, and none of them more than passable. Sophia has spots, too.'

'I do not consider Augusta hopeless,' said Louisa fairly. 'Amelia, too, may improve.'

'Squints!' said George.

'A slight cast in one eye,' corrected Louisa. 'However, we are not concerned with that. Melissa is an extremely handsome creature. No one can deny *that*!'

'And such a desirable connection!' sighed Lady Wyndham. 'Quite one of the best families!'

'They tell me Saar won't last another five years, not at the rate he's going now,' said George. 'Everything mortgaged up to the hilt, and Saar drinking himself into his grave! They say his father did the same.'

Both ladies regarded him with disfavour. 'I hope, George, you do not mean to imply that Melissa is addicted to the bottle?' said his wife.

'Oh no, no! Lord, no, I never thought of such a thing! I'm sure she's an excellent young woman. But this I will say, Louisa: I don't blame Richard if he don't want her!' said George defiantly. 'Myself, I'd as soon marry a statue!'

'I must say,' conceded Louisa, 'she is a trifle cold, perhaps. But it is a very delicate position for her, you'll allow. It has been understood since both were children that she and Richard would make a match of it, and *she* knows that as well as *we* do. And here is Richard, behaving in the most odious way! I am out of all patience with him!'

George rather liked his brother-in-law, but he knew that it would be foolhardy to defend him, so he held his peace. Lady Wyndham took up the tale of woe. 'Heaven forbid that I should force my only son to a disagreeable marriage, but I live in hourly dread of his bringing home some dreadful, low-born creature on his arm, and expecting me to welcome her!'

A vision of his brother-in-law crossed George's mind's eye. He said doubtfully: 'Really, you know, I don't think he'll do that, ma'am.'

'George is quite right,' announced Louisa. 'I should think the better of Richard if he did. It quite shocks me to see him so impervious to every feminine charm! It is a great piece of nonsense for him to dislike the opposite sex, but one thing is certain: dislike females he may, but he owes a duty to the name, and marry he must! I am sure I have been at pains to introduce him to every eligible young woman in town, for I am by no means set on his marrying Melissa Brandon. Well! He would not look twice at any of them, so if that is the mind he is in, Melissa will suit him very well.'

'Richard thinks they all want him for his money,' ventured George.

'I dare say they may. What has that to say to anything, pray? I imagine you do not mean to tell me that Richard is romantic!'

No, George was forced to admit that Richard was not romantic.

'If I live to see him suitably married, I can die content!' said Lady Wyndham, who had every expectation of living for another thirty years. 'His present course fills my poor mother's heart with foreboding!'

Loyalty forced George to expostulate. 'No, really, ma'am! Really, I say! There's no harm in Richard, not the least in the world, 'pon my honour!'

'He puts me out of all patience!' said Louisa. 'I love him dearly, but I despise him with all my heart! Yes, I do, and I do not care who hears me say so! He cares for nothing but the set of his cravat, the polish on his boots, and the blending of his snuff!'

'His horses!' begged George unhappily.

'Oh, his horses! Very well! Let us admit him to be a famous whip! He beat Sir John Lade in their race to Brighton! A fine achievement indeed!'

'Very handy with his fives!' gasped George, sinking but game.

'*You* may admire a man for frequenting Jackson's Saloon, and Cribb's Parlour! *I* do not!'

'No, my love,' George said. 'No, indeed, my love!'

'And I make no doubt you see nothing reprehensible in his addiction to the gaming-table! But I had it on the most excellent authority that he dropped three thousand pounds at one sitting at Almack's!'

Lady Wyndham moaned, and dabbed at her eyes. 'Oh, do not say so!'

'Yes, but he's so devilish wealthy it can't signify!' said George.

'Marriage,' said Louisa, 'will put a stop to such fripperies.'

The depressing picture this dictum conjured up reduced George to silence. Lady Wyndham said, in a voice dark with mystery: 'Only a mother could appreciate my anxieties. He is at a dangerous age, and I live from day to day in dread of what he may do!'

George opened his mouth, encountered a look from his wife, shut it again, and tugged unhappily at his cravat.

The door opened; a Corinthian stood upon the threshold, cynically observing his relatives. 'A thousand apologies,' said the Corinthian, bored but polite. 'Your very obedient servant, ma'am. Louisa, yours! My poor George! Ah—was I expecting you?'

'Apparently not!' retorted Louisa, bristling.

'No, you weren't. I mean, they took it into their heads —*I* couldn't stop them!' said George heroically.

'I thought I was not,' said the Corinthian, closing the door, and advancing into the room. 'But my memory, you know, my lamentable memory!'

George, running an experienced eye over his brother-in-law, felt his soul stir. 'B'gad, Richard, I like that! That's a devilish well-cut coat, 'pon my honour, it is! Who made it?'

Sir Richard lifted an arm, and glanced at his cuff. 'Weston, George, only Weston.'

'George!' said Louisa awfully.

Sir Richard smiled faintly, and crossed the room to his mother's side. She held out her hand to him, and he bowed over it with languid grace, just brushing it with his lips. 'A thousand apologies, ma'am!' he repeated. 'I trust my people have looked after you—er—*all* of you?' His lazy glance swept the room. 'Dear me!' he said. 'George, you are near to it: oblige me, my dear fellow, by pulling the bell!'

'We do not need any refreshment, I thank you, Richard,' said Louisa.

The faint, sweet smile silenced her as none of her husband's expostulations had ever done. 'My dear Louisa, you mistake—I assure you, you mistake! George is in the most urgent need of—er—stimulant. Yes, Jeffries, I rang. The Madeira—oh, ah! and some ratafia, Jeffries, if you please!'

'Richard, that's the best Waterfall I've ever seen!' exclaimed George, his admiring gaze fixed on the intricate arrangement of the Corinthian's cravat.

'You flatter me, George; I fear you flatter me.'

'Pshaw!' snapped Louisa.

'Precisely, my dear Louisa,' agreed Sir Richard amiably.

'Do not try to provoke me, Richard!' said Louisa, on a warning note. 'I will allow your appearance to be everything that it should be—admirable, I am sure!'

'One does one's poor best,' murmured Sir Richard.

Her bosom swelled. 'Richard, I could hit you!' she declared.

The smile grew, allowing her a glimpse of excellent white teeth. 'I don't think you could, my dear.'

George so far forgot himself as to laugh. A quelling glance was directed upon him. 'George, be quiet!' said Louisa.

'I must say,' conceded Lady Wyndham, whose maternal

pride could not be quite overborne, 'there is no one, except Mr Brummell, of course, who looks as well as you do, Richard.'

He bowed, but he did not seem to be unduly elated by this encomium. Possibly he took it as his due. He was a very notable Corinthian. From his Wind-swept hair (most difficult of all styles to achieve), to the toes of his gleaming Hessians, he might have posed as an advertisement for the Man of Fashion. His fine shoulders set off a coat of superfine cloth to perfection; his cravat, which had excited George's admiration, had been arranged by the hands of a master; his waistcoat was chosen with a nice eye; his biscuit-coloured pantaloons showed not one crease; and his Hessians with their jaunty gold tassels, had not only been made for him by Hoby, but were polished, George suspected, with a blacking mixed with champagne. A quizzing-glass on a black ribbon hung round his neck; a fob at his waist; and in one hand he carried a Sèvres snuff-box. His air proclaimed his unutterable boredom, but no tailoring, no amount of studied nonchalance, could conceal the muscle in his thighs, or the strength of his shoulders. Above the starched points of his shirt-collar, a weary, handsome face showed its owner's disillusionment. Heavy lids drooped over grey eyes which were intelligent enough, but only to observe the vanities of the world; the smile which just touched that resolute mouth seemed to mock the follies of Sir Richard's fellow men.

Jeffries came back into the room with a tray, and set it upon a table. Louisa waved aside the offer of refreshment, but Lady Wyndham accepted it, and George, emboldened, by his mother-in-law's weakness, took a glass of Madeira.

'I dare say,' said Louisa, 'that you are wondering what we are here for.'

'I never waste my time in idle speculation,' replied Sir Richard gently. 'I feel sure that you are going to tell me what you are here for.'

'Mama and I have come to speak to you about your marriage,' said Louisa, taking the plunge.

'And what,' enquired Sir Richard, 'has George come to speak to me about?'

'That too, of course!'

'No, I haven't!' disclaimed George hurriedly. 'You know I said I'd have nothing to do with it! I never wanted to come at all!'

'Have some more Madeira,' said Sir Richard soothingly.

'Well, thank you, yes, I will. But don't think I'm here to badger you about something which don't concern me, because I'm not!'

'Richard!' said Lady Wyndham deeply, 'I dare no longer meet Saar face to face!'

'As bad as that, is he?' said Sir Richard. 'I haven't seen him myself these past few weeks, but I'm not at all surprised. I fancy I heard something about it, from someone —I forget whom. Taken to brandy, hasn't he?'

'Sometimes,' said Lady Wyndham, 'I think you are utterly devoid of sensibility!'

'He is merely trying to provoke you, Mama. You know perfectly well what Mama means, Richard. When do you mean to offer for Melissa?'

There was a slight pause. Sir Richard set down his empty wine-glass, and flicked with one long finger the petals of a flower in a bowl on the table. 'This year, next year, sometime—or never, my dear Louisa.'

'I am very sure she considers herself as good as plighted to you,' Louisa said.

Sir Richard was looking down at the flower under his hand, but at this he raised his eyes to his sister's face, in an oddly keen, swift look. 'Is that so?'

'How should it be otherwise? You know very well that Papa and Lord Saar designed it so years ago.'

The lids veiled his eyes again. 'How medieval of you!' sighed Sir Richard.

'Now, don't, pray, take me up wrongly, Richard! If you don't like Melissa, there is no more to be said. But you do like her—or if you don't, at least *I* never heard you say so! What Mama and I feel—and George, too—is that it is time and more that you were settled in life.'

A pained glanced reproached Lord Trevor. '*Et tu, Brute?*' said Sir Richard.

'I swear I never said so!' declared George, choking over

his Madeira. 'It was all Louisa. I dare say I may have agreed with her. *You* know how it is, Richard!'

'I know,' agreed Sir Richard, sighing. 'You too, Mama?'

'Oh Richard, I live only to see you happily married, with your children about you!' said Lady Wyndham, in trembling tones.

A slight, unmistakable shudder ran through the Corinthian. 'My children about me . . . Yes. Precisely, ma'am. Pray continue!'

'You owe it to the name,' pursued his mother. 'You are the last of the Wyndhams, for it's not to be supposed that your Uncle Lucius will marry at this late date. There is Melissa, dear girl, the very wife for you! So handsome, so distinguished—birth, breeding: everything of the most desirable!'

'Ah—your pardon, ma'am, but do you include Saar, and Cedric, not to mention Beverley, under that heading?'

'That's exactly what I say!' broke in George. ' "It's all very well," I said, "and if a man likes to marry an iceberg it's all one to me, but you can't call Saar a desirable father-in-law, damme if you can! While as for the girl's precious brothers," I said, "they'll ruin Richard inside a year!" '

'Nonsense!' said Louisa. 'It is understood, of course, that Richard would make handsome settlements. But as for his being responsible for Cedric's and Beverley's debts, I'm sure I know of no reason why he should!'

'You comfort me, Louisa,' said Sir Richard.

She looked up at him not unaffectionately. 'Well, I think it is time to be frank, Richard. People will be saying next that you are playing fast and loose with Melissa, for you must know the understanding between you is an open secret. If you had chosen to marry someone else, five, ten years ago, it would have been a different thing. But so far as I am aware your affections have never even been engaged, and here you are, close on thirty, as good as pledged to Melissa Brandon, and nothing settled!'

Lady Wyndham, though in the fullest agreement with her daughter, was moved at this point to defend her son, which she did by reminding Louisa that Richard was only twenty-nine after all.

'Mama, Richard will be thirty in less than six months.

For I,' said Louisa with resolution, 'am turned thirty-one.'

'Louisa, I am touched!' said Sir Richard. 'Only the deepest sisterly devotion, I am persuaded, could have wrung from you such an admission.'

She could not repress a smile, but said with as much severity as she could muster: 'It is no laughing matter. You are no longer in your first youth, and you know as well as I do that it is your duty to think seriously of marriage.'

'Strange,' mused Sir Richard, 'that one's duty should be invariably so disagreeable.'

'I know,' said George, heaving a sigh. 'Very true! very true indeed!'

'Pooh! nonsense! What a coil you make of a simple matter!' Louisa said. 'Now, if I were to press you to marry some romantical miss, always wanting you to make love to her, and crying her eyes out every time you chose to seek your amusements out of her company, you might have reason to complain. But Melissa—yes, an iceberg, George, if you like, and what else, pray, is Richard?—Melissa, I say, will never plague you in *that* way.'

Sir Richard's eyes dwelled inscrutably upon her face for a moment. Then he moved to the table and poured himself out another glass of Madeira.

Louisa said defensively: 'Well, you don't *wish* her to cling about your neck, I suppose?'

'Not at all.'

'And you are not in love with any other woman, are you?'

'I am not.'

'Very well, then! To be sure, if you were in the habit of falling in and out of love, it would be a different matter. But, to be plain with you, you are the coldest, most indifferent, selfish creature, alive, Richard, and you will find in Melissa an admirable partner.'

Inarticulate clucking sounds from George, indicative of protest, caused Sir Richard to wave a hand towards the Madeira. 'Help yourself, George, help yourself!'

'I must say, I think it most unkind in you to speak to your brother like that,' said Lady Wyndham. 'Not but what you *are* selfish, dear Richard. I'm sure I have said so over and over again. But so it is with the greater part of the world! Everywhere one turns one meets with nothing but ingratitude!'

'If I have done Richard an injustice, I will willingly ask his pardon,' said Louisa.

'Very handsomely said, my dear sister. You have done me no injustice. I wish you will not look so distressed, George: your pity is quite wasted on me, I assure you. Tell me, Louisa: have you reason to suppose that Melissa expects me to—er—pay my addresses to her?'

'Certainly I have. She has been expecting it any time these five years!'

Sir Richard looked a little startled. 'Poor girl!' he said. 'I must have been remarkably obtuse.'

His mother and sister exchanged glances. 'Does that mean that you will think seriously of marriage?' asked Louisa.

He looked thoughtfully down at her. 'I suppose it must come to that.'

'Well, for my part,' said George, defying his wife, 'I would look around me for some other eligible female! Lord, there are dozens of 'em littering town! Why, I've seen I don't know how many setting their caps at you! Pretty ones, too, but you never notice them, you ungrateful dog!'

'Oh yes, I do,' said Sir Richard, with a curl of the lips.

'*Must* George be vulgar?' asked Lady Wyndham tragically.

'Be quiet, George! And as for you, Richard, I consider it in the highest degree nonsensical for you to take up that attitude. There is no denying that you're the biggest catch on the Marriage Mart—Yes, Mama, that is vulgar too, and I beg your pardon—but you have a lower opinion of yourself than I credit you with if you can suppose that your fortune is the only thing about you which makes you a desirable *parti*. You are generally accounted handsome— indeed, no one, I believe, could deny that your person is such as must please; and when you will take the trouble to be conciliating there is nothing in your manners to disgust the nicest taste.'

'This encomium, Louisa, almost unmans me,' said Sir Richard, much moved.

'I am perfectly serious. I was about to add that you often

spoil everything by your odd humours. I do not know how you should expect to engage a female's affection when you never bestow the least distinguishing notice upon any woman! I do not say that you are uncivil, but there is a languor, a reserve in your manner, which must repel a woman of sensibility.'

'I am a hopeless case indeed,' said Sir Richard.

If you want to know what I think, which I do not suppose you do, so you need not tell me so, it is that you are spoilt, Richard. You have too much money, you have done everything you wished to do before you are out of your twenties; you have been courted by match-making Mamas, fawned on by toadies, and indulged by all the world. The end of it is that you are bored to death. There! I have said it, and though you may not thank me for it, you will admit that I am right.'

'Quite right,' agreed Sir Richard. 'Hideously right, Louisa!'

She got up. 'Well, I advise you to get married and settle down. Come, Mama! We have said all we meant to say, and you know we are to call in Brook Street on our way home. George, do you mean to come with us?'

'No,' said George. 'Not to call in Brook Street. I daresay I shall stroll up to White's presently.'

'Just as you please, my love,' said Louisa, drawing on her gloves again.

When the ladies had been escorted to the waiting barouche, George did not at once set out for his club, but accompanied his brother-in-law back into the house. He preserved a sympathetic silence until they were out of earshot of the servants, but caught Sir Richard's eye then, in a very pregnant look, and uttered the one word: 'Women!'

'Quite so,' said Sir Richard.

'Do you know what I'd do if I were you, my boy?'

'Yes,' said Sir Richard.

George was disconcerted. 'Damn it, you can't know!'

'You would do precisely what I shall do.'

'What's that?'

'Oh—offer for Melissa Brandon, of course,' said Sir Richard.

'Well, I wouldn't,' said George positively. 'I wouldn't

marry Melissa Brandon for fifty sisters! I'd find a cosier armful, 'pon my soul I would!'

'The cosiest armful of my acquaintance was never so cosy as when she wanted to see my purse-string untied,' said Sir Richard cynically.

George shook his head. 'Bad, very bad! I must say, it's enough to sour any man. But Louisa's right, you know: you ought to get married. Won't do to let the name die out.' An idea occurred to him. 'You wouldn't care to put it about that you'd lost all your money, I suppose?'

'No,' said Sir Richard, 'I wouldn't.'

'I read somewhere of a fellow who went off to some place where he wasn't known. Devil of a fellow he was: some kind of a foreign Count, I think. I don't remember precisely, but there was a girl in it, who fell in love with him for his own sake.'

'There would be,' said Sir Richard.

'You don't like it?' George rubbed his nose, a little crestfallen. 'Well, damme if I know what to suggest!'

He was still pondering the matter when the butler announced Mr. Wyndham, and a large, portly, and convivial-looking gentleman rolled into the room, ejaculating cheerfully: 'Hallo, George! You here? Ricky, my boy, your mother's been at me again, confound her! Made me promise I'd come round to see you, though what the devil she thinks I can do is beyond me!'

'Spare me!' said Sir Richard wearily. 'I have already sustained a visit from my mother, not to mention Louisa.'

'Well, I'm sorry for you, my boy, and if you take my advice you'll marry that Brandon-wench, and be done with it. What's that you have there? Madeira? I'll take a glass.'

Sir Richard gave him one. He lowered his bulk into a large armchair, stretched his legs out before him, and raised the glass. 'Here's a health to the bridegroom!' he said, with a chuckle. 'Don't look so glum, nevvy! Think of the joy you'll be bringing into Saar's life!'

'Damn you,' said Sir Richard. 'If you had ever had a shred of proper feeling, Lucius, you would have got married fifty years ago, and reared a pack of brats in your image. A horrible thought, I admit, but at least I should not now be cast for the rôle of Family Sacrifice.'

'Fifty years ago,' retorted his uncle, quite unmoved by these insults, 'I was only just breeched. This is a very tolerable wine, Ricky. By the way, they tell me young Beverley Brandon's badly dipped. You'll be a damned public benefactor if you marry that girl. Better let your lawyer attend to the settlements, though. I'd be willing to lay you a monkey Saar tries to bleed you white. What's the matter with you, George? Got the toothache?'

'I don't like it,' said George. 'I told Louisa so at the outset, but you know what women are! Myself, I wouldn't have Melissa Brandon if she were the last woman left single.'

'What, she ain't the spotty one, surely?' demanded Lucius, concerned.

'No, that's Sophia.'

'Oh, well, nothing to worry about then! You marry the girl, Ricky: you'll never have any peace if you don't. Fill up your glass, George, and we'll have another toast!'

'What is it this time?' enquired Sir Richard, replenishing the glasses. 'Don't spare me!'

'To a pack of brats in your image, nevvy: here's to 'em!' grinned his uncle.

⋙ *Chapter II* ⋘

LORD SAAR lived in Brook Street with his wife, and his family of two sons and four daughters. Sir Richard Wyndham, driving to his prospective father-in-law's house twenty-four hours after his interview with his own parent, was fortunate enough to find Saar away from home, and Lady Saar, the butler informed him, on her way to Bath with the Honourable Sophia. He fell instead into the arms of the Honourable Cedric Brandon, a rakish young gentlemen of lamentable habits, and a disastrous charm of manner.

'Ricky, my only friend!' cried the Honourable Cedric, dragging Sir Richard into a small saloon at the back of the house. 'Don't tell me you've come to offer for Melissa! They say good news don't kill a man, but *I* never listen to gossip!

M'father says ruin stares us in the face. Lend me the money, dear boy, and I'll buy myself a pair of colours, and be off to the Peninsula, damme if I won't! But listen to me, Ricky! *Are* you listening?' He looked anxiously at Sir Richard, appeared satisfied, and said, wagging a solemn finger: 'Don't do it! There isn't a fortune big enough to settle *our* little affairs; take my word for it! Have nothing to do with Beverley! They say Fox gamed away a fortune before he was twenty-one. Give you my word, he was nothing to Bev, nothing at all. Between ourselves, Ricky, the old man has taken to brandy. H'sh! Not a word! Mustn't tell tales about m'father! But run, Ricky! That's my advice to you: *run!*'

'Would you buy yourself a pair of colours, if I gave you the money?' asked Sir Richard.

'Sober, yes; drunk, no!' replied Cedric, with his wholly disarming smile. 'I'm very sober now, but I shan't be so for long. Don't give me a groat, dear old boy! Don't give Bev a groat! He's a bad man. Now, when I'm sober I'm a good man—but I ain't sober above six hours out of the twenty-four, so you be warned! Now I'm off. I've done my best for you, for I like you, Ricky, but if you go to perdition in spite of me, I'll wash my hands of you. No, damme, I'll sponge on you for the rest of my days! Think, dear boy, think! Bev and your very obedient on your doorstep six days out of seven—duns—threats—wife's brothers done-up—pockets to let—wife in tears—nothing to do but pay! Don't do it! Fact is, we ain't worth it!'

'Wait!' Sir Richard said, barring his passage. 'If I settle your debts, will you go to the Peninsula?'

'Ricky, it's you who aren't sober. Go home!'

'Consider, Cedric, how well you would look in Hussar uniform!'

An impish smile danced in Cedric's eyes. 'Wouldn't I just! But at this present I'd look better in Hyde Park. Out of the way, dear boy! I've a very important engagement. Backed a goose to win a hundred-yard race against a turkey-cock. Can't lose! Greatest sporting event of the season!'

He was gone on the words, leaving Sir Richard, not, indeed, to run, as advised, but to await the pleasure of the Honourable Melissa Brandon.

She did not keep him waiting for long. A servant came

to request him to step upstairs, and he followed the man up the wide staircase to the withdrawing-room on the first floor.

Melissa Brandon was a handsome, dark-haired young woman, a little more than twenty-five years old. Her profile was held to be faultless, but in full face her eyes were discovered to be rather too hard for beauty. She had not, in her first seasons, lacked suitors, but none of the gentlemen attracted by her undeniable good looks, had ever, in the cock-fighting phrase of her graceless elder brother, come up to scratch. As he bowed over her hand, Sir Richard remembered George's iceberg smile, and at once banished it from his obedient mind.

'Well, Richard?'

Melissa's voice was cool, rather matter-of-fact, just as her smile seemed more a mechanical civility than a spontaneous expression of pleasure.

'I hope I see you well, Melissa?' Sir Richard said formally.

'Perfectly, I thank you. Pray sit down! I apprehend that you have come to discuss the question of our marriage.'

He regarded her from under slightly raised brows. 'Dear me!' he said mildly. 'Someone would appear to have been busy.'

She was engaged upon some stitchery, and went on plying her needle with unruffled composure. 'Do not let us beat about the bush!' she said. 'I am certainly past the age of being missish, and you, I believe, may rank as a sensible man.'

'Were you ever missish?' enquired Sir Richard.

'I trust not. I have no patience with such folly. Nor am I romantic. In that respect, we must be thought to be well-suited.'

'Must we?' said Sir Richard, gently swinging his gold-handled quizzing-glass to and fro.

She seemed amused. 'Certainly! I trust you have not, at this late date, grown sentimental! It would be quite absurd!'

'Senility,' pensively observed Sir Richard, 'often brings sentiment in its train. Or so I have been informed.'

'We need not concern ourselves with that. I like you very well, Richard, but there is just a little nonsense in your disposition which makes you turn everything to jest. I myself am of a more serious nature.'

'Then, in *that* respect, we cannot be thought to be well-suited,' suggested Sir Richard.

'I do not consider the objection insuperable. The life you have chosen to lead up till now has not been such as to encourage serious reflection, after all. I dare say you may grow more dependable, for you do not want for sense. *That,* however, must be left to the future. At all events, I am not so unreasonable as to feel the difference in our natures to be an impassable barrier to marriage.'

'Melissa,' said Sir Richard, 'will you tell me something?' She looked up. 'Pray, what do you wish me to tell you?'

'Have you ever been in love?' asked Sir Richard.

She coloured slightly. 'No. From my observation, I am thankful that I have not. There is something excessively vulgar about persons under the sway of strong emotions. I do not say it is *wrong,* but I believe I have something more of fastidiousness than most, and I find such subjects extremely distasteful.'

'You do not,' Sir Richard drawled, 'envisage the possibility of—er—falling in love at some future date?'

'My dear Richard! With whom, pray?'

'Shall we say with myself?'

She laughed. 'Now you are being absurd! If you were told that it would be necessary to approach me with some show of love-making, you were badly advised. Ours would be a marriage of convenience. I could contemplate nothing else. I like you very well, but you are not at all the sort of man to arouse those warmer passions in my breast. But I see no reason, why *that* should worry either of us. If *you* were romantic, it would be a different matter.'

'I fear,' said Sir Richard, 'that I must be very romantic.'

'I suppose you are jesting again,' she replied, with a faint shrug.

'Not at all. I am so romantic that I indulge my fancy with the thought of some woman—doubtless mythical—who might desire to marry me, not because I am a very rich man, but because—you will have to forgive the vulgarity —because she loved me!'

She looked rather contemptuous. 'I should have supposed you to be past the age of fustian, Richard. I say nothing against love, but frankly, love-matches seem to me a trifle beneath us. One would say you had been hobnobbing with the bourgeoisie at Islington Spa, or some such low place! I do not forget that I am a Brandon. I dare say we are very proud; indeed, I hope we are!'

'That,' said Sir Richard dryly, 'is an aspect of the situation which, I confess, had not so far occurred to me.'

She was amazed. 'I had not thought it possible! I imagined everyone knew what we Brandons feel about our name, our birth, our tradition!'

'I hesitate to wound you, Melissa,' said Sir Richard, 'but the spectacle of a woman of your name, birth, and tradition, cold-bloodedly offering herself to the highest bidder is not one calculated to impress the world with a very strong notion of her pride.'

'This is indeed the language of the theatre!' she exclaimed. "My duty to my family demands that I should marry well, but let me assure you that even *that* could not make me stoop to ally myself with one of inferior breeding.'

'Ah, this is pride indeed!' said Sir Richard, faintly smiling.

'I do not understand you. You must know that my father's affairs are in such case as—in short——'

'I am aware,' Sir Richard said gently. 'I apprehend it is to be my privilege to—er—unravel Lord Saar's affairs.'

'But of course!' she replied, surprised out of her statuesque calm. 'No other consideration could have prevailed upon me to accept your suit!'

'This,' said Sir Richard, pensively regarding the toe of one Hessian boot, 'becomes a trifle delicate. If frankness is to be the order of the day, my dear Melissa, I must point out to you that I have not yet—er—proffered my suit.'

She was quite undisturbed by this snub, but replied coldly: 'I did not suppose that you would so far forget what is due to our positions as to approach *me* with an offer. We do not belong to *that* world. You will no doubt seek an interview with my father.'

'I wonder if I shall?' said Sir Richard.

'I imagine that you most certainly will,' responded the lady, snipping her thread. 'Your circumstances are as well known to me as mine are to you. If I may say so bluntly, you are fortunate to be in a position to offer for a Brandon.'

He looked meditatively at her, but made no remark. After a pause, she continued: 'As for the future, neither of us, I trust, would make great demands upon the other. You have your amusements: they do not concern me, and however much my reason may deprecate your addition to pugilism, curricle-racing, and deep basset——'

'Pharaoh,' he interpolated.

'Very well, pharaoh: it is all one. However much I may deprecate such follies, I say, I do not desire to interfere with your tastes.'

'You are very obliging,' bowed Sir Richard. 'Bluntly, Melissa, I may do as I please if I will hand you my purse?'

'That is putting it bluntly indeed,' she replied composedly. She folded up her needlework, and laid it aside. 'Papa has been expecting a visit from you. He will be sorry to hear that you called while he was away from home. He will be with us again to-morrow, and you may be sure of finding him, if you care to call at—shall we say eleven o'clock?'

He rose. 'Thank you, Melissa. I feel that my time has not been wasted, even though Lord Saar was not here to receive me.'

'I hope not, indeed,' she said, extending her hand. 'Come! We have had a talk which must, I feel, prove valuable. You think me unfeeling, I dare say, but you will do me the justice to admit that I have not stooped to unworthy pretence. Our situation is peculiar, which is why I overcame my reluctance to discuss the question of our marriage with you. We have been as good as betrothed these five years, and more.'

He took her hand. 'Have you considered yourself betrothed to me these five years?' he enquired.

For the first time in their interview her eyes failed to meet his. 'Certainly,' she replied.

'I see,' said Sir Richard, and took his leave of her.

He put in a belated appearance at Almack's that evening. No one, admiring his *point-de-vice* appearance, or listening to his lazy drawl, could have supposed him to be on the eve of making the most momentous decision of his life. Only his uncle, rolling into the club some time after midnight, and observing the dead men at his elbow, guessed that the die had been cast. He told George Trevor, whom he found just rising from the basset-table, that Ricky was taking it hard, a pronouncement which distressed George, and made him say: 'I have not exchanged two words with him. Do you tell me he has actually offered for Melissa Brandon?'

'I'm not telling you anything,' said Lucius. 'All I say is that he's drinking hard and plunging deep.'

In great concern, George seized the first opportunity that offered of engaging his brother-in-law's attention. This was not until close on three o'clock, when Sir Richard at last rose from the pharaoh-table, and Sir Richard was not, by that time, in the mood for private conversation. He had lost quite a large sum of money, and had drunk quite a large quantity of brandy, but neither of these circumstances was troubling him.

'No luck, Ricky?' his uncle asked him.

A somewhat hazy but still perfectly intelligent glance mocked him. 'Not at cards, Lucius. But think of the adage!'

George knew that Sir Richard could carry his wine as well as any man of his acquaintance, but a certain reckless note in his voice alarmed him. He plucked at his sleeve, and said in a lowered tone: 'I wish you will let me have a word with you!'

'Dear George—my very dear George!' said Sir Richard, amiably smiling. 'You must be aware that I am not—quite —sober. No words to-night.'

'I shall come round to see you in the morning, then,' said George, forgetting that it was already morning.

'I shall have the devil of a head,' said Sir Richard.

He made his way out of the club, his curly-brimmed hat at an angle on his head, his ebony cane tucked under one arm. He declined the porter's offer to call up a chair, remarking sweetly: 'I am devilish drunk, and I shall walk.'

The porter grinned. He had seen many gentlemen in all the various stages of inebriety, and he did not think that Sir Richard, who spoke with only the faintest slurring of his words, and who walked with quite wonderful balance, was in very desperate straits. If he had not known Sir Richard well, he would not, he thought, have seen anything amiss with him, beyond his setting off in quite the wrong direction for St James's Square. He felt constrained to call Sir Richard's attention to this, but begged pardon when Sir Richard said: 'I know. The dawn is calling me, however. I am going for a long, long walk.'

'Quite so, sir,' said the porter, and stepped back.

Sir Richard, his head swimming a little from sudden contact with the cool air, strolled aimlessly away in a northerly direction.

His head cleared after a while. In a detached manner, he reflected that it would probably begin to ache in a short time, and he would feel extremely unwell, and not a little sorry for himself. At the moment, however, while the fumes of brandy still wreathed about his brain, a curious irresponsibility possessed him. He felt reckless, remote, divorced from his past and his future. The dawn was spreading a grey light over the quiet streets, and the breeze fanning his cheeks was cool, and fresh enough to make him glad of his light evening cloak. He wandered into Brook Street, and laughed up at the shuttered windows of Saar's house. 'My gentle bride!' he said, and kissed his fingers in the direction of the house. 'God, what a damned fool I am!'

He repeated this, vaguely pleased with the remark, and walked down the long street. It occurred to him that his gentle bride would scarcely be flattered, if she could see him now, and this thought made him laugh again. The Watch, encountered at the north end of Grosvenor Square, eyed him dubiously, and gave him a wide berth. Gentlemen in Sir Richard's condition not infrequently amused themselves with a light-hearted pastime known as Boxing the Watch, and this member of that praiseworthy force was not anxious to court trouble.

Sir Richard did not notice the Watch, nor, to do him justice, would he have felt in the least tempted to molest him if he had noticed him. Somewhere, in the recesses of his brain, Sir Richard was aware that he was the unluckiest dog alive. He felt very bitter about this, as though all the world were in league against him; and, as he branched off erratically down a quiet side street, he was cynically sorry for himself, that in ten years spent in the best circles he had not had the common good fortune to meet one female whose charms had cost him a single hour's sleep. It did not seem probable that he would be more fortunate in the future. 'Which, I suppose,' remarked Sir Richard to one of the new gas-lamps, 'is a—is a consummation devoutly to be wished, since I am about to offer for Melissa Brandon.'

It was at this moment that he became aware of a peculiar circumstance. Someone was climbing out of a second-storey window of one of the prim houses on the opposite side of the street.

Sir Richard stood still, and blinked at this unexpected sight. His divine detachment still clung to him; he was interested in what he saw, but by no means concerned with it. 'Undoubtedly a burglar,' he said, and leaned nonchalantly on his cane to watch the end of the adventure. His somewhat sleepy gaze discovered that whoever was escaping from the prim house was proposing to do so by means of knotted sheets, which fell disastrously short of the ground. '*Not* a burglar,' decided Sir Richard, and crossed the road.

By the time he had reached the opposite kerbstone, the mysterious fugitive had arrived, somewhat fortuitously, at the end of his improvised rope, and was dangling precariously above the shallow area, trying with one desperate foot to find some kind of a resting-place on the wall of the house. Sir Richard saw that he was a very slight youth, only a boy, in fact, and went in a leisurely fashion to the rescue.

The fugitive caught sight of him as he descended the area-steps, and gasped with a mixture of fright and thankfulness: 'Oh! Could you help me, please? I didn't know it was so far. I thought I should be able to jump, only I don't think I can.'

'My engaging youth,' said Sir Richard, looking up at the flushed face peering down at him. 'What, may I ask, are you doing on the end of that rope?'

'*Hush!*' begged the fugitive. 'Do you think you could catch me, if I let go?'

'I will do my poor best,' promised Sir Richard.

The fugitive's feet were only just above his reach, and in another five seconds the fugitive descended into his arms with a rush that made him stagger, and almost lose his balance. He retained it by a miracle, clasping strongly to his chest an unexpectedly light body.

Sir Richard was not precisely sober, but although the brandy fumes had produced in his brain a not unpleasant sense of irresponsibility, they had by no means fuddled his intellect. Sir Richard, his chin tickled by curls, and his arms full of fugitive, made a surprising discovery. He set the fugitive down, saying in a matter-of-fact voice: 'Yes, but I don't think you are a youth, after all.'

'No, I'm a girl,' replied the fugitive, apparently undismayed by his discovery. 'But, please, will you come away before they wake up?'

"Who?' asked Sir Richard.

'My aunt—all of them!' whispered the fugitive. 'I am very much obliged to you for helping me—and do you think you could untie this knot, if you please? You see, I had to tie my bundle on my back, and now I can't undo it. And where is my hat?'

'It fell off,' said Sir Richard, picking it up, and dusting it on his sleeve. 'I am not quite sober, you know—in fact, I am drunk—but I cannot help feeling that this is all a trifle— shall we say irregular?'

'Yes, but there was nothing else to be done,' explained the fugitive, trying to look over her own shoulder at what Sir Richard was doing with the recalcitrant knot.

'Oblige me by standing still!' requested Sir Richard.

'Oh, I am sorry! I can't think how it worked right round me like that. Thank you! I am truly grateful to you!'

Sir Richard was eyeing the bundle through his quizzing-glass. '*Are* you a burglar?' he enquired.

A chuckle, hastily choked, greeted this. 'No, of course I'm not. I couldn't manage a bandbox, so I had to tie all my things up in a shawl. And now I think I must be going, if you please.'

'Drunk I undoubtedly am,' said Sir Richard, 'but some remnants of sanity still remain with me. You cannot, my good child, wander about the streets of London at this hour of night, and dressed in those clothes. I believe I ought to ring that bell, and hand you over to your—aunt, did you say?'

Two agitated hands clasped his arm. 'Oh, *don't!*' begged the fugitive. *'Please* don't!'

'Well, what am I to do with you?' asked Sir Richard.

'Nothing. Only tell me the way to Holborn!'

'Why Holborn?'

'I have to go to the White Horse Inn, to catch the stage-coach for Bristol.'

'That settles it,' said Sir Richard. 'I will not set you a foot on your way until I have the whole story from you. It's my belief you are a dangerous criminal.'

'I am not!' said the fugitive indignantly. 'Anyone with the veriest speck of sensibility would feel for my plight! I am escaping from the most odious persecution.'

'Fortunate child!' said Sir Richard, taking her bundle from her. 'I wish I might do the same. Let us remove from this neighbourhood. I have seldom seen a street that depressed me more. I can't think how I came here. Do you feel that our agreeable encounter would be improved by an exchange of names, or are you travelling incognita?'

'Yes, I shall have to make up a name for myself. I hadn't thought of that. My real name is Penelope Creed. Who are you?'

'I,' said Sir Richard, 'am Richard Wyndham, wholly at your service.'

'Beau Wyndham?' asked Miss Creed knowledgeably.

'Beau Wyndham,' bowed Sir Richard. 'Is it possible that we can have met before?'

'Oh no, but of course I have heard of you. My cousin tries to tie his cravat in a Wyndham Fall. At least, that is what he says it is, but it looks like a muddle to me.'

'Then it is *not* a Wyndham Fall,' said Sir Richard firmly.

'No, that's what I thought. My cousin tries to be a dandy, but he has a face like a fish. They want me to marry him.'

'What a horrible thought!' said Sir Richard, shuddering.

'I told you you would feel for my plight!' said Miss Creed. 'So would you now set me on my way to Holborn?'

'No,' replied Sir Richard.

'But you must!' declared Miss Creed, on a note of panic. 'Where are we going?'

'I cannot walk about the streets all night. We had better repair to my house to discuss this matter.'

'No!' said Miss Creed, standing stock-still in the middle of the pavement.

Sir Richard sighed. 'Rid yourself of the notion that I cherish any villainous designs upon your person,' he said. 'I imagine I might well be your father. How old are you?'

'I am turned seventeen.'

'Well, I am nearly thirty,' said Sir Richard.

Miss Creed worked this out. 'You couldn't possibly be my father!'

'I am far too drunk to solve arithmetical problems. Let it suffice that I have not the slightest intention of making love to you.'

'Well, then, I don't mind accompanying you,' said Miss Creed handsomely. 'Are you really drunk?'

'Vilely,' said Sir Richard.

'No one would credit it, I assure you. You carry your wine very well.'

'You speak as one with experience in these matters,' said Sir Richard.

'My father was used to say that it was most important to see how a man behaved when in his cups. My cousin becomes excessively silly.'

'You know,' said Sir Richard, knitting his brows, 'the more I hear of this cousin of yours the more I feel you should not be allowed to marry him. Where are we now?'

'Piccadilly, I think,' replied Miss Creed.

'Good! I live in St James's Square. Why do they want you to marry your cousin?'

'Because,' said Miss Creed mournfully, 'I am cursed with a large fortune!'

Sir Richard halted in the middle of the road. 'Cursed with a large fortune?' he repeated.

'Yes, indeed. You see, my father had no other children, and I believe I am most fabulously wealthy, besides having a house in Somerset, which they won't let me live in. When he died I had to live with Aunt Almeria. I was only twelve years old, you see. And now she is persecuting me to marry my cousin Frederick. So I ran away.'

'The man with a face like a fish?'

'Yes.'

'You did quite right,' said Sir Richard.

'Well, I think I did.'

'Not a doubt of it. Why Holborn?'

'I told you,' replied Miss Creed patiently. 'I am going to get on the Bristol coach.'

'Oh! Why Bristol?'

'Well, I'm not going to Bristol precisely, but my house is in Somerset, and I have a very great friend there. I haven't seen him for nearly five years, but we used to play together, and we pricked our fingers—mixing the blood, you know —and we made a vow to marry one another when we were grown-up.'

'This is all very romantic,' commented Sir Richard.

'Yes, isn't it?' said Miss Creed enthusiastically. 'You are not married, are you?'

'No. Oh, my God!'

'Why, what is the matter?'

' I've just remembered that I am going to be.'

'Don't you want to be?'

'No.'

'But no one could force *you* to be married!'

'My good girl, you do not know my relatives,' said Sir Richard bitterly.

'Did they talk to you, and talk to you, and *talk* to you? And say it was your duty? And plague your life out? And cry at you?' asked Miss Creed.

'Something of the sort,' admitted Sir Richard. 'Is that what your relatives did to you?'

'Yes. So I stole Geoffrey's second-best suit, and climbed out of the window.'

'Who is Geoffrey?'

'Oh, he is my other cousin! He is at Harrow, and his clothes fit me perfectly. Is this your house?'

'This is my house.'

'But wait!' said Miss Creed. 'Will not the porter be sitting up to open the door to you?'

'I don't encourage people to sit up for me,' said Sir Richard, producing from his pocket a key, and fitting it into the lock.

'But I expect you have a valet,' suggested Miss Creed, hanging back. 'He will be waiting to help you to bed.'

'True,' said Sir Richard. 'But he will not come to my room until I ring the bell. You need have no fear.'

'Oh, in that case——!' said Miss Creed, relieved, and followed him blithely into the house.

A lamp was burning in the hall, and a candle was placed on a marble-topped table, in readiness for Sir Richard. He kindled it by thrusting it into the lamp, and led his guest into the library. Here there were more candles, in chandeliers fixed to the wall. Sir Richard lit as many of these as seemed good to him, and turned to inspect Miss Creed.

She had taken off her hat, and was standing in the middle of the room, looking interestedly about her. Her hair, which clustered in feathery curls on the top of her head, and was somewhat raggedly cut at the back, was guinea-gold; her eyes were a deep blue, very large and trustful, and apt at any moment to twinkle with merriment. She had a short little nose, slightly freckled, a most decided chin, and a pair of dimples.

Sir Richard, critically observing her, was unimpressed by these charms. He said: 'You look the most complete urchin indeed!'

She seemed to take this as a tribute. She raised her candid eyes to his face, and said: 'Do I? Truly?'

His gaze travelled slowly over her borrowed raiment. 'Horrible!' he said. 'Are you under the impression that you have tied that—that travesty of a cravat in a Wyndham Fall?'

'No, but the thing is I have never tied a cravat before,' she explained.

'That,' said Sir Richard, 'is obvious. Come here!'

She approached obediently, and stood still while his expert fingers wrought with the crumpled folds round her neck.

'No, it is beyond even my skill,' he said at last. 'I shall have to lend you one of mine. Never mind; sit down, and let us talk this matter over. My recollection is none of the clearest, but I fancy you said you were going into Somerset to marry a friend of your childhood.'

'Yes, Piers Luttrell,' nodded Miss Creed, seating herself in a large arm-chair.

'Furthermore, you are just seventeen.'

'Turned seventeen,' she corrected.

'Don't quibble! And you propose to undertake this journey as a passenger on an Accommodation coach?'

'Yes,' agreed Miss Creed.

'And, as though this were not enough, you are going alone?'

'Of course I am.'

'My dear child,' said Sir Richard, 'drunk I may be, but not so drunk as to acquiesce in this fantastic scheme, believe me.'

'I don't think you are drunk,' said Miss Creed. 'Besides, it has nothing to do with you! You cannot interfere in my affairs merely because you helped me out of the window.'

'I didn't help you out of the window. Something tells me I ought to restore you to the bosom of your family.'

Miss Creed turned rather white, and said in a small, but very clear voice: 'If you did that it would be the most cruel —the most treacherous thing in the world!'

'I suppose it would,' he admitted.

There was a pause. Sir Richard unfobbed his snuff-box with a flick of one practised finger, and took a pinch. Miss Creed swallowed, and said: 'If you had ever *seen* my cousin, you would understand.'

He glanced down at her, but said nothing.

'He was a wet mouth,' said Miss Creed despairingly.

'That settles it,' said Sir Richard, shutting his snuff-box. 'I will escort you to your childhood's friend.'

Miss Creed blushed. 'You? But you can't!'

'Why can't I?'

'Because—because I don't know you, and I can very well go by myself, and—well, it's quite absurd! I see now that you *are* drunk.'

'Let me inform you,' said Sir Richard, 'that missish airs don't suit those clothes. Moreover, I don't like them. Either you will travel to Somerset in my company, or you will go back to your aunt. Take your choice!'

'Do please consider!' begged Miss Creed. 'You know I am obliged to travel in the greatest secrecy. If you went with me, no one would know what had become of you.'

'No one would know what had become of me,' repeated Sir Richard slowly. 'No one—my girl, you have no longer any choice: I am going with you to Somerset!'

⋅§ *Chapter III* ⋅⋅

As no argument produced the least effect on Sir Richard's suddenly reckless mood, Miss Creed abandoned her conscientious attempt to dissuade him from accompanying her on her journey, and owned that his protection would be welcome. 'It is not that I am afraid to go by myself,' she explained, 'but, to tell you the truth, I am not quite used to do things all alone.'

'I should hope,' said Sir Richard, 'that you are not quite used to travelling in the common stage either.'

'No, of course I am not. It will be quite an adventure! Have you ever travelled by stage-coach?'

'Never. We shall travel post.'

'Travel post? You must be mad!' exclaimed Miss Creed. 'I dare say you are known at every posting-inn on the Bath road. We should be discovered in a trice. Why, I had thought of all that even before you made up your mind to join me! My cousin Frederick is too stupid to think of anything, but my Aunt Almeria is not, and I make no doubt she will guess that I have run away to my own home, and follow me. This is one of the reasons why I made up my mind to journey in the stage. She will enquire for me at the posting-houses, and no one will be able to give her the least news of me. And just think what a bustle there would be if it were discovered that we had been travelling about the country together in a post-chaise!'

'Does it seem to you that there would be less impropriety in our travelling in the stage?' enquired Sir Richard.

'Yes, much less. In fact, I do not see that it is improper at all, for how can I prevent your booking a seat in a public vehicle, if you wish to do so? Besides, I have not enough money to hire a post-chaise.'

'I thought you said you were cursed with a large fortune?'

'Yes, but they won't let me have anything but the most paltry allowance until I come of age, and I've spent most of this month's pin-money.'

'I will be your banker,' said Sir Richard.

Miss Creed shook her head vigorously. 'No, indeed you will not! One should never be beholden to strangers. I shall pay everything for myself. Of course, if you are set against travelling by the stage, I do not see what is to be done. Unless——' she broke off as an idea occurred to her, and said, with sparkling eyes: 'I have a famous notion! You are a notable whip, are you not?'

'I believe I am accounted so,' replied Sir Richard.

'Well, supposing you were to drive in your own curricle? Then I could get up behind, and pretend to be your Tiger, and hold the yard of tin, and blow up for the change and——'

'No!' said Sir Richard.

She looked disappointed. 'I thought it would be exciting. However, I dare say you are right.'

'I am right,' said Sir Richard. 'The more I think of it, the more I see that there is much to be said for the stage-coach. At what hour did you say that it leaves town?'

'At nine o'clock, from the White Horse Inn, in Fetter Lane. Only we must go there long before that, on account of your servants. What is the time now?'

Sir Richard consulted his watch. 'Close on five,' he replied.

'Then we have not a moment to lose,' said Miss Creed. 'Your servants will be stirring in another hour. But you can't travel in those clothes, can you?'

'No,' he said, 'and I can't travel with that cravat of yours either, or that abominable bundle. And, now I come to look at you more particularly, I never saw hair worse cut.'

'You mean the back, I expect,' said Miss Creed, unresentful of these strictures. 'Luckily, it has always been short in front. I had to chop the back bits off myself, and I could not well see what I was about.'

'Wait here!' commanded Sir Richard, and left the room.

When he returned it was more than half an hour later, and he had shed his evening-dress for buckskin breeches, and top-boots, and a coat of blue superfine cloth. Miss Creed greeted him with considerable relief. 'I began to fear you had forgotten me, or fallen asleep!' she told him.

'Nothing of the sort!' said Sir Richard, setting a small cloak-bag and a large portmanteau down on the floor. 'Drunk or sober, I never forget my obligations. Stand up, and I will see what I can do towards making you look more presentable.'

He had a snowy white cravat over one arm, and a pair of scissors in his hand. A few judicious snips greatly improved the appearance of Miss Creed's head, and by the time a comb had been ruthlessly dragged through her curls, forcing rather than coaxing them into a more manly style, she began to look quite neat, though rather watery-eyed. Her crumpled cravat was next cast aside, and one of Sir Richard's own put round her neck. She was so anxious to see how he was arranging it that she stood on tiptoe to catch a glimpse of herself in the mirror hanging above the mantelpiece, and got her ears boxed.

'*Will* you stand still?' said Sir Richard.

Miss Creed sniffed, and subsided into dark mutterings. However, when he released her, and she was able to see the result of his handiwork, she was so pleased that she forgot her injuries, and exclaimed: 'Oh, how nice I look! Is it a Wyndham Fall?'

'Certainly not!' Sir Richard replied. 'The Wyndham Fall is not for scrubby schoolboys, let me tell you.'

'I am not a scrubby schoolboy!'

'You look like one. Now put what you have in that bundle into the cloak-bag, and we'll be off.'

'I have a very good mind not to go with you,' said Miss Creed, glowering.

'No, you haven't. You are now my young cousin, and we are wholly committed to a life of adventure. What did you say your name was?'

'Penelope Creed. Most people call me Pen, but I ought to have a man's name now.'

'Pen will do very well. If it occasions the least comment, you will say that it is spelt with two N's. You were named after that Quaker fellow.'

'Oh, that is a very good idea! What shall I call you?'

'Richard.'

'Richard who?'

'Smith—Jones—Brown.'

She was engaged in transferring her belongings from the Paisley shawl to the cloak-bag. 'You don't look like any of those. What shall I do with this shawl?'

'Leave it,' replied Sir Richard, gathering up some gleaming scraps of guinea-gold hair from the carpet, and casting them to the back of the fireplace. 'Do you know, Pen Creed, I fancy you have come into my life in the guise of Providence?'

She looked up enquiringly. 'Have I?' she said doubtfully.

'That, or Disaster,' said Sir Richard. 'I shall know which when I am sober. But, to tell you the truth, I don't care a jot! *En avant, mon cousin!*'

It was past midday when Lady Trevor, accompanied by her reluctant husband, called at her brother's house in St James's Square. She was admitted by the porter, obviously big with news, and handed on by him to the butler. 'Tell Sir Richard that I am here,' she commanded, stepping into the Yellow Saloon.

'Sir Richard, my lady, is not at home,' said the butler, in a voice pregnant with mystery.

Louisa, who had extracted from her lord a description of Sir Richard's proceedings at Almack's on the preceding night, snorted. 'You will tell him that his sister desires to see him,' she said.

'Sir Richard, my lady, is not upon the premises,' said the butler, working up to his climax.

'Sir Richard has trained you well,' said Louisa dryly. 'But I am not to be put off so! Go and tell him that I wish to see him!'

'Sir Richard, my lady, did not sleep in his bed last night!' announced the butler.

George was surprised into indiscreet comment. 'What's that? Nonsense! He wasn't as foxed as that when *I* saw him!'

'As to that, my lord,' said the butler, with dignity, 'I have no information. In a word, my lord, Sir Richard has vanished.'

'Good Gad!' ejaculated George.

'Fiddle-de-dee!' said Louisa tartly. 'Sir Richard, as I suppose, is in his bed!'

'No, my lady. As I informed your ladyship, Sir Richard's bed has not been slept in.' He paused, but Louisa only stared at him. Satisfied with the impression he had made, he continued: 'The evening attire which Sir Richard was wearing yesterday was found by his man, Biddle, upon the floor of his bedroom. Sir Richard's second-best top-boots, a pair of buckskins, a blue riding-coat, his drab overcoat, and a fawn coloured beaver, have all disappeared. One is forced to the conclusion, my lady, that Sir Richard was called away unexpectedly.'

'Gone off without his valet?' George demanded in a stupefied tone.

The butler bowed. 'Precisely so, my lord.'

'Impossible!' George said, from the heart.

Louisa, who had been frowning over these tidings, said in a brisk voice: 'It is certainly very odd, but there is no doubt some perfectly reasonable explanation. Pray, are you certain that my brother left no word with *any* member of his household?'

'None whatsoever, my lady.'

George heaved a deep sigh, and shook his head. 'I warned you, Louisa! I *said* you were driving him too hard!'

'You said nothing of the sort!' snapped Louisa, annoyed with him for talking so indiscreetly before a palpably interested servant. 'To be sure, he may well have mentioned to us that he was going out of town, and we have forgotten the circumstance.'

'How can you say so?' asked George, honestly puzzled. 'Why, didn't you have it from Melissa Brandon herself that he was to call——'

'That will do, George!' said Louisa, quelling him with a look so terrible that he quailed under it. 'Tell me, Porson,' she resumed, turning again to the butler, 'has my brother gone in his post-chaise, or is he driving himself?'

'None of Sir Richard's vehicles, my lady, sporting or otherwise, is missing from the tables,' said Porson, relishing the cumulative effect of his disclosures.

'He is riding, then!'

'I have ascertained from the head groom, my lady, that none of Sir Richard's horses has been abstracted. The head groom has not seen Sir Richard since yesterday morning.'

'Good Gad!' muttered George, his eyes starting with dismay at the hideous thought which presented itself to him. 'No, no, he would not do that!'

'Be quiet, George! For heaven's sake, be quiet!' Louisa cried sharply. 'Why, what nonsensical notion have you taken into your head? I am sure it is most provoking of Richard to slip off like this, but as for—I won't have you say such things! Ten to one, he has gone off to watch some odious sporting event: prize-fighting, I dare say! He will be home presently.'

'But he didn't sleep at home!' George reminded her. 'And I'm bound to say he wasn't cold stone sober when he left Almack's last night. I don't mean he was badly foxed, but you know what he's like when he's——'

'I am thankful to say that I know nothing of the kind!' retorted Louisa. 'If he was not sober, it would account for his erratic behaviour.'

'Erratic behaviour! I must say, Louisa, that is a fine way to talk when poor Ricky may be at the bottom of the river,' exclaimed George, roused to noble courage.

She changed colour, but said faintly: 'How can you be so absurd? Don't say such things, I beg of you!'

The butler coughed. 'I beg your lordship's pardon, but if I might say so, Sir Richard would hardly change his raiment for the execution of—of what I apprehend your lordship means.'

'No. No, very true! He would not, of course!' agreed George, relieved.

'Moreover, my lord, Biddle reports that Sir Richard's drawers and wardrobe have been ransacked, and various articles of clothing abstracted. Upon going to rouse Sir Richard this morning, Biddle found his room in the greatest disorder, as though Sir Richard had made his preparations for a journey in haste. Furthermore, my lord, Biddle informed me that a portmanteau and a small cloak-bag are missing from the cupboard in which they are customarily kept.'

George gave a sudden croak of laughter. 'Bolted, by Gad! Yoicks! gone awa-ay!'

'*George!*'

'I don't care!' said George defiantly. 'I'm devilish glad he has bolted!'

'But there was no need!' Louisa said, forgetting that Porson was in the room. 'No one was constraining him to marry——' she caught Porson's eye, and stopped short.

'I should inform your ladyship,' said Porson, apparently deaf to her indiscreet utterance, 'that there were several other Peculiar Circumstances attached to Sir Richard's disappearance.'

'Good heavens, you talk as though he has been spirited away by magic!' said Louisa impatiently. 'What circumstances, my good man?'

'If your ladyship will excuse me, I will fetch them for your inspection,' said Porson, and bowed himself out.

Husband and wife were left to stare at one another in perplexity.

'Well!' said George, not without satisfaction, 'you see now what comes of plaguing a man out of his mind!'

'I didn't! George, it is unjust of you to say so! Pray, how could *I* force him to offer for Melissa if he did not wish to? I am persuaded his flight has nothing whatever to do with that affair.'

'No man will bear being teased to do something he don't want to do,' said George.

'Then all I have to say is that Richard is a bigger coward than I would have believed possible! I am sure, if only he had told me frankly that he did not wish to marry Melissa I should not have said another word about it.'

'Ha!' ejaculated George, achieving a sardonic laugh.

He escaped reproof by Porson's coming back into the room, bearing certain articles which he laid carefully upon the table. In great astonishment, Lord and Lady Trevor gazed at a Paisley shawl, a crumpled cravat, and some short strands of guinea-gold hair, curling appropriately enough into a shape resembling a question-mark.

'What in the world——?' exclaimed Louisa.

'These articles, my lady, were discovered by the under-footman upon his entering the library this morning,' said

Porson. 'The shawl, which neither Biddle nor myself can remember to have seen before, was lying on the floor; the cravat had been thrown into the grate; and the—er—lock of hair—was found under the shawl.'

'Well, upon my word!' said George, putting up his glass the better to inspect the articles. He pointed his glass at the cravat. 'That tells its own tale! Poor Ricky must have come in last night in a bad state. I dare say his head was aching: mine would have been, if I had drunk half the brandy he tossed off yesterday. I see it all. There he was, pledged to call on Saar this morning—no way out of it— head on fire! He tugged at his cravat, felt as though he must choke, and ruined the thing—and no matter how far gone he was, Ricky would never wear a crumpled necktie! There he was, sitting in a chair, very likely, and running his hands through his hair, in the way a man does——'

'Richard never yet disarranged his hair, and no matter how drunk he may have been, he did not pull a curl of *that* colour out of his own head!' interrupted Louisa. 'Moreover, it has been cut off. Anyone can see that!'

George levelled his glass at the gleaming curl. A number of emotions flitted across his rather stolid countenance. He drew a breath. 'You're quite right,' Louisa,' he said. 'Well, I never would have believed it! The sly dog!'

'You need not wait, Porson!' Louisa said sharply.

'Very good, my lady. But I should perhaps inform your ladyship that the under-footman found the candles burning in the library when he entered it this morning.'

'I cannot see that it signifies in the least,' replied Louisa, waving him aside.

He withdrew. George, who was holding the curl in the palm of his hand, said: 'Well, *I* can't call anyone to mind with hair of this colour. To be sure, there were one or two opera-dancers, but Ricky's not at all the sort of man to want 'em to cut off their hair for him. But there's no doubt about one thing, Louisa: this curl was a keepsake.'

'Thank you, George, I had already realized that. Yet I thought I knew all the respectable women of Richard's acquaintance! One would say that kind of keepsake must have belonged to his salad days. I am sure he is much too unromantic now to cherish a lock of hair!'

'And he threw it away,' George said, shaking his head. 'You know, it's devilish sad, Louisa, upon my word it is! Threw it away, because he was on the eve of offering for that Brandon-iceberg!'

'Very affecting! And having thrown it away, he then ran away himself—not, you will admit, making any offer at all! And where did the shawl come from?' She picked it up as she spoke, and shook it out. 'Extremely creased! Now why?'

'Another keepsake,' George said. 'Crushed it in his hands, poor old Ricky—couldn't bear the recollections it conjured up—flung it away!'

'Oh, fiddle!' said Louisa, exasperated. 'Well, Porson, what is it now?'

The butler, who had come back into the room, said primly: 'The Honourable Cedric Brandon, my lady, to see Sir Richard. I thought perhaps your ladyship would wish to receive him.'

'I don't suppose he can throw the least light on this mystery, but you may as well show him in,' said Louisa. 'Depend upon it,' she added to her husband, when Porson had withdrawn himself again, 'he will have come to learn why Richard did not keep his engagement with Saar this morning. I am sure I do not know what I am to say to him!'

'If you ask me, Cedric won't blame Richard,' said George. 'They tell me he was talking pretty freely at White's yesterday. Foxed, of course. How you and your mother can want Ricky to marry into that family is what beats me!'

'We have known the Brandons all our lives,' Louisa said defensively. 'I don't pretend that——' She broke off, as the Honourable Cedric walked into the room, and stepped forward, with her hand held out. 'How do you do, Cedric? I am afraid Richard is not at home. We—think he must have been called away suddenly on urgent affairs.'

'Taken my advice, has he?' said Cedric, saluting her hand with careless grace. ' "You run, Ricky! Don't do it!" that's what I told him. Told him I'd sponge on him for the rest of his days, if he was fool enough to let himself by caught.'

'I wonder that you should talk in that vulgar way!' said Louisa. 'Of course he has not *run!* I dare say he will be back any moment now. It was excessively remiss of him not to have sent a note round to inform Lord Saar that he could not wait on him this morning, as he had engaged himself to do, but——'

'You've got that wrong,' interrupted Cedric. 'No engagement at all. Melissa told him to call on m'father; he didn't say he would. Wormed it out of Melissa myself an hour ago. Lord, you never saw anyone in such a rage! What's all this?' His roving eye had alighted on the relics laid out upon the table. 'A lock of hair, by Jove! Devilish pretty hair too!'

'Found in the library this morning,' said George portentously, ignoring his wife's warning frown.

'Here? Ricky?' demanded Cedric. 'You're bamming me!'

'No, it is perfectly true. We cannot understand it.'

Cedric's eyes danced. 'By all that's famous! Who'd have thought it, though? Well, that settles our affairs! Devilish inconvenient, but damme, I'm glad he's bolted! Always liked Ricky—never wanted to see him bound for perdition with the rest of us! But we're done-up now, and no mistake! The diamonds have gone.'

'What?' Louisa cried. 'Cedric, not the Brandon necklace?'

'That's it. Last sheet-anchor thrown out to the windward —gone like that!' He snapped his fingers in the air, and laughed. 'I came to tell Ricky I'd accept his offer to buy me a pair of colours, and be off to the Wars.'

'But how? Where?' gasped Louisa.

'Stolen. My mother took it to Bath with her. Never would stir without the thing, more's the pity! *I* wonder m'father didn't sell it years ago. Only thing he didn't sell, except Saar Court, and that'll have to go next. My mother wouldn't hear of parting with the diamonds.'

'But Cedric, how stolen? Who took it?'

'Highwaymen. My mother sent off a courier post-haste to m'father. Chaise stopped somewhere near Bath—two fellows with masks and horse-pistols—Sophia screeching like a hen—my mother swooning—outriders taken by surprise—one of 'em winged. And off went the necklace. Which is what I can't for the life of me understand.'

'How terrible! Your poor Mama! I am so sorry! It is an appalling loss!'

'Yes, but how the devil did they find the thing?' said Cedric. 'That's what I want to know.'

'But surely if they took Lady Saar's jewel-case——'

'The necklace wasn't in it. I'll lay my last shilling on that. My mother had a hiding-place for it—devilish cunning notion—always put it there when she travelled. Secret pocket behind one of the squabs.'

'Good Gad, do you mean to say someone divulged the hiding-place to the rascals?' said George.

'Looks mightly like it, don't it?'

'Who knew of it? If you can discover the traitor, you may yet get the necklace back. Are you sure of all your servants?'

'I'm sure none of them—Lord, I don't know!' Cedric said, rather hastily. 'My mother wants the Bow Street Runners set on to it, but m'father don't think it's the least use. And now here's Ricky bolted, on top of everything! The old man will go off in an apoplexy!'

'Really, Cedric, you must not talk so of your Papa!' Louisa expostulated. 'And we don't know that Richard has—has *bolted!* Indeed, I am sure it's no such thing!'

'He'll be a fool if he hasn't,' said Cedric. 'What do you think, George?'

'I don't know,' George answered. 'It is very perplexing. I own, when I first heard of his disappearance—for you must know that he did not sleep in his bed last night, and when *I* saw him he was foxed—I felt the gravest alarm. But——'

'Suicide, by God!' Cedric gave a shout of laughter. 'I must tell Melissa that! Driven to death! Ricky! Oh, by all that's famous!'

'Cedric, you are quite abominable!' said Louisa roundly. 'Of course Richard has not committed suicide! He has merely gone away. I'm sure I don't know where, and if you say anything of the sort to Melissa I shall never forgive you! In fact, I beg you will tell Melissa nothing more than that Richard has been called away on an urgent matter of business.'

'What, can't I tell her about the lock of yaller hair? Now, don't be a spoil-sport, Louisa!'

'Odious creature!'

'We believe the lock of hair to be a relic of some long-forgotten affair,' said George. 'Possibly a boy-and-girl attachment. It would be gross impropriety to mention it beyond these walls.'

'If it comes to that, old fellow, what about the gross impropriety of poking and prying into Ricky's drawers?' asked Cedric cheerfully.

'We did no such thing!' Louisa cried. 'It was found upon the floor in the library!'

'Dropped? Discarded? Seems to me Ricky's been leading a double life. I'd have said myself he never troubled much about females. Won't I roast him when I see him!'

'You will do nothing of the sort. Oh dear, I wish to heaven I knew where he has gone, and what it all means!'

'I'll tell you where he's gone!' offered Cedric. 'He's gone to find the yaller-haired charmer of his youth. Not a doubt of it! Lord, I'd give a monkey to see him, though. Ricky on a romantic adventure!'

'Now you are being absurd!' said Louisa. 'If one thing is certain, it is that Richard has not one grain of romance in his disposition, while as for adventure——! I dare say he would shudder at the mere thought of it. Richard, my dear Cedric, is first, last, and always a man of fashion, and he will never do anything unbefitting a Corinthian. You may take my word for *that!*'

⋆§ *Chapter IV* §⋆

THE man of fashion, at that precise moment, was sleeping heavily in one corner of a huge green-and-gold Accommodation coach, swaying and rocking on its ponderous way

to Bristol. The hour was two in the afternoon, the locality
Calcot Green, west of Reading and the dreams troubling
the repose of the man of fashion were extremely uneasy.
He had endured some waking moments, when the coach
had stopped with a lurch and a heave to take up or to set
down passengers, to change horses, or to wait while a lag-
gardly pike-keeper opened a gate upon the road. These
moments had seemed to him more fraught with nightmare
even than his dreams. His head was aching, his eyeballs
seemed to be on fire, and a phantasmagoria of strange, un-
welcome faces swam before his outraged vision. He had
shut his eyes again with a groan, preferring his dreams to
reality, but when the coach stopped at Calcot Green to put
down a stout woman with a tendency to asthma, sleep
finally deserted him, and he opened his eyes, blinked at
the face of a precise-looking man in a suit of neat black,
seated opposite him, ejaculated: 'Oh, my God!' and sat up.

'Is your head *very* bad?' asked a solicitous and vaguely
familiar voice in his ear.

He turned his head, and encountered the enquiring gaze
of Miss Penelope Creed. He looked at her in silence for a
few moments; then he said: 'I remember. Stage-coach—
Bristol. Why, oh why, did I touch the brandy?'

An admonitory pinch made him recollect his surroundings. He found that there were three other persons in the
coach, seated opposite to him, and that all were regarding
him with interest. The precise-looking man, whom he
judged to be an attorney's clerk, was frankly disapproving;
a woman in a poke-bonnet and a paduasoy shawl nodded
to him in a motherly style, and said that he was like her
second boy, who could not abide the rocking of the coach
either; and a large man beside her, whom he took to be
her husband, corroborated this statement by enunciating in
a deep voice: 'That's right!'

Instinct took Sir Richard's hand to his cravat; his fingers
told him that it was considerably crumpled, like the tails
of his blue coat. His curly-brimmed beaver seemed to add
to the discomfort of his aching head; he took it off, and
clasped his head in his hands, trying to throw off the lin-
gering wisps of sleep. 'Good God!' he said thickly. 'Where
are we?'

'Well, I am not quite sure, but we have passed Reading,' replied Pen, rather anxiously surveying him.

'Calcot Green, that's where we are,' volunteered the large man. 'Stopped to set down someone. They ain't a-worriting theirselves over the time-bill, that's plain. I dare say the coachman's stepped down for a drink.'

'Ah, well!' said his wife tolerantly. 'It'll be thirsty work, setting up on the box in the sun like he has to.'

'That's right,' agreed the large man.

'If the Company was to hear of it he would be turned off, and very rightly!' said the clerk, sniffing. 'The behaviour of these stage-coachmen is becoming a scandal.'

'I'm sure there's no call for people to get nasty if a man falls behind his time-bill a little,' said the woman. 'Live and let live, that's what I say.'

Her husband assented to this in his usual fashion. The coach lurched forward again, and Pen said, under cover of the noise of the wheels and the horses' hooves: 'You kept on telling me that you were drunk, and now I see that you were. I was afraid you would regret coming with me.'

Sir Richard raised his head from his hands. 'Drunk I most undoubtedly must have been, but I regret nothing except the brandy. When does this appalling vehicle reach Bristol?'

'It isn't one of the fast coaches, you know. They don't engage to cover much above eight miles an hour. I think we ought to be in Bristol by eleven o'clock. We seem to stop such a number of times, though. Do you mind very much?'

He looked down at her. 'Do you?'

'To tell you the truth,' she confided, 'not a bit! I am enjoying myself hugely. Only I don't want you to be made uncomfortable all for my sake. I quite see that you are sadly out-of-place in a stage-coach.'

'My dear child, you had nothing whatever to do with my present discomfort, believe me. As for *my* being out-of-place, what, pray, are you?'

The dimples peeped. 'Oh, *I* am only a scrubby schoolboy, after all!'

'Did I say that?' She nodded. 'Well, so you are,' said

Sir Richard, looking her over critically. 'Except for——— Did I tie that cravat? Yes, I thought I must have. What in the world have you got there?'

'An apple,' replied Pen, showing it to him. 'The fat woman who got out just now gave it to me.'

'You are not going to sit there munching it, are you?' demanded Sir Richard.

'Yes, I am. Why shouldn't I? Would you like a bit of it?'

'I should not!' said Sir Richard.

'Well, I am excessively hungry. That was the one thing we forgot.'

'What was?'

'Food,' said Pen, digging her teeth into the apple. 'We ought to have provided ourselves with a basket of things to eat on the journey. I forgot that the stage doesn't stop at posting-houses, like the mail-coaches. At least, I didn't forget exactly, because I never knew it.'

'This must be looked to,' said Sir Richard. 'If you are hungry, you must undoubtedly be fed. What are you proposing to do with the core of that apple?'

'Eat it,' said Pen.

'Repellent brat!' said Sir Richard, with a strong shudder.

He leaned back in his corner, but a tug at his sleeve made him incline his head towards his companion.

'I told these people that you were my tutor,' whispered Pen.

'Of course, a young gentleman in his tutor's charge *would* be travelling in the common stage,' said Sir Richard, resigning himself to the rôle of usher.

At the next stage, which was Woolhampton, he roused himself from the languor which threatened to possess him, alighted from the coach, and showed unexpected competence in procuring from the modest inn a very tolerable cold meal for his charge. The coach awaited his pleasure, and the attorney's clerk, whose sharp eyes had seen Sir Richard's hand go from his pocket to the coachman's ready palm, muttered darkly of bribery and corruption on the King's Highway.

'Have some chicken,' said Sir Richard amiably.

The clerk refused this invitation with every evidence of contempt, but there were several other passengers, notably a small boy with adenoids, who were perfectly ready to share the contents of the basket on Pen's knees.

Sir Richard had good reason to know that Miss Creed's disposition was extremely confiding; during the long day's journey he discovered that she was friendly to a fault. She observed all the passengers with a bright and wholly unselfconscious gaze; conversed even with the clerk; and showed an alarming tendency to become the life and soul of the party. Questioned about herself, and her destination, she wove, zestfully, an entirely mendacious story, which she embroidered from time to time with outrageous details. Sir Richard was ruthlessly applied to for corroboration, and, entering into the spirit of the adventure, added a few extempore details himself. Pen seemed pleased with these, but was plainly disappointed at his refusal to join her in keeping the small boy with adenoids amused.

He leaned back in his corner, lazily enjoying Miss Creed's flights into the realms of fancy, and wondering what his mother and sister would think if they knew that he was travelling to an unknown destination, by stage-coach, accompanied by a young lady as unembarrassed by this circumstance as by her male attire. A laugh shook him, as he pictured Louisa's face. His head had ceased aching, but although the detachment fostered by brandy had left him, he still retained a feeling of delightful irresponsibility. Sober, he would certainly not have set forth on this absurd journey, but having done so, drunk, he was perfectly willing to continue it. He was, moreover, curious to learn more of Pen's history. Some farrago she had told him last night: his recollection of it was a trifle hazy, but there had surely been something about an aunt, and a cousin with a face like a fish.

He turned his head slightly on the dingy squabs of the coach, and watched, from under drooping eyelids, the animated little face beside him. Miss Creed was listening, apparently keenly interested, to a long and involved recital of the illness which had lately prostrated the motherly woman's youngest-born. She shook her head over the folly of the apothecary, nodded wisely at the efficiency of an age-old nostrum compounded of strange herbs, and was on the point of capping this recipe with one in use in her own family when Sir Richard's foot found her's and trod on it.

It was certainly time to check Miss Creed. The motherly woman stared at her, and said that it was queer-and-all to meet a young gentleman so knowledgeable.

'My mother,' said Pen, blushing, 'has been an invalid for many years.'

Everyone looked solicitous, and a desiccated female in the far corner of the coach said that no one could tell *her* anything about illness.

This remark had the effect of diverting attention from Pen, and as the triumphant lady plunged into the history of her sufferings, she sat back beside Sir Richard, directing up at him a look quite as mischievous as it was apologetic.

The lawyer's clerk, who had not yet forgiven Sir Richard for bribing the coachman, said something about the license allowed to young persons in these days. He contrasted it unfavourably with his own upbringing, and said that if he had a son he would not pamper him by giving him a tutor, but would send him to school. Pen said meekly that Mr Brown was very strict, and Sir Richard, correctly identifying Mr Brown with himself, lent colour to her assertion by telling her sternly not to chatter.

The motherly woman said that she was sure the young gentleman brightened them all up, and for her part she did not hold with people being harsh with children.

'That's right,' agreed her spouse. 'I never wanted to break any of *my* young 'uns' spirits: I like to see 'em up-and-coming.'

Several of the passengers looked reproachfully at Sir Richard, and, that no doubt of his severity might linger in their minds, Pen subsided into crushed silence, folding her hands on her knees, and casting down her eyes.

Sir Richard saw that he would figure for the rest of the journey as an oppressor, and mentally rehearsed a speech which was destined for Miss Creed's sole edification.

She disarmed him by falling asleep with her cheek against his shoulder. She slept between one stage and the next, and when roused by the coach's halting with its usual lurch, opened her eyes, smiled drowsily up at Sir Richard and murmured: 'I'm glad you came. Are you glad you came?'

'Very. Wake up!' said Sir Richard, wondering what more imprudent remarks might be hovering on her tongue.

She yawned, and straightened herself. An altercation seemed to be in progress between the guard and someone standing in the inn-yard. A farmer, who had boarded the coach at Calne, and was seated beside Pen, said that he thought the trouble was that the would-be passenger was not upon the way-bill.

'Well, he cannot come inside, that is certain!' said the thin woman. 'It is shocking, the way one is crowded already!'

'Where are we?' enquired Pen.

'Chippenham,' responded the farmer. 'That's where the Bath road goes off, see?'

She sat forward to look out of the window. 'Chippenham already? Oh yes, so it is! I know it well.'

Sir Richard cocked an amused eye at her. '*Already?*' he murmured.

'Well, I have been asleep, so it seems soon to me. Are you very weary, sir?'

'By no means. I am becoming entirely resigned.'

The new passenger, having apparently settled matters with the guard, at this moment pulled open the door, and tried to climb up into the coach. He was a small, spare man, in a catskin waistcoat, and jean-pantaloons. He had a sharp face, with a pair of twinkling, lashless eyes set deep under sandy brows. His proposed entrance into the coach was resolutely opposed. The thin woman cried out that there was no room; the lawyer's clerk said that the way the Company over-loaded its vehicles was a scandal; and the farmer recommended the newcomer to climb on to the roof.

'There ain't an inch of room up there,' protested the stranger. 'Lord, I don't take up much space! Squeeze up, coves!'

'Full-up! Try the boot!' said the farmer.

'Cast your winkers over me, cull: I don't take up no more room than what a bodkin would!' pleaded the stranger. 'Besides, there's a set of flash young coves on the roof. I'd be mortal afraid to sit with 'em, so I would!'

Sir Richard, casting an experienced eye over the man, mentally wrote him down as one probably better known to the Bow Street Runners than to himself. He was not surprised, however, to hear Miss Creed offering to squeeze up to make room, for he had, by this time, formed a very fair estimate of his charge's warmheartedness.

Pen, edging close to Sir Richard, coaxed the farmer to see for himself that there was room enough for one more passenger. The man in the catskin waistcoat grinned at her, and hopped into the coach. 'Dang me if I didn't think you was a flash cull too!' he said, squeezing himself into the vacant place. 'I'm obliged to ye, young shaver. When coves do Jimmy Yarde a service he don't forget it neither.'

The lawyer, who seemed to have much the same opinion of Mr Yarde as that held by Sir Richard, sniffed, and folded his hands tightly on the box which he held on his knees.

'Lord bless you!' said Mr Yarde, observing this gesture with a tolerant smile, '*I* ain't no boman prig!'

'What's a boman prig?' asked Pen innocently.

'There, now! If you ain't a werry suckling!' said Mr Yarde, almost disconcerted. 'A boman prig, young gentleman, is what I trust you'll never be. It's a cove as ends up in Rumbo—ah, and likely on the Nubbing Cheat afore he's much older!'

Much intrigued, Pen demanded a translation of these strange terms. Sir Richard, having pondered and discarded the notion of commanding her to exchange places with him, lay back and listened with lazy enjoyment to her initiation into the mysteries of thieves' cant.

A party of young gentlemen, who had been spectators of a cock-fight held in the district, had been taken up at Chippenham, and had crowded on to the roof. From the sounds preceding thence, it seemed certain that they had been refreshing themselves liberally. Ther was a good deal of shouting, some singing, and much drumming with heels upon the roof. The motherly woman and the thin spinster began to look alarmed, and the lawyer's clerk said that the behaviour of modern young men was disgraceful. Pen was too deeply engaged in conversation with Jimmy Yarde to pay much heed to the commotion, but when, after the coach had rumbled on for another five miles, the pace was suddenly accelerated, and the top-heavy vehicle bounced over ruts and pot-holes, and swung perilously first to one side and then to the other, she broke off her enthralling discourse, and looked enquiringly at Sir Richard.

A violent lurch flung her into his arms. He restored her to her own seat, saying dryly: 'More adventure for you. I hope you are enjoying it?'

'But what is happening?'

'I apprehend that one of the would-be sprigs of fashion above has taken it into his head to tool the coach,' he replied.

'Lord ha' mercy!' exclaimed the motherly woman. 'Do you mean that one of they pesky, drunken lads is a-driving of us, sir?'

'So I should suppose, ma'am.'

The spinster uttered a faint shriek. 'Good God, what will become of us?'

'We shall end, I imagine, in the ditch,' said Sir Richard, with unruffled calm.

Babel at once broke forth, the spinster demanding to be let out at once, the motherly woman trying to attract the coachman's notice by hammering against the roof with her sunshade, the farmer sticking his head out of the window to shout threats and abuse, Jimmy Yarde laughing, and the lawyer's clerk angrily demanding of Sir Richard why he did not *do* something?

'What would you wish me to do?' asked Sir Richard, steadying Pen with a comfortingly strong arm.

'Stop the coach! Oh, sir, pray stop it!' begged the motherly woman.

'Bless your heart, ma'am, it'll stop of its own this gait!' grinned Jimmy Yarde.

Hardly had he spoken than a particularly sharp bend in the road proved to be too much for the amateur coachman's skill. He took the corner too wide, the near-hind wheels mounted a slight bank, and skidded down the farther side into a deep ditch, and everyone inside the vehicle was flung rudely over. There were screams from the women, oaths from the farmer, the cracking noise of split wood, and the shatter of broken glass. The coach lay at a crazy angle with sprigs of thorn-hedge thrusting in through the broken windows.

Pen, whose face was smothered in the many capes of Sir Richard's drab driving-coat, gasped, and struggled to free herself from a hold which had suddenly clamped her to Sir Richard's side. He relaxed it, saying: 'Hurt, Pen?'

'No, not in the least! Thank you so very much for holding me! Are you hurt?'

A splinter of glass had cut his cheek slightly, but since he had been holding on to the leather arm-rest hanging in the corner of the coach, he had not been thrown, like everyone else, off his seat. 'No, only annoyed,' he replied. 'My good woman, this is neither the time nor the place for indulging in a fit of the vapours!'

This acid rider was addressed to the spinster, who, finding herself pitch-forked on top of the lawyer's clerk, had gone off into strong hysterics.

'Here, let me get my dabblers on to that there door!' said Jimmy Yarde, hoisting himself up by seizing the opposite arm-rest. 'Dang me if next time I travel in a rattler I don't ride on the roof, flash-culls or no!'

The coach not having collapsed quite on to its side, but being supported by the bank and the hedge bordering the ditch, it was not difficult to force open the door, or to climb out through it. The spinster had indeed to be lifted out, since she had stiffened all over, and would do nothing but scream and drum her heels, but Pen scrambled out with an agility which scorned helping hands, and the motherly woman said that provided every gentleman would turn his back upon her she would engage to get out by herself too.

It was now considerably after nine o'clock, but although the sun had gone, the summer sky was still light, and the air warm. The travellers found themselves on a deserted stretch of road, a couple of miles short of the little town of Wroxhall, and rather more than thirty miles from Bristol. The most cursory inspection of the coach was enough to convince them that it would need extensive repairs before being able to take the road again; and Sir Richard,

who had gone immediately to the horses, returned to Pen's
side in a few moments with the news that one of the
wheelers had badly strained a tendon. He had been right
in thinking that the reins had been handed over to one of
the outside passengers. To tool the coach was a common
enough pastime amongst young men who aspired to be
whips, but that any paid coachman could have been foolish enough to relinquish his seat to an amateur far gone in
drink was incomprehensible, until the coachman's own
condition had been realized.

Pen, who was sitting on Sir Richard's portmanteau, received the news of complete breakdown with perfect
equanimity, but all the other inside passengers burst into
vociferous complaint, and besieged the guard with demands to be instantly conveyed to Bristol, by means un-
specified. Between his indignation at his colleague's gross
misconduct, and his exasperation at being shouted at by
six or seven persons at once, the unfortunate man was for
some time incapable of collecting his wits, but presently
it was suggested that if the travellers would only be patient, he would ride back on one of the leaders to Chippenham, and there try to procure some sort of a vehicle to
convey them to Wroxhall, where they would be obliged to
remain until the next Accommodation coach to Bristol
picked them up there early on the following morning.

Several persons decided to set forward on foot for
Wroxhall at once, but the spinster was still having hysterics, the motherly woman said that her corns would not
permit of her tramping two miles, and the lawyer's clerk
held to it that he had a right to be conveyed to Bristol that
night. There was a marked tendency in one or two persons
to turn to Sir Richard, as being plainly a man accustomed
to command. This tendency had the effect of making Sir
Richard, not in the least gratified, walk over to Pen's side,
and say languidly, but with decision: 'This, I fancy, is
where we part company with our fellow-travellers.'

'Yes, do let us!' assented Pen blithely. 'You know, I
have been thinking, and I have a much better scheme now.
We won't go to Bristol at all!'

'This is very sudden,' said Sir Richard. 'Do I understand

you to mean that you have made up your mind to return to London?'

'No, no, of course not! Only now that we have broken down I think it would be silly to wait for another coach, because very likely we should be overtaken by my aunt. And I never really wanted to go to Bristol, after all.'

'In that case, it seems perhaps a pity that we came so far upon the road to it,' said Sir Richard.

Her eyes twinkled. 'Stupid! I mean, my home is not in Bristol, but near to it, and I think it would be much better, besides being like a real adventure, to walk the rest of the way.'

'Where is your home?' demanded Sir Richard.

'Well, it is near Queen Charlton, not far from Keynsham, you know.'

'I don't,' said Sir Richard. 'This is your country, not mine. How far, in your judgment, is Queen Charlton from where we now are?'

'I'm not *entirely* sure,' replied Pen cautiously. 'But I shouldn't think it could be above fifteen, or, at the most twenty miles, going 'cross country.'

'Are you proposing to walk twenty miles?' said Sir Richard.

'Well, I dare say it is not as much. As the crow flies, I expect it is only about ten miles off.'

'You are not a crow,' said Sir Richard dampingly. 'Nor, I may add, am I. Get up from that portmanteau!'

She rose obediently. 'I think I could quite well walk twenty miles. Not all at once, of course. What *are* we going to do?'

'We are going to retrace our steps along the road until we come to an inn,' replied Sir Richard. 'As I remember, there was one, about a couple of miles back. Nothing would induce me to make one of this afflictive coach-party!'

'I must own, I am a little tired of them myself,' admitted Pen. 'Only I won't go to a posting-house!'

'Make yourself easy on that score!' said Sir Richard grimly. 'No respectable posting-house would open its door to us in this guise.'

This made Pen giggle. She put forward no further opposition, but picked up the cloak-bag, and set out beside Sir Richard in the direction of Chippenham.

None of the coach-passengers noticed their departure, since all were fully occupied, either in reviling the coach-man, or in planning their immediate movements. The bend in the road soon shut them off from sight of the coach, and Sir Richard then said: 'And now you may give me that cloak-bag.'

'Well, I won't,' said Pen, holding on to it firmly. 'It is not at all heavy, and you have your portmanteau to carry already. Besides, I feel more like a man every moment. What shall we do when we reach the inn?'

'Order supper.'

'Yes, and after that?'

'Go to bed.'

Pen considered this. 'You don't think we should set forward on our journey at once?'

'Certainly not. We shall go to bed like Christians, and in the morning we shall hire a conveyance to carry us to Queen Charlton. A private conveyance,' he added.

'But——'

'Pen Creed,' said Sir Richard calmly, 'you cast me for the rôle of bear-leader, and I accepted it. You drew a re-volting picture of me which led everyone in that coach to regard me in the light of a persecutor of youth. Now you are reaping the harvest of your own sowing.'

She laughed. 'Are you going to persecute me?'

'Horribly!' said Sir Richard.

She tucked a confiding hand in his arm, and gave a little skip. 'Very well, I will do as you tell me. I'm very glad I met you: we are having a splendid adventure, are we not?'

Sir Richard's lips twitched. Suddenly he burst out laugh-ing, standing still in the middle of the road, while Pen doubtfully surveyed him.

'But what is the matter with you?' she asked.

'Never mind!' he said, his voice still unsteady with mirth. 'Of course we are having a splendid adventure!'

'Well, I think we are,' she said, stepping out beside him again. 'Piers will be so surprised when he sees me!'

'I should think he would be,' agreed Sir Richard. 'You are quite sure that you don't regret coming in search of him, I suppose?'

'Oh yes, quite! Why, Piers is my oldest friend! Didn't I tell you that we made a vow to be married?'

'I have some recollection of your doing so,' he admitted. 'But I also recollect that you said you hadn't seen him for five years.'

'No, that is true, but it doesn't signify in the least, I assure you.'

'I see,' said Sir Richard, keeping his inevitable reflections to himself.

They had not more than two miles to go before they reached the inn Sir Richard had seen from the window of the coach. It was a very small hostelry, with a weather-beaten sign creaking on its chains, a thatched roof, and only one parlour, besides the common tap-room.

The landlord, upon hearing of the breakdown of the stage-coach, accepted the travellers' unconventional arrival without surprise. It was growing dark by this time, and it was not until Sir Richard had stepped into the inn, and stood in the light of a hanging lamp, that the landlord was able to obtain a clear view of him. Sir Richard had chosen for the journey a plain coat and serviceable breeches, but the cut of the blue cloth, the high polish on his top-boots, the very style of his cravat, and the superfluity of capes on his drab over-coat all proclaimed so unmistakably the gentleman of fashion that the landlord was obviously taken aback, and looked from him to Pen with considerable suspicion.

'I shall require a bedroom for myself, and another for my nephew,' said Sir Richard. 'Also some supper.'

'Yes, sir. Did your honour says you was travelling on the Bristol-stage?' asked the landlord incredulously.

'Yes,' said Sir Richard raising his brows. 'I did say so. Have you any objection?'

'Oh no, sir! no, I'm sure!' replied the landlord hastily. 'Your honour said supper! I'm afraid we—we aren't in the habit of entertaining the quality, but if your honour would condescend to a dish of ham and eggs, or maybe a slice of cold pork, I'll see to it on the instant!'

Sir Richard having graciously approved the ham and eggs, the landlord bowed him into the stuffy little parlour, and promised to have the only two guest-chambers the inn possessed immediately prepared. Pen, directing a conspiratorial look at Sir Richard, elected to follow the portmanteau and the cloak-bag upstairs. When she reappeared a slatternly maid-servant had spread supper on the table in the parlour, and Sir Richard had succeeded in forcing open two of its tiny windows. He turned, as Pen came in, and asked: 'What in heaven's name have you been doing all this time? I began to think you had deserted me.'

'Desert you! Of course I wouldn't do anything so silly! The thing was, I could see the landlord had noticed your clothes, so I thought of a famous tale to tell him. That's why I went off with him. I knew he would try to discover from me why you were travelling on the stage-coach.'

'And did he?'

'Yes, and I told him that you had reverses on 'Change and had fallen on evil times,' said Pen, drawing up her chair to the table.

'Oh!' said Sir Richard. 'Was he satisfied with that?'

'Perfectly. He said he was very sorry. And then he asked where we were bound for. I said, for Bristol, because *all* the family had lost its money, and so I had had to be taken away from school.'

'You have the most fertile imagination of anyone of my acquaintance,' said Sir Richard. 'May I ask what school you have been gracing?'

'Harrow. Afterwards I wished I had said Eton, because my cousin Geoffrey is at Harrow, and I don't like him. I wouldn't go to his school.'

'I suppose it is too late to change the school now,' Sir Richard said, in a regretful tone.

She looked up quickly, her fascinating smile crinkling the corners of her eyes. 'You are laughing at me.'

'Yes,' admitted Sir Richard. 'Do you mind?'

'Oh no, not a bit! No one laughs in my aunt's house. I like it.'

'I wish,' said Sir Richard, 'you would tell me more about this aunt of yours. Is she your guardian?'

'No, but I have had to live with her ever since my father died. I have no real guardian, but I have two trustees. On account of my fortune, you understand.'

'Of course, yes: I was forgetting your fortune. Who are your trustees?'

'Well, one is my uncle Griffin—Aunt Almeria's husband, you know—but he doesn't signify, because he does just what Aunt tells him. The other is my father's lawyer, and he doesn't signify either.'

'For the same reason?'

'I don't know, but I shouldn't wonder at it in the least. Everyone is afraid of Aunt Almeria. Even I am, a little. That's why I ran away.'

'Is she unkind to you?'

'N-no. At least, she doesn't ill-treat me, but she is the kind of woman who always gets her own way. Do you know?'

'I know,' Sir Richard said.

'She talks,' explained Pen. 'And when she is displeased with one, I must say that it is very uncomfortable. But one should always be just, and I do not blame her for being so set on my marrying Fred. They are not very rich, you see, and of course Aunt would like Fred to have all my fortune. In fact, I am very sorry to be so disobliging, particularly as I have lived with the Griffins for nearly five years. But, to tell you the truth, I didn't in the least want to, and as for marrying Fred, I could *not!* Only when I suggested to Aunt Almeria that I would much prefer to give my fortune to Fred, and *not* marry him, she flew into a passion, and said I was heartless and shameless, and cried, and talked about nourishing vipers in her bosom. I thought that was unjust of her, because it was a very handsome offer, don't you agree?'

'Very,' said Sir Richard. 'But perhaps a trifle—shall we say, crude?'

'Oh!' Pen digested this. 'You mean that she did not like my *not* pretending that Fred was in love with me?'

'I think it just possible,' said Sir Richard gravely.

'Well, I am sorry if I wounded her feelings, but truly I don't think she has the least sensibility. I only said what I thought. But it put her in such a rage that there was nothing for it but to escape. So I did.'

'Were you locked in your room?' enquired Sir Richard.

'Oh no! I daresay I should have been if Aunt had guessed what I meant to do, but she would never think of such a thing.'

'Then—forgive my curiosity!—why did you climb out of the window?' asked Sir Richard.

'Oh, that was on account of Pug!' replied Pen sunnily.

'Pug?'

'Yes, a horrid little creature! He sleeps in a basket in the hall, and he *always* yaps if he thinks one is going out. That would have awakened Aunt Almeria. There was nothing else I could do.'

Sir Richard regarded her with a lurking smile. 'Naturally not. Do you know, Pen, I owe you a debt of gratitude?'

'Oh?' she said, pleased, but doubtful. 'Why?'

'I thought I knew your sex. I was wrong.'

'Oh!' she said again. 'Do you mean that I don't behave as a delicately bred female should?'

'That is one way of putting it, certainly.'

'It is the way Aunt Almeria puts it.'

'She would, of course.'

'I am afraid,' confessed Pen, 'that I am not very well-behaved. Aunt says that I had a lamentable upbringing, because my father treated me as though I had been a boy. I ought to have been, you understand.'

'I cannot agree with you,' said Sir Richard. 'As a boy you would have been in no way remarkable; as a female, believe me, you are unique.'

She flushed to the roots of her hair. 'I *think* that is a compliment.'

'It is,' Sir Richard said, amused.

'Well, I wasn't sure, because I am not out yet, and I do not know any men except my uncle and Fred, and they don't pay compliments. That is to say, not like that.' She looked up rather shyly, but chancing to catch sight of someone through the window, suddenly exclaimed: 'Why, there's Mr Yarde!'

'Mr who?' asked Sir Richard, turning his head.

'You can't see him now: he has gone past the window. You *must* remember Mr Yarde sir! He was the odd little man who got into the coach at Chippenham, and used such queer words that I could not perfectly understand him. Do you suppose he can be coming to this inn?'

'I sincerely trust not!' said Sir Richard.

❧ *Chapter V* ☙

His trust was soon seen to have been misplaced, for after a few minutes the landlord came into the room, to ask apologetically whether the noble gentleman would object to giving up one of his rooms to another traveller. 'I told him as how your honour had bespoke both bedchambers, but he is very wishful to get a lodging, sir, so I told him as how I would ask your honour if, maybe, the young gentleman could share your honour's chamber—there being two beds, sir.'

Sir Richard, meeting Miss Creed's eye for one pregnant moment, saw that she was struggling with a strong desire to burst out laughing. His own lips quivered, but before he could answer the landlord, the sharp face of Mr Jimmy Yarde peered over that worthy's shoulder.

Upon recognizing the occupants of the parlour, Mr Yarde seemed to be momentarily taken aback. He recovered himself quickly, however, to thrust his way into the parlour with a very fair assumption of delight at encountering two persons already known to him. 'Well, if it ain't my young chub!' he exclaimed. 'Dang me if I didn't think the pair of you had loped off to Wroxhall!'

'No,' said Sir Richard. 'It appeared to me that Wroxhall would be over-full of travellers to-night.'

'Ay, you're a damned knowing one, ain't you? Knowed it the instant I clapped my glaziers on you. And right you are! Says I to myself, "Wroxhall's no place for you, Jimmy, my boy!" '

'Was the thin woman still having the vapours?' asked Pen.

'Lordy, young chub, she were stretched out as stiff as a corpse when I loped off, and no one knowing what to do to bring her to her senses. Ah, and mighty peevy I thought myself, to hit on the notion of coming to this ken—not knowing as you had bespoke all the rooms afore me.'

His bright face shifted to Sir Richard's unpromising countenance. 'Unfortunate!' said Sir Richard politely.

'Ah, now!' wheedled Mr Yarde, 'you wouldn't go for to out-jockey Jimmy Yarde! Lordy, it's all of eleven o'clock, and the light gone. What's to stop your doubling up with the young shaver?'

'If your honour would condescend to allow the young gentleman to sleep in the spare bed in your honour's chamber?' interpolated the landlord in an ingratiating tone.

'No,' said Sir Richard. 'I am an extremely light sleeper, and my nephew snores.' Ignoring an indignant gasp from Pen, he turned to Mr Yarde. 'Do you snore?' he asked.

Jimmy grinned. 'Not me! I sleep like a baby, so help me!'

'Then you,' said Sir Richard, 'may share my room.'

'Done!' said Jimmy promptly. 'Spoke like a rare gager, guv'nor, which I knew you was. Damme, if I don't drain a clank to your very good health!'

Resigning himself to the inevitable, Sir Richard nodded to the landlord, and bade Jimmy draw up a chair.

Not having boarded the stage-coach when Pen had announced Sir Richard to be her tutor, Jimmy apparently accepted her new relationship without question. He spoke of her to Sir Richard as 'your nevvy,' drank both their healths in gin-and-water bespoken by Sir Richard, and seemed to be inclined to make a night of it. He became rather loquacious over his second glass of daffy, and made several mysterious references to Files, and those engaged on the Dub-lay, and the Kidd. Various embittered strictures on the Flash Culls led Sir Richard to infer that he had lately been working in partnership with persons above his own social standing, and did not mean to repeat the experience.

Pen sat drinking it all in, with her eyes growing rounder and rounder, until Sir Richard said that it was time she was in bed. He escorted her out of the parlour to the foot of the stairs, where she whispered to him in the tone of one who has made a great discovery: 'Dear sir, I don't believe he is a respectable person!'

'No,' said Sir Richard. 'I don't believe it either.'

'But is he a *thief?*' asked Pen, shocked.

'I should think undoubtedly. Which is why you will lock your door, my child. Is it understood?'

'Yes, but are you sure you will be safe? It would be dreadful if he were to cut your throat in the night!'

'It would indeed,' Sir Richard agreed. 'But I can assure you he won't. You may take this for me, if you will, and keep it till the morning.'

He put his heavy purse into her hand. She nodded. 'Yes, I will. You will take great care, will you not?'

'I promise,' he said, smiling. 'Be off now, and don't tease yourself over my safety!'

He went back to the parlour, where Jimmy Yarde awaited him. Being called upon to join Mr Yarde in a glass of daffy, he raised not the slightest objection, although he very soon suspected Jimmy of trying to drink him under the table. As he refilled the glasses for the third time, he said apologetically: 'Perhaps I ought to warn you that I am accounted to have a reasonably strong head. I should not like you to waste your time, Mr Yarde.'

Jimmy was not at all abashed. He grinned, and said: 'Ah, I said you was a peevy cull! Knowed it as soon as I clapped my daylights on to you. You learned to drink Blue Ruin in Cribb's parlour!'

'Quite right,' said Sir Richard.

'Oh, I knowed it, bless your heart! "That there gentry-cove would peel remarkably well," I says to myself. "And a handy bunch of fives he's got." Never you fret, guv'nor: Jimmy Yarde's no green 'un. What snabbles me, though, is how you come to be travelling in the common rumble.'

Sir Richard gave a soft laugh suddenly. 'You see, I have lost all my money,' he said.

'Lost all your money?' repeated Jimmy, astonished.

'On 'Change,' added Sir Richard.

The light, sharp eyes flickered over his elegant person. 'Ah, you're trying to gammon me! What's the lay?'

'None at all.'

'Dang me if I ever met such a cursed rum touch!' A suspicion crossed his mind. 'You ain't killed your man, guv'nor?'

'No. Have you?'

Jimmy looked quite alarmed. 'Not me, guv'nor, not me! I don't hold with violence, any gait.'

Sir Richard helped himself to a leisurely pinch of snuff. 'Just the Knuckle, eh?'

Jimmy gave a start, and looked at him with uneasy respect. 'What would the likes of you know about the Knuckle?'

'Not very much, admittedly. I believe it means the filching of watches, snuff-boxes, and such-like from the pockets of the unsuspecting.'

'Here!' said Jimmy, looking very hard at him across the table, 'you don't work the Drop, do you?'

Sir Richard shook his head.

'You ain't a Picker-up, or p'raps a Kidd?'

'No,' said Sir Richard. 'I am quite honest—what you, I fancy, call a Flat.'

'I don't!' Jimmy said emphatically. 'I never met a flat what was so unaccountable knowing as what you are, guv'nor; and what's more I hope I don't meet one again!'

He watched Sir Richard rise to his feet, and kindle his bedroom candle at the guttering one on the table. He was frowning in a puzzled way, clearly uncertain in his mind. 'Going to bed, guv'nor?'

Sir Richard glanced down at him. 'Yes. I did warn you that I am a shockingly light sleeper, did I not?'

'Lord, you ain't got no need to fear *me!*'

'I am quite sure I have not,' smiled Sir Richard.

When Jimmy Yarde, an hour later, softly tiptoed into the low-pitched bed-chamber above the parlour, Sir Richard lay to all appearances peacefully asleep. Jimmy edged close to the bed, and stood watching him, and listening to his even breathing.

'Don't drop hot tallow on me, I beg!' said Sir Richard, not opening his eyes.

Jimmy Yarde jumped, and swore.

'Quite so,' said Sir Richard.

Jimmy Yarde cast him a look of venomous dislike, and in silence undressed, and got into the neighbouring bed.

He awoke at an early hour, to hear roosters crowing from farm to farm in the distance. The sun was up, but the day was still misty, and the air very fresh. The bed creaked under him as he sat up, but it did not rouse Sir Richard. Jimmy Yarde slid out of it cautiously, and dressed himself. On the dimity-covered table by the window, Sir Richard's gold quizzing-glass and snuff-box lay, carelessly discarded. Jimmy looked wistfully at him. He was something of a connoisseur in snuff-boxes, and his fingers itched to slip this one into his pocket. He glanced uncertainly towards the bed. Sir Richard sighed in his sleep. His coat hung over a chair within Jimmy's reach. Keeping his eyes on Sir Richard Jimmy felt in its pockets. Nothing but a handkerchief rewarded his search. But Sir Richard had given no sign of returning consciousness. Jimmy picked up the snuff-box, and inspected it. Still no movement from the bed. Emboldened, Jimmy dropped it into his capacious pocket. The quizzing-glass swiftly followed it. Jimmy went stealthily towards the door. As he reached it, a yawn made him halt in his tracks, and spin round.

Sir Richard stretched and yawned again. 'You're up early, my friend,' he remarked.

'That's right,' said Jimmy, anxious to be gone before his theft could be discovered. 'I'm not one for lying abed on a fine summer's morning. I'll get a breath of air before I have my breakfast. Daresay we'll meet downstairs, eh, guv'nor?'

'I dare say we shall,' agreed Sir Richard. 'But in case we don't, I'll relieve you of my snuff-box and my eyeglass now.'

Exasperated, Jimmy let fall the modest bundle which contained his nightgear. 'Dang me, if I ever met such a leery cove in all my puff!' he said. 'You never saw me lift that lobb!'

'I warned you that I was a shockingly light sleeper,' said Sir Richard.

'Bubbled by a gudgeon!' said Jimmy disgustedly, handing over the booty. 'Here you are: there's no need for you to go calling in any harman, eh?'

'None at all,' replied Sir Richard.

'Damme, you're a blood after my own fancy, guv'nor! No hard feeling?'

'Not the least in the world.'

'I wish I knew what your lay might be,' Jimmy said wistfully, and departed, shaking his head over the problem.

Downstairs he found Pen Creed, who had also awakened early. She bade him a cheerful good-morning, and said that she had been out, and was of the opinion that it was going to be a hot day. When he asked her if she and her uncle meant to board the next stage-coach to Bristol, she replied prudently that her uncle had not yet told her what they were going to do.

'You are bound for Bristol, ain't you?' enquired Jimmy.

'Oh yes!' said Pen, with a beautiful disregard for the truth.

They were standing in the taproom, which, at that hour of the morning, was empty, and just as Pen was beginning to say that she wanted her breakfast, the landlady came through the door leading from the kitchen, and asked them if they had heard the news.

'What news?' Pen asked uneasily.

'Why, everyone's in quite a pucker up at Wroxhall, us being quiet folk, and not used to town-ways. But there's my boy Jim come in saying there's one of they Bow Street Runners come down by the Mail. What he may want, surely to goodness there's none of us knows! They do say as how he stopped off at Calne, and come on easy-like to Wroxhall. And there he be, poking his nose into respectable houses, and asking all manner of questions! Well, what I say is, *we've* nothing to hide, and he may come here if he pleases, but he will learn nothing.'

'Is he coming here?' asked Pen, in a faint voice.

'Going to all the inns hereabout, by what they tell me,' responded the landlady. 'Jim took the notion into his head it's all along of the stage-coach which you and your good uncle was on, sir, for seemingly he's been asking a mort of questions about the passengers. Our Sam looks to see him here inside of half an hour. "Well," I says, "let him come, for I'm an honest woman, and there's never been a word said against the house, not to my knowledge!" Your breakfast will be on the table in ten minutes, sir.'

She bustled into the parlour, leaving Pen rather pale, and Jimmy Yarde suddenly thoughtful. 'Runners, eh?' said that worthy, stroking his chin. 'There now!'

'I have never seen one,' said Pen, with a creditable show of nonchalance. 'It will be most interesting. I wonder what he can want?'

'There's no telling,' replied Jimmy, his lashless eyes dwelling upon her in a considering stare. 'No telling at all. Seems to me, though, he won't be wanting a flash young chub like you.'

'Why, of course not!' replied Pen, forcing a laugh.

'That's what I thought,' said Jimmy, transferring his gaze to the long coat which had been flung across one of the tables. 'Might that be your toge, young shaver?'

'Yes, but I didn't need it after all. It is much warmer outside than I thought it would be.'

He picked it up, shook out its folds, and gave it to her. 'Don't you go leaving things about in common taprooms!' he said austerely. 'There's plenty of files—ah, even in these quiet parts!—would be glad to get their dabblers on to a good toge like that.'

'Oh yes! Thank you! I'll take it upstairs!' said Pen, glad of an opportunity to escape.

'You couldn't do better,' approved Jimmy. 'Then we'll have a bit of food, and though I don't hold with harmen in general—which is to say, with Law-officers, young shaver —why, I'm a peaceable man, and if any such be wishful to search me, they're welcome.'

He strolled into the parlour, with the air of one whose conscience is clean, and Pen hurried off upstairs, to tap urgently on Sir Richard's door.

His voice called to her to come in, and she entered to find him putting the finishing touches to his cravat. He met her eyes in the mirror, and said: 'Well, brat?'

'Sir, we must leave this place instantly!' said Pen impetuously. 'We are in the greatest danger!'

'Why? Has your aunt arrived?' asked Sir Richard, preserving his calm.

'Worse!' Pen declared. 'A Bow Street Runner!'

'Ah, I thought you were a house-breaker in the first place!' said Sir Richard, shaking his head.

'I am not a house-breaker! You know I am not!'

'If the Runners are after you, it is obvious to me that you are a desperate character,' he replied, slipping his snuff-box into his pocket. 'Let us go downstairs, and have some breakfast.'

'Please, dear sir, be serious! I am sure that my Aunt must have set the Runner on to me!'

'My dear child, if there is any one thing more certain than another it is that Bow Street has never heard of your existence. Don't be silly!'

'Oh!' She heaved a sigh of relief. 'I do trust you are right, but it is just the sort of thing Aunt Almeria would do!'

'You are the best judge of that, no doubt, but you may take it from me that it is not in the least the sort of thing a Bow Street Runner would do. You will probably find that the man he wants is our friend Mr Yarde.'

'Yes, at first I thought that too, but he says the Runner is welcome to search him if he wants to.'

'Then it is safe to assume that Mr Yarde has disposed of whatever booty it was he ran off with. Breakfast!'

In considerable trepidation, Pen followed him down to the parlour. They found Jimmy Yarde discussing a plate of cold beef. He greeted Sir Richard with a grin and a wink, obviously quite unabashed by his previous encounter with him that morning, to which he referred in the frankest terms. 'When I meet up with a leery cove, I don't bear malice,' he announced, raising a tankard of ale. 'So here's your wery good health, guv'nor, and no hard feelings!'

Sir Richard seemed to be rather bored, and merely nodded. Jimmy Yarde fixed him with a twinkling eye, and said: 'And no splitting to any harman about poor old Jimmy boning your lobb, because he never did, and you know well it's in your pocket at this wery moment. What's more,' he added handsomely, 'I wouldn't fork you now I has your measure, guv'nor, not for fifty Yellow Boys!'

'I'm glad of that,' said Sir Richard.

'No splitting?' Jimmy said, his head on one side.

'Not if I am allowed to eat my breakfast in peace,' replied Sir Richard wearily.

'All's bowman then!' said Jimmy, 'and not another word

will you hear from me, guv'nor, till we gets to Bristol. Damme if I don't ride outside the rattler, just to oblige you!'

Sir Richard looked meditatively at him, but said nothing. Pen sat down facing the window, and watched the road for signs of a Bow Street Runner.

Contrary to the landlady's expectations, the Runner did not reach the inn until some little time after the breakfast covers had been removed, and Jimmy Yarde had strolled out to lounge at his ease on a bench set against the wall of the hostelry.

The Runner entered the inn by way of the yard at the back of it, and the first person he encountered was Sir Richard, who was engaged in settling his account with the landlord. Miss Creed, at his elbow, drew his attention to the Runner's arrival by urgently twitching his coat sleeve. He looked up, with raised brows, saw the newcomer, and lifted his quizzing-glass.

'Beg your pardon, sir,' said the Runner, touching his hat. 'Me not meaning to intrude, but being wishful to speak with the landlord.'

'Certainly,' said Sir Richard, his brows still expressive of languid surprise.

'At your convenience, sir: no hurry, sir!' said the Runner, retreating to a discreet distance.

The sigh which escaped Miss Creed was one of such profound relief that it was plain her alarms had not until that moment been allayed. Sir Richard finished paying his shot, and with a brief: 'Come, Pen!' tossed over his shoulder, left the taproom.

'He didn't come to find me!' breathed Pen.

'Of course he didn't.'

'I couldn't help being a little alarmed. What shall we do now, sir?'

'Shake off your very undesirable travelling-acquaintance,' he replied briefly.

She gave a gurgle. 'Yes, but how? I have *such* a fear that he means to go with us to Bristol.'

'But we are not going to Bristol. While he is being interrogated by that Runner, we, my child, are going to walk quietly out by the back door, and proceed by ways, which

I trust will not prove as devious as the tapster's description of them, to Colerne. There we shall endeavour to hire a vehicle to carry us to Queen Charlton.'

'Oh, famous!' cried Pen. 'Let us go at once!'

Five minutes later they left the inn unobtrusively, by way of the yard, found themselves in a hayfield, and skirted it to a gate leading into a ragged spinney.

The village of Colerne was rather less than three miles distant, but long before they had reached it Sir Richard was tired of his portmanteau. 'Pen Creed, you are a pestilent child!' he told her.

'Why, what have I done?' she asked, with one of her wide, enquiring looks.

'You have hailed me from my comfortable house——'

'I didn't! It was you who *would* come!'

'I was drunk.'

'Well, that was not my fault,' she pointed out.

'Don't interrupt me! You have made me travel for miles in a conveyance smelling strongly of dirt and onions——'

'That was the fat woman's husband,' interpolated Pen. 'I noticed it myself.'

'No one could have failed to notice it. And I am not partial to onions. You drew a portrait of me which led everyone in the coach to regard me in the light of an oppressor of innocent youth——'

'Not the thin, disagreeable man. *He* wanted me to be oppressed.'

'He was a person of great discrimination. Not content with that, you pitchforked me into what threatens to be a life-friendship with a pickpocket, to escape from whose advances I am obliged to tramp five miles, carrying a pormanteau which is much heavier than I had supposed possible. It only remains for me to become embroiled in an action for kidnapping, which I feel reasonably assured your aunt will bring against me.'

'Yes, and now I come to think of it, I remember that you said you were going to be married,' said Pen, quite unimpressed by these strictures. 'Will she be very angry with you?'

'I hope she will be so very angry that she will wish never to see my face again,' said Sir Richard calmly. 'In fact, brat, that reflection so far outweighs all other considerations that I forgive you the rest.'

'I think you are a very odd sort of person,' said Pen. 'Why did you ask her to marry you, if you did not wish to?'

'I didn't. During the past two days that is the only folly I have not committed.'

'Well, why did you mean to ask her, then?'

'You should know.'

'But you are a man! No one could make you do anything you did not choose to do!'

'They came mighty near it. If you had not dropped out of the window into my arms, I have little doubt that I should at this moment be receiving the congratulations of my acquaintance.'

'Well, I must say I do not think you are at all just to me, then, to call me a pestilent child! I saved you—though, indeed, I didn't know it—from a horrid fate.'

'True. But need I have been saved in a noisome stage-coach?'

'That was part of the adventure. Besides, I explained to you at the outset why I was travelling on the stage. You must own that we are having a very exciting time! And, what is more, you have had more adventure than I, for you actually shared a room with a real thief!'

'So I did,' said Sir Richard, apparently much struck by this circumstance.

'And I can plainly see a cottage ahead of us, so I expect we have reached Colerne,' she said triumphantly.

In a few moments, she was found to have been right. They walked into the village, and fetched up at the best-looking inn.

'Now, what particular lie shall we tell here?' asked Sir Richard.

'A wheel came off our post-chaise,' replied Pen promptly.

'Are you never at a loss?' he enquired, regarding her in some amusement.

'Well, to tell you the truth I haven't had very much experience,' she confided.

'Believe me, no one would suspect that.'

'No, I must say I think I was quite born to be a vaga-bond,' she said seriously.

The story of the faulty wheel was accepted by the land-lord of the Green Man without question. If he thought it strange that the travellers should have left the main high-way to brave the perils of rough country lanes, his mild surprise was soon dissipated by the announcement that they were on their way to Queen Charlton, and had attempted to find a shorter road. He said that they would have done better to have followed the Bristol road to Cold Ashton, but that perhaps they were strangers in these parts?

'Precisely,' said Sir Richard. 'But we are going to visit friends at Queen Charlton, and we wish to hire some sort of a vehicle to carry us there.'

The smile faded from the landlord's face when he heard this, and he shook his head. There were no vehicles for hire at Colerne. There was, in fact, only one suitable car-riage, and that his own gig. 'Which I'd be pleased to let out to your honour if I had but a man to send with it. But the lads is all out haymaking, and I can't go myself. Maybe the blacksmith could see what's to be done to patch up your chaise, sir?'

'Quite useless!' said Sir Richard truthfully. 'The wheel is past repairing. Moreover, I instructed my postilion to ride back to Wroxhall. What will you take for lending your gig to me without a man to go with it?'

'Well, sir, it ain't that so much, but how will I get it back?'

'Oh, one of Sir Jasper's grooms will drive it back!' said Pen. 'You need have no fear on that score!'

'Would that be Sir Jasper Luttrell, sir?'

'Yes, indeed, we are going on a visit to him.'

The landlord was plainly shaken. Sir Jasper was appar-ently well-known to him; on the other hand Sir Richard was not. He cast him a doubtful, sidelong look, and slowly shook his head.

'Well, if you won't let out your gig on hire, I suppose I shall have to buy it,' said Sir Richard.

'Buy my gig, sir?' gasped the landlord, staggered.

'And the horse too, of course,' added Sir Richard, pull-ing out his purse.

The landlord blinked at him. 'Well, I'm sure, sir! If that's the way it is, I don't know but what I could let you drive the gig over yourself—seeing as how you're a friend of Sir Jasper. Come to think of it, I won't be needing it for a couple of days. Only you'll have to rest the old horse afore you send him back, mind!'

Sir Richard raised no objection to this, and after coming to terms with an ease which led to the landlord's expressing the wish that there were more gentlemen like Sir Richard to be met with, the travellers had only to wait until the cob had been harnessed to the gig, and led round to the front of the inn.

The gig was neither smart nor well-sprung, and the cob's gait was more sure than swift, but Pen was delighted with the whole equipage. She sat perched up beside Sir Richard, enjoying the hot sunshine, and pointing out to him the manifold superiorities of the Somerset countryside over any other county.

They did not reach Queen Charlton until dusk, since the lay to it was circuitous, and often very rough. When they came within sight of the village, Sir Richard said: 'Well, brat, what now? Am I to drive you to Sir Jasper Luttrell's house?'

Pen, who had become rather silent during the last five miles of their drive, said with a little gasp: 'I have been thinking that perhaps it would be better if I sent a message in the morning! It is not Piers, you know, but, though I did not think of her at the time, it—it has occurred to me that perhaps Lady Luttrell may not perfectly understand . . .'

Her voice died away unhappily. She was revived by Sir Richard's saying in matter-of-fact tones: 'A very good notion. We will drive to an inn.'

'The George was always accounted the best,' offered Pen. 'I have never actually been inside it, but my father was used to say its cellars were excellent.'

The George was discovered to be an ancient half-timbered hostelry with beamed ceilings, and wainscoted parlours. It was a rambling house, with a large yard, and many chintz-hung bedrooms. There was no difficulty in procuring a private parlour, and by the time Pen had washed the dust of the roads from her face, and unpacked the cloak-bag, her spirits, which had sunk unaccountably, had begun to lift again. Dinner was served in the parlour, and neither the landlord·nor his wife seemed to recognize in the golden-haired stripling the late Mr Creed's tomboyish little girl.

'If only my aunt does not discover me before I have found Piers!' Pen said, helping herself to some more raspberries.

'We will circumvent her. But touching the question of Piers, do you—er—suppose that he will be able to extricate you from your personal difficulties?'

'Well, he will have to, if I marry him, won't he?'

'Undoubtedly. But—you must not think me an incorrigible wet blanket—it is not precisely easy to be married at a moment's notice.'

'Isn't it? I didn't know,' said Pen innocently. 'Oh well, I dare say we shall fly to Gretna Green then! We used to think· that would be a splendid adventure.'

'Gretna Green in those clothes?' enquired Sir Richard, levelling his quizzing-glass at her.

'Well, no, I suppose not. But when Piers has explained it all to Lady Luttrell, I expect she will be able to get some proper clothes for me.'

'You do not entertain any doubts of Lady Luttrell's—er—receiving you as her prospective daughter-in-law?'

'Oh no! She was always most kind to me! Only I did think that perhaps it would be better if I saw Piers first.'

Sir Richard, who had so far allowed himself to be borne along resistless on the tide of this adventure, began to perceive that it would shortly be his duty to wait upon Lady Luttrell, and to give her an account of his dealings with Miss Creed. He glanced at that young lady, serenely finishing the last of the raspberries, and reflected, with a wry smile, that the task was not going to be an easy one.

A servant came in to clear away the dishes presently. Pen at once engaged him in conversation and elicited the news that Sir Jasper Luttrell was away from home.

'Oh! But not Mr Piers Luttrell?'

'No, sir, I saw Mr Piers yesterday. Going to Keynsham, he was. I do hear as he has a young gentleman staying with him—a Lunnon gentleman, by all accounts.'

'Oh!' Pen's voice sounded rather blank. As soon as the man had gone away, she said: 'Did you hear that, sir? It makes it just a little awkward, doesn't it?'

'Very awkward,' agreed Sir Richard. 'It seems as though we have now to eliminate the gentleman from London.'

'I wish we could. For I am sure my aunt will guess that I have come home, and if she finds me before I have found Piers, I am utterly undone.'

'But she will not find you. She will only find me.'

'Do you think you will be able to fob her off?'

'Oh, I think so!' Sir Richard said negligently. 'After all, she would scarcely expect you to be travelling in my company, would she? I hardly think she will demand to see my nephew.'

'No, but what if she does?' asked Pen, having no such dependence on her aunt's forbearing.

Sir Richard smiled rather sardonically. 'I am not, perhaps, the best person in the world of whom to make—ah—impertinent demands.'

Pen's eyes lit with sudden laughter. 'Oh, I do hope you will talk to her like that, and look at her just *so!* And if she brings Fred with her, he will be quite overcome, I dare say, to meet you face to face. For you must know that he admires you excessively. He tries to tie his cravat in a Wyndham Fall, even!'

'That, in itself, I find an impertinence,' said Sir Richard.

She nodded, and lifted a hand to her own cravat. 'What do you think of mine, sir?'

'I have carefully refrained from thinking about it at all. Do you really wish to know?'

'But I have arranged it just as you did!'

'Good God!' said Sir Richard faintly. 'My poor deluded child!'

'You are teasing me! At least it was not ill enough tied to make you rip it off my neck as you did when you first met me!'

'You will recall that we left the inn in haste this morning,' he explained.

'I am persuaded *that* would not have weighed with you. But you put me in mind of a very important matter. You paid my reckoning there.'

'Don't let that worry you, I beg.'

'I am determined to pay everything for myself,' Pen said firmly. 'It would be a shocking piece of impropriety if I were to be beholden for money to a stranger.'

'True. I had not thought of that.'

She looked up with her sudden bright look of enquiry. 'You are laughing at me again!'

He showed her a perfectly grave countenance. 'Laughing? I?'

'I know very well you are. You may make your mouth prim, but I have noticed several times that you laugh with your eyes.'

'Do I? I beg your pardon!'

'Well, you need not, for I like it. I would not have come all this way with you if you had not had such smiling eyes. Isn't it odd how one knows if one can trust a person, even if he is drunk?'

'Very odd,' he said.

She was hunting fruitlessly through her pockets. 'Where can I have put my purse? Oh, I think I must have put it in my overcoat!'

She had flung this garment down on a chair, upon first entering the parlour, and stepped across the room to feel in the capacious pockets.

'Are you seriously proposing to count a few miserable shillings into my hand?'

'Yes, indeed I am. Oh, here it is!' She pulled out a leather purse with a ring round its neck, from one pocket, stared at it, and exclaimed: 'This is not my purse!'

Sir Richard looked at it through his glass. 'Isn't it? It is certainly not mine, I assure you.'

'It is very heavy. I wonder how it can have come into my pocket? Shall I open it?'

'By all means. Are you quite sure it is not your own?'

'Oh yes, quite!' She moved to the table, tugging at the ring. It was a little hard to pull off, but she managed it after one or two tugs, and shook out into the palm of her hand a diamond necklace that winked and glittered in the light of the candles.

'*Richard!*' gasped Miss Creed, startled into forgetting the proprieties again. 'Oh, I beg your pardon! But look!'

'I am looking, and you have no need to beg my pardon. I have been calling you Pen these two days.'

'Oh, that is another matter, because you are so much older!'

He looked at her somewhat enigmatically. 'Am I? Well, never mind. Do I understand that this gaud does not belong to you?'

'Good gracious, no! I never saw it before in my life!'

'Oh!' said Sir Richard. 'Well, it is always agreeable to have problems solved. Now we know why your friend Mr Yarde had no fear of the Bow Street Runner.'

◄§ *Chapter VI* §►

PEN let the necklace slip through her fingers on to the table. 'You mean that he stole it, and then—and then put it in *my* pocket? But, sir, this is terrible? Why— why, that Runner will next come after us!'

'I think it more likely that Mr Yarde will come after us.'

'Good God!' Pen said, quite pale with dismay. 'What are we to do?'

He smiled rather maliciously. 'Didn't you desire to meet with a real adventure?'

'Yes, but—— Oh, do not be absurd and teasing, I beg of you! What shall we do with the necklace? Couldn't we throw it away somewhere, or hide it in a ditch?'

'We could, of course, but it would surely be a trifle unfair to the owner?'

'I don't care about that,' confessed Pen. 'It would be dreadful to be arrested for thieving, and I know we shall be!'

'Oh, I trust not!' Sir Richard said. He straightened the necklace, where it lay on the table, and looked down at it with a slight frown creasing his brow. 'Yes,' he said meditatively. 'I have seen you before. Now, *where* have I seen you before?'

'Do please put it away!' begged Pen. 'Only think if a servant were to come into the room!'

He picked it up. 'My lamentable memory! Alas, my lamentable memory! Where, oh, *where* have I seen you?'

'Dear sir, if Jimmy Yarde finds us, he will very likely cut our throats to get the necklace back!'

'On the contrary, I have his word for it that he is opposed to all forms of violence.'

'But when he does not discover it in my pocket, where he placed it—and now I come to think of it, he actually had my coat in his hands—he must guess that we have discovered it!'

'Very likely he will, but I cannot see what profit there would be in his cutting our throats.' Sir Richard restored the necklace to its leather purse, and dropped it into his pocket. 'We have now nothing to do but to await the arrival of Jimmy Yarde. Perhaps—who knows?—we may induce him to divulge the ownership of the necklace. Meanwhile, this parlour is very stuffy, and the night remarkably fine. Do you care to stroll out with me to admire the stars, brat?'

'I suppose,' said Pen defiantly, 'that you think I am very poor-spirited!'

'Very,' agreed Sir Richard, his eyes glinting under their heavy lids.

'I am not afraid of anything,' Pen announced. 'Merely, I am *shocked!*'

'A waste of time, believe me. Are you coming?'

'Yes, but it seems to me as though you have put a live coal in your pocket! What if some dishonest person were to steal it from you?'

'Then we shall be freed from all responsibility. Come along!'

She followed him out into the warm night. He appeared to have banished all thought of the necklace from his mind. He pointed various constellations out to her, and, drawing her hand through his arm, strolled with her down the street, past the last straggling cottages, into a lane redolent of meadowsweet.

'I suppose I was poor-spirited,' Pen confided presently. 'Shall you feel obliged to denounce poor Jimmy Yarde to the Runner?'

'I hope,' said Sir Richard dryly, 'that Mr Piers Luttrell is a gentleman of resolute character.'

'Why?'

'That he may be able to curb your somewhat reckless friendliness.'

'Well, I haven't seen him for five years, but it was always I who thought of things to do.'

'That is what I feared. Where does he live?'

'Oh, about two miles farther down this road! *My* home is on the other side of the village. Should you like to see it?'

'Immensely, but not at the moment. We will now retrace our steps, for it is time that you were in bed.'

'I shan't sleep a wink.'

'I trust that you are mistaken, my good child—in fact, I am reasonably certain that you are.'

'And to add to everything,' said Pen, unheeding, 'Piers has got a horrid man staying with him! I don't know what is to be done.'

'In the morning,' said Sir Richard soothingly, 'we will attend to all these difficulties.'

'In the morning, very likely, Aunt Almeria will have discovered me.'

On this gloomy reflection, they retraced their steps to the inn. Its shuttered windows cast golden gleams out into the quiet street, several of them standing open to let in the cool night air. Just as they were about to pass one of them on their way to the inn door, a voice spoke inside the room, and to her astonishment, Sir Richard suddenly gripped Pen's arm, and brought her to a dead halt. She started to enquire the reason for this sudden stop, but his hand across her mouth choked back the words.

The voice from within the house said with a slight stammer: 'You c-can't come up to C-Crome Hall, I tell you! It's b-bad enough as it is. G-Good God, man, if anyone were to see me sneaking off to meet you here they'd p-precious soon smell a rat!'

A more robust voice answered: 'Maybe I've been smelling rats myself, my young buck. Who was it foisted a partner on to me, eh? Were the pair of ye meaning to cheat Horace Trimble? Were ye, my bonny boy?'

'You fool, you let yourself be b-bubbled!' the stammerer

said furiously. 'Then you c-come here—enough to ruin everything! I tell you I d-daren't say! And don't come up to C-Crome Hall again, damn you! I'll m-meet you tomorrow, in the spinney down the road. 'Sblood, he can't have g-gone far! Why don't you go to B-Bristol if he didn't b-break back to London? Instead of c-coming here to insult me!'

'I insult you! By the powers, that's rich!' A full-throated laugh followed the words, and the sound of a chair being dashed back on a wooden floor.

'Damn your impudence! You've b-bungled everything, and now you c-come blustering to me! *You* were to arrange everything! *I* was to l-leave all to you! Finely you've ar-ranged it! And n-now you expect m-me to set all to rights!'

'Softly, my buck! softly! You're crowing mighty loud, but I did my part of the business all right and tight. It was the man you were so set on that bubbled me, and that makes me think, d'ye hear? It makes me think mighty hard. Maybe you'd better think too—and if you've a notion in your head that Horace Trimble's a green 'un, get rid of it! See?'

'Hush, for G-God's sake! You d-don't know who may be listening! I'll m-meet you to-morrow, at eleven, if I c-can shake off y-young Luttrell. We must think what's to be done!'

A door opened and was hastily shut again. Sir Richard pulled Pen back into the shadows beyond the window, and, a moment later, a slight, cloaked figure came out of the inn, and strode swiftly away into the darkness.

The warning pressure on Pen's arm held her silent, al-though she was by this time agog with excitement. Sir Richard waited until the dwindling sound of footsteps had died in the distance, and then strolled on with Pen's hand still tucked in his arm, past the open window to the inn-door. Not until they stood in their own parlour again did Pen allow herself to speak, but as soon as the door was shut behind them, she exclaimed: 'What did it mean? He spoke of "Young Luttrell"—did you hear him? It must be the man who is staying with him! But who was the other man, and what were they talking about?'

Sir Richard did not appear to be attending very closely. He was standing by the table, a frown between his eyes, and his mouth rather grim. Suddenly his gaze shifted to Pen's face, but what he said seemed to her incomprehensible. 'Of course!' he muttered softly. 'So *that* was it!'

'Oh, *do* tell me!' begged Pen. '*What* was it, and why did you stop when you heard the stammering-man speak? Do you—is it possible that you know him?'

'Very well indeed,' replied Sir Richard.

'Good heavens! And it is he who is visiting Piers! Dear sir, does it seem to you that everything is becoming a trifle awkward?'

'Extremely so,' said Sir Richard.

'Well, that is what I thought,' said Pen. 'First we are saddled with a stolen necklace, and now we discover that a friend of yours is staying with Piers!'

'Oh no, we do not!' said Sir Richard. 'That young gentleman is no friend of mine! Nor, I fancy, is his presence in this neighbourhood unconnected with that necklace. If I do not mistake, Pen, we have become enmeshed in a plot from which it will take all my ingenuity to extricate us.'

'I have ingenuity too,' said Miss Creed, affronted.

'Not a scrap,' responded Sir Richard calmly.

She swallowed this, saying in a small voice: 'Very well, if I haven't, I haven't, but I wish you will explain.'

'I feel sure you do,' said Sir Richard: 'But the truth is that I cannot. Not only does it appear to me to be a matter of uncommon delicacy, but it is also for the moment—a little obscure.'

She sighed. 'It does not seem fair, because it was I who found the necklace, after all! Who is the stammering-man? You may just as well tell me that, because Piers will, you know.'

'Certainly. The stammering-man is the Honourable Beverley Brandon.'

'Oh! I don't know him,' said Pen, rather disappointed.

'You are to be congratulated.'

'Is he an enemy of yours?'

'An enemy! No!'

'Well, you seem to dislike him very cordially.'

'That does not make him my enemy. To be exact, he is the younger brother of the lady to whom I was to have been betrothed.'

Pen looked aghast. 'Good God, sir, can he have come in search of you?'

'No, nothing of that kind. Indeed, Pen, I can't tell you more, for the rest is conjecture.' He met her disappointed look, and smiled down at her, gently pinching her chin. 'Poor Pen! Forgive me!'

A little colour stole up to the roots of her hair. 'I do not mean to tease you. I expect you will tell me all about it when—when it isn't conjecture.'

'I expect I shall,' he agreed. 'But that will not be tonight, so be off with you to bed, child!'

She went, but was back again a few minutes later, round-eyed and breathless. 'Richard! He has found us! I have seen him! I am certain it was he!'

'Who?' he asked.

'Jimmy Yarde, of course! It was so hot in my room that I drew back the curtains to open the window, and the moon was so bright that I stood looking out for a minute. And there he was, directly below me! I could not mistake. And the worst is that I fear he saw me, for he drew back at once into the shadow of the house!'

'Did he indeed?' There was a gleam in Sir Richard's eye. 'Well, he is here sooner than I expected. A resourceful gentleman, Mr Jimmy Yarde!'

'But what are we going to do? I am not in the least afraid, but I should like to be told what you wish me to do!'

'That is very easily done. I wish you to exchange bed-chambers with me. Show yourself again at the window of your own room, if you like, but on no account pull back the blinds in mine. I have a very earnest desire to meet Mr Jimmy Yarde.'

Her dimples peeped. 'I see! like the fairy-story! "Oh, Grandma, what big teeth you have!" *What* an adventure we are having! But you will take care, won't you, sir?'

'I will.'

'And you will tell me all about it afterwards?'

'Perhaps.'

'If you don't,' said Pen, with deep feeling, 'it will be the most unjust thing imaginable!'

He laughed, and, seeing that there was no more to be got out of him, she went away again.

An hour later, the candlelight vanished from the upper room with the open casements and the undrawn blinds, but it was two hours before Mr Yarde's head appeared above the window-sill, and not a light shone in the village.

The moon, sailing across a sky of deepest sapphire, cast a bar of silver across the floor of the chamber, but left the four-poster bed in shadow. The ascent, by way of the porch-roof, a stout drain-pipe, and a gnarled branch of wistaria, had been easy, but Mr Yarde paused before swinging a leg over the sill. His eye, trying to penetrate the darkness, encountered a drab driving-coat, hanging over the back of a chair placed full in the shaft of moonlight. He knew that coat, and a tiny sigh escaped him. He hoisted himself up, and noiselessly slid into the room. He had left his shoes below, and his stockinged-feet made no sound on the floor, as he crept across it.

But there was no heavy leather sack-purse in the pocket of the driving-coat.

He was disappointed, but he had been prepared for disappointment. He stole out of the moonlight to the bedside, listening to the sound of quiet breathing. No tremor disturbed its regularity, and after listening to it for a few minutes, he bent, and began cautiously to slide his hand under the dimly-seen pillow. The other, his right, grasped a muffler, which could be readily clapped over a mouth opened to utter a startled cry.

The cry, hardly more than a croak, strangled at birth, was surprised out of himself, however, for, just as his sensitive fingers felt the object for which they were seeking, two iron hands seized him by the throat, and choked him.

He tore quite unavailingly at the hold, realizing through the drumming in his ears, the bursting of his veins, and the pain in his temples, that he had made a mistake, that the hands crushing the breath out of him certainly did not belong to any stripling.

Just as he seemed to himself to be losing possession of his senses, the grip slackened, and a voice he was learning to hate, said softly: 'Your error, Mr Yarde!'

He felt himself shaken and suddenly released, and, being quite powerless to help himself, fell to the floor and stayed there, making odd crowing noises as he got his wind back.

By the time he had recovered sufficiently to struggle on to one elbow, Sir Richard had cast off the coverlet, and sprung out of bed. He was dressed in his shirt and breeches, as Mr Yarde's suffused eyes saw, as soon as Sir Richard had relit the candle by his bed.

Sir Richard laid aside the tinder-box, and glanced down at Mr Yarde. Jimmy's vision was clearing; he was able to see that Sir Richard's lips had curled into a somewhat contemptuous smile. He began gingerly to massage his throat, which felt badly bruised, and waited for Sir Richard to speak.

'I warned you that I was a shockingly light sleeper,' Sir Richard said.

Jimmy cast him a malevolent look, but made no answer.

'Get up!' Sir Richard said. 'You may sit on that chair, Mr Yarde, for we are going to enjoy a heart-to-heart talk.'

Jimmy picked himself up. A glance in the direction of the window was enough to convince him that he would be intercepted before he could reach it. He sat down and drew the back of his hand across his brow.

'Don't let us misunderstand one another!' Sir Richard said. 'You came to find a certain diamond necklace, which you hid in my nephew's coat this morning. There are just three things I can do with you. I can deliver you up to the Law.'

'You can't prove I come to fork the necklace, guv'nor,' Jimmy muttered.

'You think not? We may yet see. Failing the Bow Street Runner—but I feel he would be happy to take you into custody—I fancy a gentleman of the name of Trimble—ah, Horace Trimble, if my memory serves!—would be even happier to relieve me of you.'

The mention of this name brought an expression of great uneasiness into Jimmy's sharp countenance. 'I don't know him! Never heard of any such cove!'

'Oh yes, I think you have!' said Sir Richard.

'I ain't done you any harm, guv'nor, nor intended any! I'll cap downright——'

'You needn't: I believe you.'

Jimmy's spirits began to lift. 'Dang me if I didn't say you was a leery cove! You wouldn't be hard on a cull!'

'That depends on the—er—cull. Which brings me, Mr
Yarde, to the third course I might—I say, might, Mr Yarde
—pursue. I can let you go.'

Jimmy gasped, swallowed, and muttered hoarsely: 'Spoke
like the gentry-cove you are, guv'nor!'

'Tell me what I want to know, and I will let you go,' said
Sir Richard.

A wary look came into Jimmy's eyes. 'Split, eh? Lord
bless you, there ain't anything to tell you!'

'It will perhaps make it easier for you if I inform you
that I am already aware that you have been working in—
somewhat uneasy partnership—with Mr Horace Trimble.'

'Cap'n Trimble,' corrected Jimmy.

'I should doubt it. He, I take it, is the—er—flash cull—
whom you referred to last night.'

'I don't deny it.'

'Furthermore,' said Sir Richard, 'the pair of you were
working for a young gentleman with a pronounced stammer.
Ah, for a Mr Brandon, to be precise.'

Jimmy had changed colour. 'Stow your whids and plant
'em!' he growled. 'You're too leery for me, see? Damme if
I know what your lay is!'

'That need not concern you. Think it over, Mr Yarde!
Will you be handed over to Captain Trimble, or do you
choose to go as you came, through that window?'

Jimmy sat for a moment, still gently rubbing his throat,
and looking sideways at Sir Richard. 'Damn all flash culls!'
he said at last. 'I'll whiddle the whole scrap. I ain't a bridle-
cull, see? What *you* calls the High Toby. That ain't my lay:
I'm a rum diver. Maybe I've touched the rattler now and
then, but I never went on the bridle-lay, not till a certain
gentry-cove, which we knows of, tempted me. And I wish I
hadn't, see? Five hundred Yellow Boys I was promised, but
not a grig will I get! He's a rare gager, that gentry-cove!
Dang me if I ever works with such again! He's a bad 'un,
guv'nor, you can lay your last megg on that!'

'I am aware. Go on!'

'There's an old gentry-mort going to Bath, see? Lord love
you, she was his own mother! Now, that's what I don't hold
with, but it ain't none of my business. Me and Cap'n
Trimble holds up the chaise by Calne, or thereabouts. The

necklace is in a hiding-place behind one of the squabs—ah, and rum squabs they was, all made out of red silk!'

'Mr Brandon knew of this hiding-place, and told you?'

'Lord love you, he made naught of that, guv'nor! We was to snaffle the necklace, and pike on the bean, see?'

'Not entirely.'

'Lope off as fast we could. Now, I don't hold with violence, any gait, nor that stammering young chub neither. But Cap'n Trimble looses off his pops, and one of the outriders gets it in the wing. While the Cap'n's a-covering the coves with his pops, I dubs the jigger—opens the door— and finds a couple of gentry-morts, hollering fit to rouse the countryside. I don't take nothing but the necklace, see? I'm a peevy cove, and this ain't my lay. I don't like it. We pikes, and Cap'n Trimble he pushes his pop into my belly, and says to hand over the necklace. Well, I does so. I'm a peevy cove. I don't hold with violence. Now, the lay is that we take them sparklers to that flash young boman prigs, which is taking cover down here, with a regular green 'un, which he gets to know at Oxford. All's Bob, then! But I'm leery, see? Seems to me I'm working with a flash file, and if he makes off with the sparklers, which I suspicion he will, my young chub don't tip me my earnest. I forks the cove. Bristol's the place for me, I thinks, and I gets on to the werry same rattler which you and your nevvy's a-riding in. When that harman from Bow Street comes along, I thinks there's a fastner out for me, and I tips the cole to Adam Tiler, as you might say.'

'You placed the necklace in my nephew's pocket?'

'That's it, guv'nor. No harman won't suspicion a young shaver like him, I thinks. But you and he lopes off unbeknownst, and I comes to this place. Oh, I knew you was a peevy cull! So I touts the case, see?'

'No.'

'Runs my winkers over the house,' said Jimmy impatiently. 'I see your young shaver at this werry window— I should have remembered that you was a peevy cove, guv'nor.'

'You should indeed. However, you have told me what I wish to know, and you are now at liberty to—er—pike on the bean.'

'Spoke like the gentry-cove you are!' said Jimmy hoarsely. 'I'm off! And no hard feelings!'

It did not take him long to climb out of the window. He waved his hand with cheerful impudence, and disappeared from Sir Richard's sight.

Sir Richard undressed, and went to bed.

The boots, who brought up his blue coat in the morning, and his top-boots, was a little surprised to find that he had exchanged bedchambers with his supposed nephew, but accepted his explanation that he disliked his original apartment with only an inward shrug. The Quality, he knew, were full of whims and oddities.

Sir Richard looked though his glass at his coat, which he had sent downstairs to be pressed, and said he felt sure the unknown presser had done his best. He next levelled the eyeglass at his top-boots, and sighed. But when he was asked if there were anything amiss, he said No, nothing: it was good for a man to be removed occasionally from civilisation.

The top-boots stood side by side, glossily black and without a speck upon them of dust, or mud. Sir Richard shook his head sadly, and sighed again. He was missing his man, Biddle, in whose ingenious brain lay the secret of polishing boots so that you could see your face reflected in them.

But to anyone unacquainted with the art of Biddle Sir Richard's appearance, when he presently descended the stairs, left little to be desired. There were no creases in the blue coat, his cravat would have drawn approval from Mr Brummell himself, and his hair was brushed into that state of cunning disorder known as the Windswept Style.

As he rounded the bend in the stair-case, he heard Miss Creed exchanging friendly salutations with a stranger. The stranger's voice betrayed his identity to Sir Richard, whose eyes managed, for all their sleepiness, to take very good stock of Captain Trimble.

Sir Richard came down the last flight in a leisurely fashion, and interrupted Miss Creed's harmless remarks, by saying in his most languid tone: 'My good boy, I wish you will not converse with strangers. It is a most lamentable habit. Rid yourself of it, I beg!'

Pen looked round in surprise. It occurred to her that she

had not known that her protector could sound so haughty, or look so—yes, so insufferably proud!

Captain Trimble turned too. He was a fleshy man, with a coarse, florid sort of good-looks, and a rather loud taste in dress. He said jovially: 'Oh, I don't mind the lad's talking to me!'

Sir Richard's hand sought his quizzing-glass, and raised it. It was said in *haut-ton* circles that the two deadliest weapons against all forms of pretension were Mr Brummell's lifted eyebrow, and Sir Richard Wyndham's quizzing-glass. Captain Trimble, though thick-skinned, was left in no doubt of its blighting message. His cheeks grew dark, and his jaw began to jut belligerently.

'And who might you be, my fine buck?' he demanded.

'I might be a number of different persons,' drawled Sir Richard.

Pen's eyes were getting rounder and rounder, for it appeared to her that this new and haughty Sir Richard was deliberately trying to provoke Captain Trimble into quarrelling with him.

For a moment it seemed as though he would succeed. Captain Trimble started forward, with his fists clenched, and an ugly look on his face. But just as he was about to speak, his expression changed, and he stopped in his tracks, and ejaculated: 'You're Beau Wyndham! Well, I'll be damned!'

'The prospect,' said Sir Richard, bored, 'leaves me unmoved.'

With the discovery of Sir Richard's identity, the desire to come to blows with him seemed to have deserted the Captain. He gave a somewhat unconvincing laugh, and said that there was no offence.

The quizzing-glass focused upon his waistcoat. A shudder visibly shook Sir Richard. 'You mistake—believe me, you mistake, sir. That waistcoat is an offence in itself.'

'Oh, I know you dandies!' said the Captain waggishly. 'You're full of quips. But we shan't quarrel over a little thing like that. Oh, no!'

The quizzing-glass fell. 'I am haunted by waistcoats,' Sir Richard complained. 'There was something with tobine stripes at Reading, horrible to any person of taste. There was a mustard-coloured nightmare at—Wroxham was it? No. I fancy, if memory serves me, Wroxham was rendered hideous by a catskin disaster with pewter buttons. The mustard-coloured nightmare came later. And now, to crown all——'

'Catskin?' interrupted Captain Trimble, his eyes fixed intently upon that disdainful countenance. 'Catskin, did you say?'

'Pray do not keep on repeating it!' said Sir Richard. 'The very thought of it——'

'Look'ee, sir, I'm by way of being interested in a catskin waistcoat myself! Are you sure it was at Wroxham you saw it?'

'A catskin waistcoat on its way to Bristol,' said Sir Richard dreamily.

'Bristol! Damme, I never thought—I thank you, Sir Richard! I thank you very much indeed!' said Captain Trimble, and plunged down the passage leading to the stable-yard at the back of the inn.

Sir Richard watched him go, a faint, sweet smile on his lips. 'There, now!' he murmured. 'An impetuous gentleman, I fear. Let it be a lesson to you, brat, not to confide too much in strangers.'

'I didn't!' said Pen. 'I merely——'

'But he did,' Sir Richard said. 'A few chance words let fall from my tongue, and our trusting acquaintance is already calling for his horse. I want my breakfast.'

'But why have you sent him to Bristol?' Pen demanded.

'Well, I wanted to get rid of him,' he replied, strolling into the parlour.

'I thought you were trying to pick a quarrel with him.'

'I was, but he unfortunately recognized me. A pity. It would have given me a good deal of pleasure to have put him to sleep. However, I dare say it has all turned out for the best. I should have been obliged to have tied him up somewhere, which would have been a nuisance, and might have led to future complications. I shall be obliged to leave you for a short space this morning, by the way.'

'Do, please, sir, stop being provoking!' begged Pen. 'Did you see Jimmy Yarde last night, and what happened?'

'Oh yes, I saw him! Really, I don't think anything of particular moment happened.'

'He didn't try to murder you?'

'Nothing so exciting. He tried merely to recover the diamonds. When he—er—failed to do so, we enjoyed a short conversation, after which he left the inn, as unobtrusively as he had entered it.'

'Through the window, you mean. Well, I am glad you let him go, for I could not help liking him. But what are we going to do now, if you please?'

'We are now going to eliminate Beverley,' replied Sir Richard, carving the ham.

'Oh, the stammering-man! How shall we do that? He sounded very disagreeable, but I don't think we should eliminate him in a rough way, do you?'

'By no means. Leave the matter in my hands, and I will engage for it that he will be eliminated without the least pain or inconvenience to anyone.'

'Yes, but then there is the necklace,' Pen pointed out. 'I feel that before we attend to anything else we ought to get rid of it. Only fancy if you were to be found with it in your pocket!'

'Very true. But I have arranged for that. The necklace belongs to Beverley's mother, and he shall restore it to her.'

Pen laid down her knife and fork. 'Then that explains it all! I thought that stammering-man had more to do with it than you would tell me. I suppose he hired Jimmy Yarde, and that other person, to steal the necklace?' She wrinkled her brow. 'I don't wish to say rude things about your friends, Richard, but it seems to me very wrong of him— most improper!'

'Most,' he agreed.

'Even *dastardly!*'

'I think we might call it dastardly.'

'Well, that is what it seems to me. I see now that there is a great deal in what Aunt Almeria says. She considers that there are terrible pitfalls in Society.'

Sir Richard shook his head sadly. 'Alas, too true!'

'And vice,' said Pen awfully. 'Profligacy, and extravagance, you know.'

'I know.'

She picked up her knife and fork again. 'It must be very exciting,' she said enviously.

'Far be it from me to destroy your illusions, but I feel I should inform you that stealing one's mother's diamonds is not the invariable practice of members of the *haut ton*.'

'Of course not. I know *that!*' said Pen with dignity. She added in persuasive tones: 'Shall I come with you when you go to meet the stammering-man?'

'No,' answered Sir Richard, not mincing matters.

'I thought you would say that. I wish I were really a man.'

'I still should not take you with me.'

'Then you would be very selfish, and disagreeable, and altogether abominable!' declared Pen roundly.

'I think I am,' reflected Sir Richard, recalling his sister's homily.

The large eyes softened instantly, and as they scanned Sir Richard's face a slight flush mounted to Pen's cheeks. She bent over her plate again, saying in a gruff little voice: 'No, you are not. You are very kind, and obliging, and I am sorry I teased you.'

Sir Richard looked at her. He seemed to be about to speak, but she forestalled him, adding buoyantly: 'And when I tell Piers how well you have looked after me, he will be most grateful to you, I assure you.'

'Will he?' said Sir Richard, at his dryest. 'I am afraid I was forgetting Piers.'

⋖§ *Chapter VII* §⋗

THE spinney down the road, referred to by Beverley in his assignation with Captain Trimble, was not hard to locate. A careless question put to one of the ostlers elicited the information that it formed part of the grounds of Crome Hall. Leaving Pen to keep a sharp look-out for signs of an invasion by her relatives, Sir Richard set out shortly be-

fore eleven o'clock, to keep Captain Trimble's appointment.
The impetuous Captain had indeed called for his horse,
and had set off in the direction of Bristol, with his cloak-
bag strapped on to the saddle. He had paid his shot, so
it did not seem as though he contemplated returning to
Queen Charlton.

At the end of a ten-minute walk, Sir Richard reached
the outskirts of the spinney. A gap in the hedge showed
him a trodden path through the wood, and he followed
this, glad to be out of the strong sunlight. The path led to
a small clearing, where a tiny stream ran between clumps
of rose-bay willow herb in full flower. Here a slightly built
young gentleman, dressed in the extreme of fashion, was
switching pettishly with his cane at the purple heads of the
willow-herb. The points of his collar were so monstrous as
to make it almost impossible for him to turn his head, and
his coat fitted him so tightly that it seemed probable that it
must have needed the combined efforts of three strong
men to force him into it. Very tight pantaloons of a delicate
biscuit-hue encased his rather spindly legs, and a pair of
tasselled Hessians sneered at their sylvan surroundings.

The Honourable Beverley Brandon was not unlike his
sister Melissa, but the classic cast of his features was
spoiled by a pasty complexion, and a weakness about
mouth and chin not shared by Melissa. He turned, as he
heard the sound of approaching footsteps, and started
forward, only to be fetched up short by the sight, not of
Captain Trimble's burly figure, but of a tall, well-built
gentleman in whom he had not the slightest difficulty in
recognizing his prospective brother-in-law.

He let his malacca cane drop from suddenly nerveless
fingers. His pale eyes stared at Sir Richard. 'W-w-what the
d-devil?' he stammered.

Sir Richard advanced unhurriedly across the clearing.
'Good-morning, Beverley,' he said, in his pleasant, drawl-
ing voice.

'W-what are *you* d-doing here?' Beverley demanded, the
wildest surmises chasing one another through his brain.

'Oh, enjoying the weather, Beverly, enjoying the weather!
And you?'

'I'm staying with a friend. F-fellow I knew up at Oxford!'

'Indeed?' Sir Richard's quizzing-glass swept the glade, as though in search of Mr Brandon's host. 'A delightful rendezvous! One would almost suspect you of having an assignation with someone!'

'N-no such thing! I was j-just taking the air!'

The quizzing-glass was levelled at him. Sir Richard's pained eye ran over his person. 'Putting the countryside to scorn, Beverley? Strange that you who care so much about your appearance should achieve such lamentable results! Now, Cedric cares nothing for his, but—er—always looks the gentleman.'

'You have a d-damned unpleasant tongue, Richard, b-but you needn't think I'll put up with it j-just because you've known me for y-years!'

'And how,' enquired Sir Richard, faintly interested, 'do you propose to put a curb on my tongue?'

Beverley glared at him. He knew quite as well as Captain Trimble that Sir Richard's exquisite tailoring and languid bearing were deceptive; that he sparred regularly with Gentleman Jackson, and was accounted one of the best amateur heavyweights in England. 'W-what are you d-doing here?' he reiterated weakly.

'I came to keep your friend Trimble's appointment with you,' said Sir Richard, removing a caterpillar from his sleeve. Ignoring a startled oath from Mr Brandon, he added: 'Captain Trimble—by the way, you must tell me sometime where he acquired that unlikely title—found himself obliged to depart for Bristol this morning. Rather a hasty person, one is led to infer.'

'D-damn you, Richard, you mean you sent him off! W-what do you know about Trimble, and why did———'

'Yes, I fear that some chance words of mine may perhaps have influenced him. There was a man in a catskin waistcoat—dear me, there seems to be a fatal spell attached to that waistcoat! You look quite pale, Beverley.'

Mr Brandon had indeed changed colour. He shouted: 'S-stop it! So Yarde split, d-did he? Well, w-what the d-devil has it to do with you, hey?'

'Altruism, Beverley, sheer altruism. You see, your friend Yarde—you know, I cannot congratulate you on your choice of tools—saw fit to hand the Brandon diamonds into my keeping.'

Mr Brandon looked quite stupefied. 'Handed them to *you?* Yarde d-did that? B-but how d-did you know he had them? How *c-could* you have known?'

'Oh, I didn't!' said Sir Richard, taking snuff.

'B-but if you didn't know, why d-did you constrain him —oh, what the d-devil does all this m-mean?'

'You have it wrong, my dear Beverley. I didn't constrain him. I was, in fact, an unwitting partner in the crime. I should perhaps explain that Mr Yarde was being pursued by a Runner from Bow Street.'

'A Runner!' Mr Brandon began to look ashen. 'Who set them on? G-god damn it, I——'

'I have no idea. Presumably your respected father, possibly Cedric. In Mr Yarde's picturesque but somewhat obscure language, he—er—tipped the cole to Adam Tiler. Have I that right?'

'How the d-devil should I know?' snapped Brandon.

'You must forgive me. You seem to me to be so familiar with—er—thieves and—er—swashbucklers, that I assumed that you were conversant also with thieving cant.'

'D-don't keep on talking about thieves!' Beverley said, stamping his foot.

'It is an ugly word, isn't it?' agreed Sir Richard.

Beverley ground his teeth, but said in a blustering voice: 'Very well! I *did* t-take the damned necklace! If you m-must know, I'm d-done up, ruined! But you n-needn't take that psalm-singing t-tone with me! If I d-don't sell it, my father will soon enough!'

'I don't doubt you, Beverley, but I must point out to you that you have forgotten one trifling circumstance in your very engaging explanation. The necklace belongs to your father.'

'I c-consider it's family property. It's folly to keep it w-when we're all of us aground! D-damn it, I was forced to take the thing! *You* don't know w-what it is to be in the p-power of a d-damned cent-per-cent! If the old m-man would have p-parted, this wouldn't have happened! I told him a m-month ago I hadn't a feather to fly with, but the old fox wouldn't c-come up to scratch. I tell you, I've no c-compunction! He lectured me as though he himself w-weren't under hatches, which, by God, he is! Deep b-basset's been *his* ruin; m-myself, I prefer to g-go to per- dition with a d-dice-box.' He gave a reckless laugh, and suddenly sat down on the moss-covered stump of a felled tree, and buried his face in his hands.

'You are forgetting women, wine, and horses,' said Sir Richard unemotionally. 'They also have played not incon- siderable rôles in this dramatic progress of yours. Three years ago you were once again under the hatches. I forget what it cost to extricate you from your embarrassments, but I do seem to recall that you gave your word you would not again indulge in——er——quite so many excesses.'

'Well, I'm n-not expecting *you* to raise the w-wind for me this time,' said Beverley sulkily.

'What's the figure?' Sir Richard asked.

'How should I know? I'm n-not a damned b-banking clerk! T-twelve thousand or so, I dare say. If you hadn't spoiled my g-game, I c-could have settled the whole thing.'

'You delude yourself. When I encountered your friend Yarde he was making for the coast with the diamonds in his pocket.'

'Where are they now?'

'In my pocket,' Sir Richard said coolly.

Beverley lifted his head. 'L-listen, Richard, you're not a b-bad fellow! Who's to know you ever had the d-diamonds in your hands? It ain't your affair: give them to m-me, and forget all about the rest! I swear I'll n-never breathe a w-word to a soul!'

'Do you know, Beverley, you nauseate me? As for giv- ing you the diamonds, I have come here with exactly that purpose.'

Beverley's hand shot out. 'I d-don't care what you think of m-me! Only hand the n-necklace over!'

'Certainly,' Sir Richard said, taking the leather purse out of his pocket. 'But you, Beverley, will give them back to your mother.'

Beverley stared at him. 'I'll be d-damned if I will! You fool, how could I?'

'You may concoct what plausible tale you please: I will

even engage myself to lend it my support. But you will give back the necklace.'

A slight sneer disfigured Beverley's face. 'Oh, j-just as you l-like! Hand it over!'

Sir Richard tossed the purse over to him. 'Ah, Beverley! Perhaps I should make it clear to you that if, when I return to town, it has not been restored to Lady Saar I shall be compelled to—er—split on you.'

'You won't!' Beverley said, stowing the purse away in an inner pocket. 'M-mighty pretty behaviour for a b-brother-in-law!'

'But I am not your brother-in-law,' said Sir Richard gently.

'Oh, you n-needn't think I don't know you're g-going to m-marry Melissa! Our scandals will become yours too. I think you'll keep your m-mouth shut.'

'I am always sorry to disappoint expectations, but I have not the smallest intention of marrying your sister,' said Sir Richard, taking another pinch of snuff.

Beverley's jaw dropped. 'You d-don't mean she w-wouldn't have you?'

'No, I don't mean that.'

'B-but it's as g-good as settled!'

'Not, believe me, by me.'

'The d-devil!' Beverley said blankly.

'So you see,' pursued Sir Richard, 'I should have no compunction whatsoever in informing Saar of this episode.'

'You w-wouldn't split on me to my f-father!' Beverley cried, jumping up from the tree-stump.

'That, my dear Beverley, rests entirely with you.'

'But, d-damn it, m-man, I *can't* give the d-diamonds back! I tell you I'm d-done—up, fast aground!'

'I fancy that to have married into your family would have cost me considerably more than twelve thousand pounds. I am prepared to settle your debts—ah, for the last time, Beverley!'

'D-devilish good of you,' muttered Beverley. 'G-give me the money, and I'll settle 'em myself.'

'I fear that your intercourse with Captain Trimble has led you to credit others with his trusting disposition. I, alas, repose not the slightest reliance on your word. You may send a statement of your debts to my town house. I think that is all—except that you will be recalled to London suddenly, and you will leave Crome Hall, if you are wise, not later than to-morrow morning.'

'Blister it, I w-won't be ordered about by y'you! I'll leave w-when I choose!'

'If you don't choose to do so in the morning, you will leave in the custody of a Bow Street Runner.'

Beverley coloured hotly. 'By G-God, I'll p-pay you for this, Richard!'

'But not, if I know you, until I have settled your debts,' said Sir Richard, turning on his heel.

Beverley stood still, watching him walk away down the path, until the undergrowth hid him from sight. It was several minutes before it occurred to him that although Sir Richard had been unpleasantly frank on some subjects, he had not divulged how or why he came to be in Queen Charlton.

Beverley frowned over this. Sir Richard might, of course, be visiting friends in the neighbourhood, but apart from a house belonging to some heiress or other, Crome Hall was the only country seat of any size for several miles. The more Beverley considered the matter, the more inexplicable became Sir Richard's presence. From a sort of sullen curiosity, he passed easily to a mood of suspicion, and began to think that there was something very odd about the whole affair, and to wonder whether any profit could be made out of it.

He was not in the least grateful to Sir Richard for promising to pay his debts. He certainly wished to silence his more rapacious creditors, but he would have considered it a stupid waste of money to settle any bill which could possibly be held over to some later date. Moreover, the mere payment of his debts would not line his pockets, and it was hard to see how he was to continue to support life in the manner to which he was accustomed.

He took the necklace out, and looked at it. It was a singularly fine specimen of the jeweller's art, and several of the stones in it were of a truly formidable size. It was worth perhaps twice twelve thousand pounds. One did not, of course, find it easy to obtain the real value of stolen goods, but even if he had been forced to sell it for as little as twenty thousand pounds he would still have been eight thousand pounds in pocket, since there was no longer the least necessity to share the proceeds with Horace Trimble. Trimble, Beverley thought, has bungled the affair, and deserved nothing. If only Richard could be silenced, Trimble need never know that the necklace had been recovered from Jimmy Yarde, and it could be sold to the sole advantage of the only one of the three persons implicated in its theft who had a real right to it.

The more he reflected on these lines, and the longer he gazed at the diamonds, the more fixed became Beverley's conviction that Sir Richard, instead of assisting him in his financial difficulties, had actually robbed him of eight thousand pounds, if not more. A burning sense of injury possessed him, and if he could at that moment have done Sir Richard an injury, without incurring any himself, he would certainly have jumped at the chance.

But short of lying in wait for him, and shooting him, there did not seem to be anything he could do to Richard, with advantage; and although he would have been very glad to have heard of Richard's sudden death, and would have thought it, quite sincerely, a judgment on him, his murderous inclination was limited, to do him justice, to a strong wish that Richard would fall out of a window, and break his neck, or be set upon by armed highwaymen, and summarily slain. At the same time, there was undoubtedly something queer about Richard's being in this remote village, and it might be worth while to discover what had brought him to Queen Charlton.

Sir Richard, meanwhile, walked back to the village, arriving at the George in time to see a couple of sweating horses being led into the stable, and a postchaise being pushed into one corner of the roomy yard. He was therefore fully prepared to encounter strangers in the inn, and any doubts of their identity were set at rest upon his stepping into the entrance-parlour, and perceiving a matron with an imposing front seated upon one of the oaken settles, and vigorously fanning her heated countenance. At her elbow stood a stockily built young gentleman with his hair brushed into a Brutus, mopping his brow. He had somewhat globular eyes of no particular colour, and when seen in profile bore a distinct likeness to a hake.

The same unfortunate resemblance was to be observed, though in a less pronounced degree, in Mrs Griffin. The lady was built on massive lines, and appeared to be feeling the heat. Possibly a travelling costume of purple satin trimmed with a quantity of sarsenet, and worn under a spencer, and a voluminous cloak of drab merino cloth, might have contributed to her discomfort. Her locks were confined in a round cap, and over this she wore a beehive bonnet of moss-straw, trimmed with enough plumes to remind Sir Richard forcibly of a hearse. The landlord was standing in front of her in an attitude of concern, and as Sir Richard stepped into the entrance-parlour, she said in tones of strong resolution: 'You are deceiving me! I demand to have this—this youth brought before me!'

'But, Mama!' said the stocky young man unhappily.

'Silence, Frederick!' pronounced the matron.

'But consider, Mama! If the—the young man the land-lord speaks of is travelling with his uncle, he could not possibly be—be my cousin, could he?'

'I do not believe a word of what this man says!' declared Mrs Griffin. 'I should not wonder if he had been bribed.'

The landlord regretfully said that no one had tried to bribe him.

'Pshaw!' said Mrs Griffin.

Sir Richard judged it to be time to call attention to his own presence. He walked forward in the direction of the staircase.

'Here is the gentleman!' said the landlord, with a good deal of relief. 'He will tell for himself that what I've said is the truth, ma'am.'

Sir Richard paused, and glanced with raised eyebrows from Mrs Griffin to her son, and from Mr Frederick Griffin to the landlord. 'I beg your pardon?' he drawled.

The attention of the Griffins instantly became focused upon him. The gentleman's eyes were riveted to his cravat; the lady, taking in his air of elegance, was plainly shaken.

'If your honour pleases!' said the landlord. 'The lady, sir, is come in search of a young gentleman, which has run away from school, the same being her ward. I've told her that I have but one young gentleman staying in the house, and him your honour's nephew, and I'd be glad if you'd bear me out, sir.'

'Really,' said Sir Richard, bored, 'I don't know whom you have staying in the house besides myself and my nephew.'

'The question is, *have* you a nephew?' demanded Mrs Griffin.

Sir Richard raised his quizzing-glass, surveyed her through it, and bowed slightly. 'I was certainly under the impression that I had a nephew, ma'am. May I ask in what way he interests you?'

'If he *is* your nephew, I have no interest in him whatsoever,' declared the matron handsomely.

'Mama!' whispered her son, anguished. 'Recollect, I beg of you! A stranger! No proof! The greatest discretion!'

'I am quite distracted!' said Mrs Griffin, shedding tears.

This had the effect of driving the landlord from the room, and of flustering Mr Griffin. Between trying to pacify his parent, and excusing such odd behaviour to the elegant stranger, he became hotter than ever, and floundered in a morass of broken phrases. The look of astonishment on Sir Richard's face, the pained lift of his brows, quite discomposed him, and he ended by saying: 'The truth is my mother is sadly overwrought!'

'My confidence has been betrayed!' interpolated Mrs Griffin, raising her face from her damp handkerchief.

'Yes, Mama: precisely so! Her confidence has been betrayed, sir, by—by the shocking conduct of my cousin, who has——'

'I have nourished a viper in my bosom!' said Mrs Griffin.

'Just so, Mama. She has nourished—at least, not quite that, perhaps, but it is very bad, very upsetting to a lady of delicate sensibility!'

'All my life,' declaimed Mrs Griffin, 'I have been surrounded by ingratitude!'

'Mama, you cannot be surrounded by—and in any case, you know it is not so! Do, pray, calm yourself! I shall claim your indulgence, sir. The circumstances are so peculiar, and my cousin's behaviour has exerted so strong an effect upon my poor mother that—in short——'

'It is the impropriety of it which is worse than anything!' said Mrs Griffin.

'Exactly so, Mama. You see, it is the impropriety, sir—I mean, my mother is not quite herself.'

'I shall never,' announced the matron, 'hold up my head again! It is my belief that this person is in league with her!'

'Mama, most earnestly I implore you——!'

'Her?' repeated Sir Richard, apparently bewildered.

'Him!' corrected Mr Griffin.

'You must forgive me if I do not perfectly understand you,' said Sir Richard. 'I apprehend that you have—er—mislaid a youth, and have come——'

'Precisely so, sir! We mis—at least, no, no, we did not mislay him, of course!'

'Ran away!' uttered Mrs Griffin, emerging from the handkerchief for a brief instant.

'Ran away,' corroborated her son.

'But in what way,' enquired Sir Richard, 'does this concern me, sir?'

'Not at all, sir, I assure you! No such suspicion is cherished by me, upon my word!'

'What suspicion?' asked Sir Richard, still more bewildered.

'None sir, none in the world! That is just what I was saying. I have no suspicion——'

'But I have!' said Mrs Griffin, in much more robust tones. 'I accuse you of concealing the truth from me!'

'Mama, do but consider! You cannot—you know you cannot insult this gentleman by insinuating——'

'In the execution of my duty there is nothing I cannot do!' responded his mother nobly. 'Besides, I do not know him. I mistrust him.'

Mr Griffin turned wretchedly to Sir Richard: 'You see, sir, my mother——'

'Mistrusts me,' supplied Sir Richard.

'No, no, I assure you! My mother is sadly put out, and scarcely knows what she is saying.'

'I am in the fullest possession of my faculties, I thank you, Frederick!' said Mrs Griffin, gathering strength.

'Of course, of course, Mama! But the agitation—the natural agitation——'

'If he is speaking the truth,' interrupted Mrs Griffin, 'let him summon his nephew to stand before me!'

'Ah, I begin to understand you!' said Sir Richard. 'Is it possible, ma'am, that you suspect my nephew of being your errant ward?'

'No, no!' said Griffin feebly.

'Yes!' declared his mother.

'But Mama, only consider what such a thought must imply!' said Mr Griffin in a frenzied aside.

'I can believe anything of that unnatural creature!'

'I should doubt very much whether my nephew is upon the premises,' said Sir Richard coldly. 'He was engaged to spend the day with friends, upon an expedition of pleasure. However, if he should not yet have left the house, I will engage to—er—allay all these heart burnings.'

'If he has run out to escape us, I shall await his return!' said Mrs Griffin. 'And so I warn you!'

'I admire your resolution, ma'am, but I must point out to you that your movements are of no possible interest to me,' said Sir Richard, stepping over to the bell, and jerking it.

'Frederick!' said Mrs Griffin. 'Will you stand by and hear your mother being insulted by one whom I strongly suspect of being a dandy?'

'But Mama, indeed, it is no concern of ours if he is!'

'Perhaps,' said Sir Richard, in arctic tones, 'it may be of service if I make myself known to you, ma'am. My name is Wyndham.'

Mrs Griffin received this information with every appearance of disdain, but its effect upon her son was staggering. His eyes seemed to be in danger of bursting out of their sockets; he started forward, and ejaculated in tones of deepest reverence: 'Sir! is this possible? Have I the honour of addressing Sir Richard Wyndham?'

Sir Richard bowed slightly.

'The celebrated Whip?' asked Mr Griffin.

Sir Richard bowed again.

'The creator of the Wyndham Fall?' pursued Mr Griffin, almost overcome.

Tired of bowing, Sir Richard said: 'Yes.'

'Sir,' said Mr Griffin, 'I am happy to make your acquaintance! My name is Griffin!'

'How do you do?' murmured Sir Richard, holding out his hand.

Mr Griffin clasped it. 'I wonder I should not have recognized you. Mama, we have been quite mistaken. This is none other than the famous Sir Richard Wyndham—the friend of Brummell, you know! You must have heard me— you must have heard him spoken of. It is quite impossible that he can know anything of my cousin's whereabouts.'

She seemed to accept this, though with obvious reluctance. She looked Sir Richard over with disfavour, and said paralysingly: 'I have the greatest dislike of all forms of dandyism, and I have ever deplored the influence exerted by the Bow-Window set upon young men of respectable upbringing. However, if you are indeed Sir Richard Wyndham, I dare say you would not object to showing my son how to arrange his cravat in what he calls the Wyndham Fall, so that he need no longer spoil every neckcloth in his drawer before achieving a result which I consider lamentable.'

'Mama!' whispered the unhappy Mr Griffin. 'I beg of you!'

The entrance of a servant, in answer to the bell's summons, came as a timely interruption. Upon being asked to discover whether Sir Richard's nephew were in the house, he was able to reply that the young gentleman had left the inn some time previously.

'Then I fear there is nothing for you to do but to await his return,' said Sir Richard addressing himself to Mrs Griffin.

'We should not dream of—Mama there can be no doubt that she—he—did not come here after all. Lady Luttrell disclaims all knowledge, remember, and *she* must certainly have known if my cousin had come into this neighbourhood.'

'If I could think that she had gone to cousin Jane, all would not yet be lost!' said Mrs Griffin. 'Yet it is possible? I fear the worst!'

'This is all very perplexing,' complained Sir Richard. 'I was under the impression that this mysterious truant was of the male sex.'

'Federick my nerves can stand no more!' said Mrs

Griffin, surging to her feet. 'If you mean to drag me the length of England again, I must insist upon being permitted the indulgence of half an hour's solitude first!'

'But Mama, it was not I who would come here!' expostulated Mr Griffin.

Sir Richard again rang the bell, and this time desired that a chambermaid should be sent to him. Mrs Griffin was presently consigned to the care of an abigail, and left the room majestically, commanding hot water to wash with, tea, and a decent bedchamber.

Her son heaved a sigh of relief. 'I must beg pardon, Sir Richard! You must allow me to beg your pardon!'

'Not at all,' said Sir Richard.

'Yes, yes, I insist! Such an unfortunate misunderstanding! An explanation is due to you! A slip of the tongue, you know, but my mother is labouring under strong emotion, and does not quite heed what she says. You noticed it: indeed, no one could wonder at your surprise! The unhappy truth, sir, is that my cousin is not a boy, but—in a word, sir—a female!'

'This explanation, Mr Griffin, is quite unnecessary, believe me.'

'Sir,' said Mr Griffin earnestly, 'as a Man of the World, I should value your opinion! Concealment is useless: the truth must be discovered in the end. What, sir, would you think of a member of the Weaker Sex who assumed the disguise of a man, and left the home of her natural protector by way of the window?'

'I should assume,' replied Sir Richard, 'that she had strong reasons for acting with such resolution.'

'She did not wish to marry me,' said Mr Griffin gloomily.

'Oh!' said Sir Richard.

'Well, I'm sure I can't see why she should be so set against me, but that's not it, sir. The thing is that here's my mother determined to find her, and to make her marry me, and so hush up the scandal. But I don't like it above half. If she dislikes the notion so much, I don't think I ought to marry her, do you?'

'Emphatically not!'

'I must say I am very glad to hear you say that, Sir Richard!' said Mr Griffin, much cheered. 'For you must

know that my mother has been telling me ever since yesterday that I must marry her now, to save her name. But I
think she would very likely make me uncomfortable, and
nothing could make up for that, in my opinion.'

'A lady capable of escaping out of a window in the guise
of a man would quite certainly make you more than uncomfortable,' said Sir Richard.

'Yes, though she's only a chit of a girl, you know. In fact,
she is not yet out. I am very happy to have had the benefit
of the opinion of a Man of the World. I feel that I can
rely on your judgment.'

'On my judgment you might, but in nothing else, I assure
you,' said Sir Richard. 'You know nothing of me, after all.
How do you know that I am not now concealing your
cousin from you?'

'Ha-ha! Very good, upon my word! Very good, indeed!'
said Mr Griffin, saluting a jest of the first water.

◆§ *Chapter VIII* §◆

THE Griffins did not leave Queen Charlton until the cool
of the afternoon, and by the time he saw their chaise off the
premises of the George, Sir Richard was heartily sick of the
company of surely one of his most devout worshippers. No
sign was seen of Pen, who had no doubt fled the house upon
the Griffins' arrival. What sustenance she had snatched up
to bear her strength up through a long day, Sir Richard had
no means of knowing.

Mrs Griffin, tottering downstairs to partake of light refreshment, found her son hanging upon Sir Richard's bored
lips. Upon hearing that he had divulged the secret of Pen's
identity, she first showed a dangerous tendency to swoon,
but upon being supplied with a glass of ratafia by Sir
Richard, revived sufficiently to pour out her wrongs into
his ear.

'What, I ask myself,' she said dramatically, 'has become
of that tiresome girl? Into what company may she have

fallen? I see that you, Sir Richard, are a person of sensibility. Conceive of my feelings! What—I say, *what* if my unfortunate niece should have fallen into the hands of some *Man?*'

'What indeed?' said Sir Richard.

'She must marry him. When I think of the care, the hopes, the maternal fondness I have lavished—but it is ever so! There is no gratitude in the world to-day.'

Upon this gloomy reflection, she ordered her chaise to be got ready to bear her instantly to Chippenham. She would have remained at Queen Charlton for the night, she explained, only that she suspected the sheets.

Sir Richard, having seen her off, walked down the street, to cool his heated brow, and to consider the intricacies of his position.

It was while he was absent that Miss Creed and the Honourable Beverley Brandon, approaching the George from widely divergent angles, but with identical circumspection, came face to face in the entrance-parlour.

They eyed one another. A few moments' conversation with the tapster had put Beverley in possession of information which he found sufficiently intriguing to make him run the risk of perhaps encountering Captain Trimble in entering the inn, and prosecuting further enquiries about Sir Richard Wyndham. Sir Richard, the tapster had told him, was putting up at the George with his nephew.

Now, Sir Richard's nephew, as Beverley knew well, was a lusty young gentleman not yet breeched. He did not mention this circumstance in the tapster, but on hearing that the mysterious nephew in question was a youth in his teens, he pricked up his ears, and penetrated from the tap room into the main parlour of the inn.

Here Pen, entering the George cautiously from the stableyard, came plump upon him. Never having seen his face, she did not at once recognize him, but when, after an intent stare, he moved towards her, saying with a slight stammer: 'How d-do you do? I think you m-must be Wyndham's n-nephew?' she had no doubt of his identity.

She was no fool, and she realized at once that anyone well-acquainted with Sir Richard must be aware that she was not his nephew. She replied guardedly: 'Well, I call him my uncle, because he is so much older than I am, but in point of fact we are cousins only. Third cousins,' she added, making the relationship as remote as she could.

A smile which she did not quite like lingered on Beverley's rather slack mouth. Mentally, he was reviewing Sir Richard's family, but he said with great affability: 'Oh, indeed? Ch-charmed to make your acquaintance, Mr-er-er?'

'Brown,' supplied Pen, regretting that she had not thought to provide herself with a more unusual surname.

'Brown,' bowed Beverley, his smile widening. 'It is a great p-pleasure to me to m-meet any connection of W-Wyndham's. In such a remote spot, too! Now d-do tell me! What b-brings you here?'

'Family affairs,' answered Pen promptly. 'Uncle Richard —Cousin Richard, I mean, only I have always been in the way of calling him uncle, you understand—very kindly undertook to come with me.'

'So it was on y-your account that he came to Queen Ch-Charlton!' said Beverley. 'That is most interesting!' His eyes ran over her in a way that made her feel profoundly ill-at-ease. 'M-*most* interesting!' he repeated. 'P-pray present my c-compliments to Wyndham, and tell him that I perfectly understand his reasons for choosing such a secluded locality!'

He bowed himself out with a flourish, leaving Pen in a state of considerable trepidation. In the tap room, he called for paper, ink, a pen, and some brandy, and sat down at a table in one corner to write a careful letter to Sir Richard. It took time, for he was not apt with a pen, and much brandy, but it was finished at last to his satisfaction. He looked round rather owlishly for wafers, but the tapster had brought him none, so he folded the note into a screw, wrote Sir Richard's name on it in a flourishing scrawl, and told the tapster to give it to Sir Richard upon his return to the inn. After that he went away, not quite steadily, but full of chuckling glee at his own ingenuity.

The tapster, who was busy serving drinks, left the twisted note on the bar while he hurried to the other end of the room with beer for a clamorous party of countrymen. It was here that Captain Trimble, coming into the taproom from the stableyard, found it.

Captain Trimble, who had spent a fruitless day in attempting to discover some trace of Jimmy Yarde in Bristol, was hot, and tired, and in no very good temper. He sat down on a high stool at the bar, and began to wipe his face with a large handkerchief. It was as he was restoring the handkerchief to his pocket that the note, and its superscription, caught his eye. He was well-acquainted with Mr Brandon's handwriting, and he recognized it at once. It did not at first surprise him that Mr Brandon should have written to Sir Richard Wyndham; he supposed them to be of the same fashionable set. But as he looked idly down at the screw of paper thoughts of the wild-goose chase upon which Sir Richard had sent him took strong possession of his mind, and he wondered, not for the first time during that exasperating day, whether Sir Richard could have had a motive in dispatching him to Bristol. The note began to assume a sinister aspect; suspicion darkened the already warm colour in the Captain's cheeks; and after staring at the note for a minute, he cast a quick look round, saw that no one was watching him, and deftly palmed it.

The tapster came back to the bar, but by the time he had recollected the note, Captain Trimble had retired to a high-backed settle by the empty fireplace, and was calling for a can of ale. At a convenient moment, he unscrewed the twist of paper, and read its contents.

'*My very dear Richard,*' had written Mr Brandon, '*I am desolated to find that you have gone out. I should like to continue our conversation. When I tell you that I have been privileged to meet your nephew, my dear Richard, I feel that you will appreciate the wisdom of meeting me again. You would not wish me to talk, but a paltry twelve thousand is not enough to close my mouth, which, however, I am willing to do, tho' not for a less sum than I have it in my power to obtain by Other Means. Should you wish to discuss this delicate matter, I shall be in the spinney at ten o'clock this evening. If you do not come there, I shall understand that you have Withdrawn your Objection to my disposing of Certain Property as I choose, and I fancy that it would be Unwise of you to mention our dealings in this matter to anyone, either now or later.*'

Captain Trimble read this missive twice before folding

it again into its original twist. The mention of Pen he found obscure, and of no particular interest. There was apparently a disreputable secret in some way connected with Sir Richard's young nephew, but the Captain did not immediately perceive what profit was to be made out of it. Far more arresting was the thinly veiled reference to the Brandon necklace. The Captain's eyes smouldered as he thought this over, and his massive jaw worked a little. He had suspected Beverley's good faith from the moment that Jimmy Yarde had been thrust on him as an accomplice. The matter seemed as clear as crystal now. Beverley and Yarde had hatched a plot to cheat him of his share in the fortune, and when Beverley had been raving against him for blundering —very convincingly he had raved too—he had actually had the necklace in his pocket. Well, Mr Brandon would have to learn that it was not wise to try to bubble Horace Trimble, and still less wise to leave unsealed notes lying about in a common taproom. As for Sir Richard, the Captain found his part in these tortuous proceeding very diffiicult to fathom. He seemed to know something about the diamonds, but he was far too wealthy a man, the Captain considered, to have the least interest in their worth in terms of guineas. But Sir Richard had undoubtedly meddled in the affair, and the Captain wished with all his heart that he could discover a way to pay him in full for his interference.

Captain Trimble was naturally a man of violence, but although he would have liked very much to spoil Sir Richard's handsome face, he wasted no more than a couple of minutes over this pleasing dream. Sir Richard, if it came to fisticuffs, would enjoy the encounter far more than would his assailant. A more determined assault, on a dark night, by a couple of stout men armed with clubs, might have a better chance of success, but even this scheme had a drawback. Sir Richard had been set upon twice before, by hardy rogues who planned to rob him. He had not been robbed, and he had not been attacked again. He was marked down by every cut-throat and robber in the Rogues' Calendar as dangerous, one who carried pistols, and could draw and fire with a speed and a deadly accuracy which made him a most undesirable man to molest.

Regretfully, the Captain decided that Sir Richard must be left alone, for the present, at all events.

By this time the tapster had discovered the loss of Mr Brandon's note. Everyone in the room disclaimed all knowledge of its whereabouts. Captain Trimble drained his can, and carried it over to the bar. As he set it down, he said: 'Isn't that a bit of paper I see?'

No one could see anything, but that might have been because the Captain bent so quickly to pick it up. When he straightened himself, the screw of paper was between his fingers. The tapster took it with a word of thanks, and gave it to one of the waiters, who had come into the taproom for a pint of burgundy, and told him to deliver it to Sir Richard. Captain Trimble, quite as well-pleased as Beverley had been, betook himself to the coffee-room, and ordered a sustaining meal.

Sir Richard, meanwhile, had returned to the inn. He found Pen awaiting him in the parlour, curled up in a big chair and eating an apple. 'This passion for munching raw fruit!' he remarked. 'You look a very urchin.'

She twinkled at him. 'Well, I am hungry. Did you—did you have a pleasant day with my Aunt Almeria, sir?'

'I hope with all my heart,' said Sir Richard, eyeing her with some severity, 'that *you* spent the day in the greatest possible discomfort. I wish it had rained.'

'I didn't. I visited my home, and I went to all the *particular* places Piers and I used to hide in, when people wanted us to do our lessons. Only I hadn't anything to eat.'

'I am glad,' said Sir Richard. 'Do you know that I have not only found myself in a position where I was forced to lie, and dissemble, and practise the most shocking deceit, but I have also been obliged to consort for five hours with one of the most commonplace young cubs it has ever been my ill-fortune to meet?'

'I knew Fred would come with my aunt! Doesn't he look just like a fish, sir?'

'Yes, a hake. But you cannot divert me from what I wish to say. Half an hour's conversation with your aunt has convinced me that you are an unprincipled brat.'

'Did she say unkind things of me?' Miss Creed wrinkled her brow. 'I don't think I am *unprincipled*, precisely.'

'You are a menace to all law-abiding and respectable citizens,' said Sir Richard.

She seemed gratified. 'I didn't think I was as important as that.'

'Look what you have done to me!' said Sir Richard.

'Yes, but I don't think you are very law-abiding or respectable,' objected Pen.

'I was once, but it seems a long time ago.'

She finished her apple. 'Well, I am sorry you are feeling cross, for I think I should tell you something which you may not be pleased about.'

He looked at her with misgiving. 'Let me know the worst!'

'It was the stammering-man,' said Pen, not very lucidly. 'Of course, I quite see that I should have been more careful.'

'You mean Beverley Brandon. What has he been doing?'

'Well, you see, he came here. And just at that very same moment, I chanced to walk into the inn, and—and we met.'

'When was this?'

'Oh, not long ago! You were gone out. Only he seemed to know me.'

'Seemed to know you?'

'Well, he said surely I must be your nephew,' Pen explained.

Sir Richard had been listening to her with a gathering frown. He said now, with a grim note which she had not before heard in his voice: 'Beverley knows very well that the only nephew I have is a child in short petticoats.'

'Oh, have you got a nephew?' enquired Pen, diverted.

'Yes. Never mind that. What did you reply?'

'Well, I think I was quite clever,' said Pen hopefully. 'Naturally, I knew who he must be, as soon as he spoke; and I guessed, of course, that he must know I am not your nephew. Because even if some people think I have no ingenuity, I am not at all stupid,' she added, with a darkling look.

'Does that rankle?' His countenance had relaxed a little. 'Never mind! go on!'

'I said that in point of fact you were not my uncle, but

I called you so because you were a great deal older than I. I said that you were my third cousin. Then he asked me why we had come to Queen Charlton, and I said it was on account of family affairs, though I would rather have pointed out that it was extremely ill-bred and inquisitive of him to ask me such questions. And after that he went away.'

'Did he indeed? Did he say what had brought him here in the first place?'

'No. But he gave me a message for you, which I did not quite like.'

'Well?'

'It sounded sinister to me,' said Pen, preparing him for the worst.

'I can well believe it.'

'And the more I think of it the more sinister it appears to me. He said I must present his compliments to you, and tell you that he perfectly understands your reason for coming to such a secluded spot.'

'The devil!' said Sir Richard.

'I was afraid you would not be excessively pleased,' Pen said anxiously. 'Do you suppose that it means that he knows who I am?'

'Not that, no,' Sir Richard replied.

'Perhaps,' suggested Pen, 'he guessed that I am not a boy?'

'Perhaps.'

She thought the matter over. 'Well, I don't see what else he could possibly have meant. But Jimmy Yarde never suspected me, and I conversed with him far more than I did with this disagreeable stammering-man. How very unfortunate it is that we should have met someone who knows you well!'

'I beg your pardon?' said Sir Richard, putting up his glass.

She looked innocently up at him. 'On account of his being aware that you have no nephew or cousin like me, I mean.'

'Oh!' said Sir Richard, lowering the glass. 'I see. Don't let it worry you!'

'Well, it does worry me, because I see now that I have

been imprudent. I should not have let you come with me. It has very likely placed you in an awkward situation.'

'That aspect of it had not occurred to me,' said Sir Richard, faintly smiling. 'The imprudence was mine. I ought to have handed you over to your aunt at our first meeting.'

'Do you wish you had?' asked Pen wistfully.

He looked down at her for an instant. 'No.'

'Well, I'm glad, because if you had tried to, I would have run away from you.' She lifted her chin from her cupped hands. 'If you are not sorry to be here, do not let us give it another thought! It is so very fatiguing to go on being sorry about something which one has done. Did you order any dinner, sir?'

'I did. Duck and peas.'

'Good!' said Pen, with profound satisfaction. 'Where has Aunt Almeria gone, do you suppose?'

'To Chippenham, and then to Cousin Jane.'

'To Cousin Jane? Good gracious, why?'

'To see whether you have taken refuge with her, I imagine.'

'With Cousin Jane!' Pen exclaimed. 'Why, she is the most odious old woman, and takes snuff!'

Sir Richard, who had just opened his own box, paused. 'Er—do you consider that an odious habit?' he asked.

'In a female, I do. Besides, she spills it on her clothes. Ugh! Oh, I did not mean you, sir!' she added, with a ripple of sudden laughter. 'You do it with such an air!'

'Thank you!' he said.

A waiter came in to lay the covers for dinner, and presented a small, twisted note to Sir Richard on a large tray.

He picked it up unhurriedly, and spread it open. Pen, anxiously watching him, could detect nothing in his face but boredom. He read the note through to the end, and consigning it to his pocket, glanced towards Pen. 'Let me see: what were we discussing?'

'Snuff,' replied Pen, in a hollow voice.

'Ah, yes! I myself use King's Martinique, but there are many who consider it a trifle light in character.'

She returned a mechanical answer, and upon the waiter's leaving the room, interrupted Sir Richard's description of the proper way to preserve snuff in good condition, by demanding impetuously: 'Who was it from, sir?'

'Don't be inquisitive!' said Sir Richard calmly.

'You can't deceive me! I feel sure it was from that hateful man.'

'It was, but there is no occasion for you to trouble your head over it, believe me.'

'Only tell me! Does he mean to do you some mischief?'

'Certainly not. It would, in all events, be a task quite beyond his power.'

'I feel very uneasy.'

'So I perceive. You will be the better for your dinner.'

The waiter came in with the duck at that opportune moment, and set it upon the table. Pen was, in fact, so hungry that her thoughts were instantly diverted. She made a very good dinner, and did not again refer to the note.

Sir Richard, maintaining a flow of easy conversation, seemed to be wholly devoid of care, but the note had annoyed him. There was very little fear, he considered, of Beverley's being able to harm Miss Creed, since he could have no knowledge of her identity; and his veiled threat of exposing Sir Richard was a matter of indifference to that gentleman. But he would certainly meet Beverley in the spinney at the proposed hour, for it now became more than ever necessary to despatch him to London immediately. While he remained in the neighbourhood there would be no question of delivering Pen into Lady Luttrell's care, and although Sir Richard had not the least desire to relinquish his self-appointed guardianship of that enterprising damsel, he was perfectly well aware that he must do so, and without any loss of time.

Accordingly, he sent her to bed shortly after half-past-nine, telling her that if she were not tired she deserved to be. She went without demur, so probably her day spent in the open had made her sleepy. He waited until a few minutes before ten o'clock, and then took his hat and walking-cane, and strolled out of the inn.

There was a full moon, and not a cloud to be seen in the sky. Sir Richard had no difficulty in seeing his way, and soon came to the track through the wood. It was darker here, for the trees held out the moonlight. A rabbit scuttled across the path, an owl hooted somewhere at hand, and there were little rustlings in the undergrowth, but Sir Richard was not of a nervous disposition, and did not find these sounds in any way disturbing.

But he was hardly prepared to come upon a lady lying stretched across the path, immediately round a bend in it. This sight was, indeed, so unexpected that it brought him up short. The lady did not move, but lay in a crumpled heap of pale muslin and darker cloak. Sir Richard, recovering from his momentary surprise, strode forward, and dropped on to his knee beside her. It was too dark under the trees for him to be able to distinguish her features clearly, but he thought she was young. She was not dead, as he had at first feared, but in a deep faint. He began to chafe her hands, and had just bethought him of the tiny stream which he had observed that morning, when she showed signs of returning consciousness. He raised her in his arms, hearing a sigh flutter past her lips. A moan succeeded the sigh; she said something he could not catch, and began weakly to cry.

'Don't cry!' Sir Richard said. 'You are quite safe.'

She caught her breath on a sob, and stiffened in his hold. He felt her little hands close on his arm. Then she began to tremble.

'No, there is nothing to frighten you,' he said in his cool way. 'You will be better directly.'

'Oh!' The exclamation sounded terrified. 'Who are you? Oh, let me go!'

'Certainly I will let you go, but are you able to stand yet? You do not know me, but I am perfectly harmless, I assure you.'

She made a feeble attempt to struggle up, and succeeded only in crouching on the path in a woebegone huddle, saying through her sobs: 'I must go! Oh, I must go! I ought not to have come!'

'That I can well believe,' said Sir Richard, still on his knee beside her. 'Why did you come? Or is that an impertinent question?'

It had the effect of redoubling her sobs. She buried her

face in her hands, shuddering, and rocking herself to and fro, and gasping out unintelligible phrases.

'Well!' said a voice behind Sir Richard.

He looked quickly over his shoulder. 'Pen! What are you doing here?'

'I followed you,' replied Pen, looking critically down at the weeping girl. 'I brought a stout stick too, because I thought you were going to meet the odious stammering-man, and I feel sure he means to do you a mischief. Who is this?'

'I haven't the slightest idea,' replied Sir Richard. 'And presently I shall have something to say to you on the subject of this idiotic escapade of yours! My good child, can't you stop crying?'

'What is she doing here?' asked Pen, unmoved by his strictures.

'Heaven knows! I found her lying on the path. How does one make a female stop crying?'

'I shouldn't think you could. She's going to have a fit of the vapours, I expect. And I do *not* see why you should hug people, if you don't know who they are.'

'I was not hugging her.'

'It looked like it to me,' argued Pen.

'I suppose,' said Sir Richard sardonically, 'you would have had me step over her, and walk on?'

'Yes, I would,' replied Pen promptly.

'Don't be a little fool! The girl had fainted.'

'Oh!' Pen moved forward. 'I wonder what made her do that? You know, it all seems extremely odd to me.'

'It seems quite as odd to me, let me tell you.' He laid his hand on the sobbing girl's shoulder. 'Come! You will not help matters by crying. Can't you tell me what has happened to upset you so?'

The girl made a convulsive effort to choke back her hysterical tears, and managed to utter: 'I was so frightened!'

'Yes, that I had realized. What frightened you?'

'There was a man!' gasped the girl. 'And I hid, and then another man came, and they began to quarrel, and I dared not move for fear they should hear me, and the big one hit the other, and he fell down and lay still, and the big one took something out of his pocket, and went away, and oh, oh, he passed so close I c-could have touched him only by stretching out my hand! The other man never moved, and I was so frightened I ran, everything went black, and I think I fainted.'

'Ran away?' repeated Pen in disgusted accents. 'What a poor-spirited thing to do! Didn't you go to help the man who was knocked down?'

'Oh no, no, no!' shuddered the girl.

'I must say, I don't think you deserve to have such an adventure. And if I were you I wouldn't continue sitting in the middle of the path. It isn't at all helpful, and it makes you look very silly.'

This severe speech had the effect of angering the girl. She reared up her head, and exclaimed: 'How dare you? You are the rudest young man I ever met in my life!'

Sir Richard put his hand under her elbow, and assisted her to her feet. 'Ah—accept my apologies on my nephew's behalf, ma'am!' he said, with only the faintest quiver in his voice. 'A sadly ill-conditioned boy! May I suggest to you that you should rest on this bank for a few moments, while I go to investigate the—er—scene of the assault you so graphically described? My nephew—who has, you perceive, provided himself with a stout stick—will charge himself with your safety.'

'I'll come with you,' said Pen mutinously.

'You will—for once in your life—do as you are told,' said Sir Richard, and, lowering the unknown on to the bank, strode on down the track towards the clearing in the wood.

Here the moonlight bathed the ground in its cold silver light. Sir Richard had no doubt that he would find Beverley Brandon, either stunned, or reovering from the effects of the blow which had felled him, but as he stepped into the clearing he saw not only one man lying still on the ground, but a second on his knees beside him.

Sir Richard trod softly, and it was not until he had approached to within a few feet of the little group that the kneeling man heard his footsteps, and looked quickly over his shoulder. The moonlight drained the world of colour, but even allowing for this the face turned towards Sir Richard was unnaturally pallid. It was the face of a very young man, and perfectly strange to Sir Richard.

'Who are you?' The question was shot out in a hushed, rather scared voice. The young man started to his feet, and took up an instinctively defensive pose.

'I doubt whether my name will convey very much to you, but for what it is worth, it is Wyndham. What has happened here?'

The boy seemed quite distracted, and replied in a shaken tone: 'I don't know. I found him here—like this. I—I think he's dead!'

'Nonsense!' said Sir Richard, putting him out of his way, and in his turn kneeling beside Beverley's inanimate body. There was a bruise on the livid brow, and when Sir Richard raised Beverley his head fell back in a way that told its own tale rather horribly. Sir Richard saw the tree-stump, and realized that Beverley's head must have struck it. He laid his body down again, and said without the least vestige of emotion: 'You are perfectly right. His neck is broken.'

The boy dragged a handkerchief out of his pocket, and wiped his brow with it. 'My God, who did it?—I—I didn't, you know!'

'I don't suppose you did,' Sir Richard replied, rising to his feet, and dusting the knees of his breeches.

'But it's the most shocking thing! He was staying with me, sir!'

'Oh!' said Sir Richard, favouring him with a long, penetrating look.

'He's Beverley Brandon—Lord Saar's younger son!'

'I know very well who he is. You, I apprehend, are Mr Piers Luttrell?'

'Yes. Yes, I am. I knew him up at Oxford. Not very well, because I—well, to tell you the truth, I never liked him much. But a week ago he arrived at my home. He had been visiting friends, I think. I don't know. But of course I—that is, my mother and I—asked him to stay, and he did. He has not been quite well—seemed to be in need of rest, and—country air. Indeed, I can't conceive how he comes to be here now, for he retired to his room with one of his sick headaches. At least, that was what he told my mother.'

'Then you did not come here in search of him?'

'No, no! I came—— The fact is, I just came out to enjoy a stroll in the moonlight,' replied Piers, in a hurry.

'I see.' There was a dry note in Sir Richard's voice.

'Why are *you* here?' demanded Piers.

'For the same reason,' Sir Richard answered.

'But you know Brandon!'

'That circumstance does not, however, make me his murderer.'

'Oh no! I did not mean—but it seems so strange that you should both be in Queen Charlton!'

'I thought it tiresome, myself. My errand to Queen Charlton did not in any way concern Beverley Brandon.'

'Of course not! I didn't suppose—Sir, since you didn't kill him, and I didn't, who—who did, do you suppose? For he did not merely trip and fall, did he? There is that bruise on his forehead, and he was lying face upwards, just as you saw him. Someone struck him down!'

'Yes, I think someone struck him down,' agreed Sir Richard.

'I suppose you do not know who it might have been, sir?'

'I wonder?' Sir Richard said thoughtfully.

Piers waited, but as Sir Richard said no more, but stood looking frowningly down at Beverley's body, he blurted out: 'What ought I to do? Really, I do not know! I have no experience in such matters. Perhaps you could advise me?'

'I do not pretend to any very vast experience myself, but I suggest that you should go home.'

'But we can't leave him here—can we?'

'No, we can't do that. I will inform the magistrate that there is—er—a corpse in the wood. No doubt he will attend to it.'

'Yes, but I don't wish to run away, you know,' Piers objected. 'It is the most devilish, awkward situation, but of course I don't dream of leaving you to—to explain it all to the magistrate. I shall have to say that it was I who found the body.'

Sir Richard, who knew that the affair was one of extreme delicacy, and who had been wondering for several minutes in what way it could be handled so as to spare the Brandons as much humiliation as possible, did not feel that the entry of Piers Luttrell into the proceedings would facilitate his task. He cast another of his searching looks over the young man, and said: 'Your doing so would serve no useful purpose, I believe. You had better leave it to me.'

'You know something about it!'

'Yes, I do. I am on terms of—er—considerable intimacy with the Brandons, and I know a good deal about Beverley's activities. There is likely to be a peculiarly distasteful scandal arising out of this murder.'

Piers nodded. 'I was afraid of that. You know, sir, he was not at all the thing, and he knew some devilish odd people. A man came up to the house, enquiring for him only yesterday—a seedy sort of bully: I dare say you may be familiar with the type. Beverley did not like it above half, I could see.'

'Were you privileged to meet this man?'

'Well, I saw him: I didn't exchange two words with him. The servant came to tell Beverley that a Captain Trimble had called to see him, and Beverley was so much put out that I—well, I fear I did rather wonder what was in the wind.'

'Ah!' said Sir Richard. 'The fact that you have met Trimble may—or may not—prove useful. Yes, I think you had better go home, and say nothing about this. No doubt the news of Beverley's death will be conveyed to you tomorrow morning.'

'But what shall I tell the constable, sir?'

'Whatever he asks you,' replied Sir Richard.

'Shall I say that I found Beverley here, with you?' asked Piers doubtfully.

'I hardly think that he will ask you that question.'

'But will he not wonder how it came about that I did not miss Beverley?'

'Did you not say that Beverley gave it out that he was retiring to bed? Why should you miss him?'

'To-morrow morning?'

'Yes, I think you might miss him at the breakfast-table,' conceded Sir Richard.

'I see. Well, if you feel it to be right, sir I—I own I would rather not divulge that I was in the wood to-night. But what must I say if I am asked if I know you?'

'You don't know me.'

'N-no. No, I don't, of course,' said Piers, apparently cheered by this reflection.

'That is a pleasure in store for you. I came into this neighbourhood for the purpose of—er—making your acquaintance, but this seems hardly the moment to enter upon a matter which I have reason to suspect may prove extremely complicated.'

'You came to see *me*?' said Piers, astonished. 'How can this be?'

'If,' said Sir Richard, 'you will come to see me at the "George" to-morrow—a very natural action on your part, in view of my discovery of your guest's corpse—I will tell you just why I came to Queen Charlton in search of you.'

'I am sure I am honoured—but I cannot conceive what your business with me may be, sir!'

'That,' said Sir Richard, 'does not surprise me nearly as much as my business is likely to surprise you, Mr Luttrell!'

❦ *Chapter IX* ❦

HAVING got rid of Piers Luttrell, who, after peering at his watch surreptitiously, and several times looking about him as though in the expectation of seeing someone hiding amongst the trees, went off, rather relieved but much bewildered, Sir Richard walked away to rejoin Pen and the unknown lady. He found only Pen, seated on the bank with an air of aloof virtue, her hands folded primly on her knees. He paused, looking her over with a comprehending eye. 'And where,' he asked in conversational tones, 'is your companion?'

'She chose to go home,' responded Pen. 'I dare say she grew tired of waiting for you to come back.'

'Ah, no doubt! Did you by any chance, suggest to her that she should do so?'

'No, because it was not at all necessary. She was very anxious to go. She said she wished she had not come.'

'Did you tell you why she had come?'

'No. I asked her, of course, but she is such a silly little missish thing that she would do nothing but cry, and say she was a wicked girl. Do you know what I think, Richard?'

'Probably.'

'Well, it's my belief she came to meet someone. She seems to me exactly the sort of female who would feel romantic just because there is a full moon. Besides, why else should she be here at this hour?'

'Why indeed?' agreed Sir Richard. 'I apprehend that you have little sympathy to spare for such folly?'

'None at all,' said Pen. 'In fact, I think it's silly, besides being improper.'

'You are severe!'

'I can tell by your voice that you are laughing at me. I expect you are thinking of my climbing out of a window. But *I* was not going to meet a lover by moonlight! Such stuff!'

'Fustian,' nodded Sir Richard. 'Did she disclose the identity of her lover?'

'No, but she said her own name was Lydia Daubenay. And no sooner had she told me that than she went off into another taking, and said she was distracted, and wished she had not told me. Really, I was quite glad when she decided to go home without waiting for you.'

'Yes, I had rather gathered the impression that her company was not agreeable to you. I suppose it hardly signifies. She did not appear to me to be the kind of young woman who could be trusted to bear a still tongue in her head.'

'Well, I don't know,' said Pen thoughtfully. 'She was so frightened I quite think she may not say a word about the adventure. I have been considering the matter, and it seems to me that she must be in love with someone whom her parents do not wish her to marry.'

'That,' said Sir Richard, 'seems to be a fair conclusion.'

'So that I shouldn't be at all surprised if she conceals the fact that she was in the wood to-night. By the way, was it the stammering-man?'

'It was, and Miss Daubenay was right in her suspicion: he is dead.'

Miss Creed accepted this with fortitude. 'Well, if he is, I can tell you who killed him. That girl told me all over again how it happened, and there is no doubt that the other man was Captain Trimble. And he did it to get the necklace!'

'Admirable!' said Sir Richard.

'It is as plain as a pikestaff. And now that I come to think of it, it may very likely be all for the best. Of course, I am sorry for the stammering-man, but you can't deny that he was a very disagreeable person. Besides, I know perfectly well that he was threatening you. That is why I followed you. Now we are rid of the whole affair!'

'Not quite, I fear. You must not think that I am unmoved by your heroic behaviour, but I could wish that you had gone to bed, Pen.'

'Yes, but I find that most unreasonable of you,' objected Pen. 'It seems to me that you want to keep all the adventure for yourself!'

'I appreciate your feelings,' said Sir Richard, 'but I would point out to you that your situation is a trifle—shall we say irregular?—and that we have been at considerable pains to excite no undue attention. Hence that abominable stage-coach. The last thing in the world I desire is to see you brought forward as a witness to this affair. If Miss Daubenay does not disclose her share in it, you may yet escape notice, but, to tell you the truth, I place little dependence on Miss Daubenay's discretion.'

'Oh!' said Pen, digesting this. 'You think there may be a little awkwardness if it should be discovered that I am not a boy? Perhaps we had better leave Queen Charlton?'

'No, that would indeed be fatal. We are now committed to this adventure. I am going to inform the local magistrate that I have discovered a corpse in this spinney. As you have encountered Miss Daubenay, upon whose discretion we have decided to place no reliance, I shall mention the fact that you accompanied me upon my evening stroll, and we must trust that no particular notice will be taken of you. By the way, brat, I think you had better become my young cousin—my remote young cousin.'

'Ah!' said Miss Creed, gratified. 'My own story!'

'Your own story.'

'Well, I must say I am glad you don't wish to run away,' she confided. 'You cannot conceive how much I am enjoying myself! I dare say it is otherwise with you, but, you see, I have had such a very dull life up till now! And I'll tell you another thing, Richard: naturally I am very anxious to find Piers, but I think we had better not send any word to him until we have finished this adventure.'

He was silent for a moment. 'Are you very anxious to find Piers?' he asked at last.

'Of course I am! Why, that is why we came!'

'Very true. I was forgetting. You will see Piers to-morrow morning, I fancy.'

She got up from the bank. 'I shall see him to-morrow? But how do you know?'

'I should have mentioned to you that I have just had the felicity of meeting him.'

'Piers?' she exclaimed. 'Here? In the wood?'

'Over Beverley Brandon's body.'

'I thought I heard voices! But how did he come to be here? And why didn't you bring him to me directly?'

Sir Richard took time over his answer. 'You see, I was under the impression that Miss Daubenay was still with you,' he explained.

'Oh, I see!' said Pen innocently. 'Yes, indeed, you did quite right! We don't want her to be included in our adventure. But did you tell Piers about me?'

'The moment did not seem to be propitious,' confessed Sir Richard. 'I told him to come to visit me at the "George" to-morrow morning, and on no account to divulge his presence in the wood to-night.'

'What a surprise it will be to him when he finds me at the "George"!' said Pen gleefully.

'Yes,' said Sir Richard. 'I think it will be—a surprise to him.'

She fell into step beside him on their way back to the road. 'I am glad you did not tell him! I suppose he had come to look for the stammering-man? I can't conceive how he could have had such a disagreeable person to visit him!'

Sir Richard, who had rarely, during the twenty-nine years of his existence, found himself at a loss, now discovered that he was totally incapable of imparting his own suspicions to his trusting companion. Apparently, it had not occurred to her that the sentiments of her old playfellow might have undergone a change; and so fixed in her mind was a five-year-old pact of betrothal that it had not entered her head to question either its durable qualities, or its desirability. She evidently considered herself plighted to Piers Luttrell, a circumstance which had no doubt had much to do with her friendly acceptance of Sir Richard's companionship. Phrases of warning half-formed themselves in Sir Richard's brain, and were rejected. Piers would have to do his explaining; Sir Richard could only hope that upon coming face to face with him after a lapse of years, Pen might discover that as he had outgrown a childhood's fancy, so too had she.

They entered the George together. Pen went up to bed at a nod from Sir Richard, but Sir Richard rang the bell for a servant. A sleepy waiter came in answer to the summons, and, upon being asked for the direction of the nearest magistrate, said that Sir Jasper Luttrell was the nearest, but was away from home. He knew of no other, so Sir Richard desired him to fetch the landlord to him, and sat down to write a short note to whom it might concern.

When the landlord came into the parlour, Sir Richard was shaking the sand off the single sheet of paper. He folded it, and sealed it with a wafer, and upon being told that Mr John Philips, of Whitchurch, was the nearest available magistrate, wrote this gentleman's name on the note. As he wrote, he said in his calm way: 'I shall be obliged to you if you will have this letter conveyed directly to Mr Philips.'

'To-night, sir?'

'To-night, Mr Philips will, I imagine, come back with your messenger. If he asks for me, show him into this room. Ah, and landlord!'

'Sir?'

'A bowl of rum punch. I will mix it myself.'

'Yes, sir! Immediately, sir!' said the landlord, relieved to receive such a normal command.

He lingered for a moment, trying to summon up sufficient resolution to ask the fine London gentleman why he wanted to see a magistrate thus urgently. Sir Richard's quizzing-glass came up, and the landlord withdrew in haste. The waiter would have followed him, but was detained by Sir Richard's uplifted forefinger.

'One moment! Who gave you the note which you delivered to me this evening?'

'It was Jem, sir—the tapster. It was when I went up to the bar for a pint of burgundy for a gentleman dining in the coffee-room that Jem gave it to me. It was Captain Trimble who picked it up off the ground, where it was a-laying. It got swep' off the bar, I dessay, sir, the taproom being crowded at the time, and Jem with his hands full.'

'Thank you,' said Sir Richard. 'That is all.'

The waiter went away considerably mystified. Sir Richard on the other hand, felt that the mystery had been satisfactorily explained, and sat down to await the landlord's return with the ingredients for a bowl of punch.

Mr Philips' residence was situated some five miles from Queen Charlton, and it was consequently some time before the clatter of horses' hooves in the street heralded his arrival. Sir Richard was squeezing the lemon into the punch bowl when he was ushered into the parlour, and looked up fleetingly to say: 'Ah, how do you do? Mr Philips, I apprehend?'

Mr. Philips was a grizzled gentleman with a harassed frown, and a slight paunch.

'Your servant, sir! Have I the honour of addressing Sir Richard Wyndham?'

'Mine, sir, is the honour,' said Sir Richard absently, intent upon his punch.

'Sir,' said Mr Philips, 'your very extraordinary communication—I may say, your unprecedented disclosure—has, as you perceive, brought me immediately to enquire into this incredible affair!'

'Very proper,' said Sir Richard. 'You will wish to visit the scene of the crime, I imagine. I can give you the direction, but no doubt the village constable is familiar with the locality. The body, Mr Philips, is—or was—lying in the clearing in the middle of the spinney, a little way down the road.'

'Do you mean to tell me, sir, that this story is true?' demanded the magistrate.

'Certainly it is true. Dear me, did you suppose me to be so heartless as to drag you out at this hour on a fool's errand? Are you in favour of adding the juice of one or of two lemons?'

Mr Philips, whose eyes had been critically observing Sir Richard's proceedings, said, without thinking: 'One! One is enough!'

'I feel sure you are right,' said Sir Richard.

'You know, sir, I must ask you some questions about this extraordinary affair!' said Philips, recollecting his errand.

'So you shall, sir, so you shall. Would you like to ask them now, or after you have disposed of the body?'

'I shall first repair to the scene of the murder,' declared Philips.

'Good!' said Sir Richard. 'I will engage to have the punch ready against your return.'

Mr Philips felt that this casual way of treating the affair was quite out of order, but the prospect of returning to a bowl of hot rum punch was so agreeable that he decided to overlook any trifling irregularity. When he returned to the inn, half an hour later, he was feeling chilled, for it was now past midnight and he had not taken his overcoat with him. Sir Richard had caused a fire to be kindled in the wainscoted parlour, and from the bowl on the table, which he was stirring with a long-handled spoon, there arose a very fragrant and comforting aroma. Mr Philips rubbed his hands together, and could not refrain from ejaculating: 'Ha!'

Sir Richard looked up, and smiled. His smile had won more hearts than Mr Philips', and it had a visible effect on that gentleman.

'Well, well, well! I won't deny that's a very welcome smell, Sir Richard! A fire, too! Upon my word, I'm glad to see it! Gets chilly at night, very chilly! A bad business, sir! a very bad business!'

Sir Richard ladled the steaming brew into two glasses, and gave one to the magistrate. 'Draw up a chair to the fire, Mr Philips. It is, as you say, a very bad business. I should tell you that I am intimately acquainted with the family of the deceased.'

Mr Philips fished Sir Richard's note out of his pocket. 'Yes, yes, just as I supposed, sir. I do not know how you would otherwise have furnished me with the poor man's name. You know him, in fact. Precisely! He was travelling in your company, perhaps?'

'No,' said Sir Richard, taking a chair on the opposite side of the fireplace. 'He was staying with a friend who lives in the neighbourhood. The name was, I think, Luttrell.'

'Indeed! This becomes more and more—— But pray continue, sir! You were not, then, together?'

'No, nothing of the sort. I came into the west country in family affairs. I need not burden you with them, I think.'

'Quite, quite! Family affairs: yes! Go on, sir! How came you to discover Mr Brandon's body?'

'Oh, by accident! But it will be better, perhaps, if I recount my share in this affair from its start.'

'Certainly! Yes! Pray do so, sir! This is a remarkable good bowl of punch, I may say.'

'I am generally thought to have something of a knack with a punch bowl,' bowed Sir Richard. 'To go back, then, to the start! You have no doubt heard, Mr Philips, of the Brandon diamonds?'

From the startled expression in the magistrate's eyes, and the slight dropping of his jaw, it was apparent that he had not. He said: 'Diamonds? Really, I fear—— No, I must confess that I had not heard of the Brandon diamonds.'

'Then, I should explain that they make up a certain famous necklace, worth, I dare say, anything you like.'

'Upon my word! An heirloom! Yes, yes, but in what way——'

'While on my way to Bristol with a young relative of mine, a slight accident befell our coach, and we were forced to put up for the night at a small inn near Wroxhall. There, sir, I encountered an individual who seemed to me—but I am not very well-versed in these matters—a somewhat questionable character. How questionable I did not know until the following morning, when a Bow Street Runner arrived at the inn.'

'Good God, sir! This is the most—— But I interrupt you!'

'Not at all,' said Sir Richard politely. 'I left the inn while the Runner was interrogating this individual. It was not until my young cousin and I had proceeded some way on our journey that I discovered in my pocket a purse containing the Brandon necklace.'

The magistrate sat bolt upright in his chair. 'You amaze me, sir! You astonish me! The necklace in your pocket? Really, I do not know what to say!'

'No,' agreed Sir Richard, rising and refilling his guest's glass. 'I was rather taken aback myself. In fact, it was some time before I could think how it came to be there.'

'No wonder, no wonder! Most understandable, indeed! You recognized the necklace?'

'Yes,' said Sir Richard, returning to his chair. 'I recognized it, but—really, I am amazed at my own stupidity! —I did not immediately connect it with the individual encountered near Wroxhall. The question was then not so much how it came to be in my possession, as how to restore it to Lord Saar with the least possible delay. I could picture Lady Saar's dismay at such an irreparable loss! Ah—a lady of exquisite sensibility, you understand!'

The magistrate nodded his comprehension. The rum punch was warming him quite as much as the fire, and he had a not unpleasant sensation of mixing with exalted persons.

'Happily—or perhaps I should say, in the light of future events, *unhappily*,' continued Sir Richard, 'I recalled that Beverley Brandon—he was Saar's younger son, I should mention—was staying in this neighbourhood. I repaired instantly to this inn, therefore, and, being fortunate enough to meet Brandon just beyond the village, gave the necklace to him without further ado.'

The magistrate set down his glass. 'You gave the necklace to him? Did he know that it had been stolen?'

'By no means. He was as astonished as I was, but engaged himself to restore it immediately to his father. I considered the matter satisfactorily settled—Saar, you know, having the greatest dislike of any kind of notoriety, such as must accrue from the theft, and the subsequent proceedings.'

'Sir!' said Mr Philips, 'do you mean to imply that this unfortunate young man was murdered for the sake of the necklace?'

'That,' said Sir Richard, 'is what I fear may have happened.'

'But this is shocking! Upon my word, sir, I am quite dumbfounded!—what—who can have known that the necklace was in his possession?'

'I should have said that no one could have known it, but, upon consideration, I imagine that the individual who hid it in my pocket may well have followed me to this place, waiting for an opportunity to get it back into his possession.'

'True! very true! You have been spied upon! Yet you have not seen that man in Queen Charlton?'

'Do you think he would—er—let me see him?' enquired Sir Richard, evading this question.

'No. No, indeed! Certainly not! But this must be looked to!'

'Yes,' agreed Sir Richard, pensively swinging his eyeglass on the end of its ribbon. 'And I think you might, with advantage, look to the sudden disappearance from this inn of a flashy person calling himself Captain Trimble, Mr Philips.'

'Really, sir! This becomes more and more—— Pray, what reason have you for supposing that this man may be implicated in the murder?'

'Well,' said Sir Richard slowly, 'some chance words which I let fall on the subject of—ah—waistcoats, sent Captain Trimble off hot-foot to Bristol.'

The magistrate blinked, and directed an accusing glance towards his half-empty glass. A horrid suspicion that the rum punch had affected his understanding was dispelled, however, by Sir Richard's next words.

'My acquaintance at the inn near Wroxhall wore a catskin waistcoat. A casual reference to this circumstance had the surprising effect of arousing the Captain's curiosity. He asked me in what direction the man in the catskin waistcoat had been travelling, and upon my saying that I believed him to be bound for Bristol, he left the inn—er—incontinent.'

'I see! yes, yes, I see! An accomplice!'

'My own feeling,' said Sir Richard, 'is that he was an accomplice who had been—er—bubbled.'

The magistrate appeared to be much struck by this. 'Yes! I see it all! Good God, this is a terrible affair! I have never been called upon to—— But you say this Captain Trimble went off to Bristol, sir?'

'He did. But I have since learned, Mr Philips, that he was back at this inn at six o'clock this evening. Ah! I should, I see, say *yesterday* evening,' he added with a glance at the clock on the mantelpiece.

Mr Philips drew a long breath. 'Your disclosures, Sir Richard, open up—are in fact, of such a nature as to—— Upon my word, I never thought—— But the murder! You discovered this, sir?'

'I discovered Brandon's body,' corrected Sir Richard.

'How came you to do this, sir? You had a suspicion? You——'

'None at all. It was a warm evening, and I stepped out to enjoy a stroll in the moonlight. Chance alone led my footsteps to the wood where I found my unfortunate young friend's body. It is only since making that melancholy discovery that I have pieced together the—er—evidence.'

Mr Philips had a hazy idea that chance had played an over-important part in Sir Richard's adventures, but he was aware that the punch he had drunk had slightly clouded his intellect. He said guardedly: 'Sir, the story you have unfolded is of a nature which—in short, it must be carefully sifted. Yes, indeed. Carefully sifted! I must request you not to remove from this neighbourhood until I have had time—pray do not misunderstand me! There is not the least suggestion, I assure you, of——'

'My dear sir, I don't misunderstand you, and I have no intention of removing from this inn,' said Sir Richard soothingly. 'I am aware that you have, so far, only my word for it that I am indeed Richard Wyndham.'

'Oh, as to that, I am sure—no suggestion of disbelieving—— But my duty is prescribed! You will appreciate my position, I am persuaded!'

'Perfectly!' said Sir Richard. 'I shall hold myself wholly at your disposal. You, as a man of the world, will, I am assured, appreciate the need of the exercise of—ah—the most delicate discretion in handling this affair.'

Mr Philips, who had once spent three weeks in London, was flattered to think that the imprint of that short sojourn was pronounced enough to be discernible to such a personage as Beau Wyndham, and swelled with pride. Native caution, however, warned him that his investigation had better be postponed to a more sober moment. He rose to his feet with careful dignity, and set his empty glass down on the table. 'I am obliged to you!' he pronounced. 'I shall wait upon you to-morrow—no, to-day! I must consider this affair. A terrible business! I think one may say, a terrible business!'

Sir Richard agreed to this, and after a meticulous exchange of courtesies, Mr Philips took his leave. Sir Richard snuffed the candles, and went up to bed, not dissatisfied with his night's work.

In the morning, Pen was first down. The day was fine, and her cravat, she flattered herself, very well tied. There was a suggestion of a prance about her gait as she sallied forth to inspect the weather. Sir Richard, no believer in early rising, had ordered breakfast for nine o'clock, and it was as yet only eight. A maid-servant was engaged in sweeping the floor of the private parlour, and a bored waiter was spreading clean cloths over the tables in the coffee-room. As Pen passed through the entrance-parlour, the landlord, who was conversing in low tones with a gentleman unknown to her, looked round, and exclaimed: 'Here is the young gentleman himself, sir!'

Mr Philips, confronted with the biggest crime ever committed within the limits of his jurisdiction, had perhaps imbibed too strong a brew of rum punch on the previous evening, but he was a zealous person, and, in spite of awaking with a very bad head, he had lost no time in getting out of his comfortable bed, and riding back to Queen Charlton to continue his investigations. As Pen paused, he stepped forward, and bade her a civil good-morning. She responded, wishing that Sir Richard would come downstairs; and upon Mr Philips' asking her, in a tone of kindly patronage, whether she was Sir Richard's young cousin, assented, and hoped that the magistrate would not ask for her name.

He did not. He said: 'Now, you were with Sir Richard when he discovered this very shocking crime, were you not, young man?'

'Well, not precisely,' said Pen.

'Oh? How is that?'

'I was, and I wasn't,' Pen explained, with an earnestness which robbed the words of flippancy. 'I didn't see the body.'

'No? Just tell me exactly what happened. No need to feel any alarm, you know! If you walked out with your cousin, how came you to have separated?'

'Well, sir, there was an owl,' confided Pen unblushingly.

'Come, come! An *owl?*'

'Yes: my cousin said that too.'

'Said what?'

'Come, come! He is not interested in bird-life.'

'Ah, I see! You collect eggs, eh? That's it, is it?'

'Yes, and also I like to watch birds.'

Mr Phillips smiled tolerantly. He wondered how old this slim boy was, and thought it a pity the young fellow should be so effeminate; but he was a country man himself, and dimly he could recall the bird-watching days of his youth. 'Yes, yes, I understand! You went off on your own to try to catch a glimpse of this owl: well, I have done the same in my time! And so you were not with your good cousin when he reached the clearing in the wood?'

'No, but I met him on his return, and of course he told me what he had found.'

'I dare say, but hearsay, my boy, is not evidence,' said Mr Phillips, nodding dismissal.

Pen made for the door, feeling that she had extricated herself from a difficult situation with aplomb. The landlord ran after her with a sealed letter. 'If I was not forgetting! I beg pardon, sir, but a young person brought this for you not an hour ago. Leastways, it was for a young gentleman of the name of Wyndham. Would that be in mistake for yourself, sir?'

Pen took the letter, and looked at it with misgiving. 'A young person?' she repeated.

'Well, sir, it was one of the servant-girls from Major Daubenay's.'

'Oh!' said Pen. 'Oh, very well! Thank you!'

She passed out into the village street, and after dubiously regarding the direction on the note, which was to—— 'Wyndham Esq.,' and written in a round schoolgirl's hand, she broke the seal, and spread open the single sheet.

'Dear Sir,' the letter began, primly enough, *The Unfortunate Being whom you befriended last night, is in Desperate Case, and begs that you will come to the little orchard next to the road at eight o'clock punctually, because it is vital that I should have Private Speech with you. Do not fail. Your obliged servant,*

'Lydia Daubenay.'

It was plain that Miss Daubenay had written this missive in considerable agitation. Greatly intrigued, Pen enquired the way to Major Daubenay's house of a baker's boy, and set off down the dusty road.

By the time she had reached the appointed rendezvous it was half-past eight, and Miss Daubenay was pacing up and down impatiently. A thick, high hedge shut the orchard off from sight of the house, and a low wall enclosed it from the road. Pen climbed on to this without much difficulty, and was greeted by an instant accusation: 'Oh, you are so late! I have been waiting ages!'

'Well, I am sorry, but I came as soon as I had read your letter,' said Pen, jumping down into the orchard. 'Why do you wish to see me?'

Miss Daubenay wrung her hands, and uttered in tense accents: 'Everything has gone awry. I am quite distracted! I don't know what to do!'

Pen betrayed no particular solicitude at this moving speech, but critically looked Miss Daubenay over.

She was a pretty child, about the same age as Pen herself, but shorter, and much plumper. She had a profusion of nut-brown ringlets, a pair of fawn-like brown eyes, and

a soft rosebud of a mouth. She was dressed in a white
muslin dress, high-waisted, and frilled about the ankles,
and with a great many pale-blue bows of ribbon with long
fluttering ends. She raised her melting eyes to Pen's face,
and breathed: 'Can I trust you?'

Miss Creed was a literal-minded female, and instead of
responding with promptness and true chivalry, she replied
cautiously: 'Well, probably you can, but I am not sure till
I know what it is that you want.'

Miss Daubenay seemed a little daunted for a moment,
and said in a soft moan: 'I am in such a taking! I have
been very, very silly!'

Pen found no difficulty in believing this. She said: 'Well,
don't stand there wringing your hands! Let us sit down
under that tree.'

Lydia looked doubtful. 'Will it not be damp?'

'No, of course not! Besides, what if it were?'

'Oh, the grass might stain my dress!'

'It seems to me,' said Pen severely, 'that if you are both-
ering about your dress you cannot be in such great trouble.'

'Oh, but I am!' said Lydia, sinking down on to the turf,
and clasping her hands at her bosom. 'I do not know what
you will say, or what you will think of me! I must have
been mad! Only you were kind to me last night, and I
thought I could trust you!'

'I dare say you can,' said Pen. 'But I wish you will tell
me what is the matter, because I have not yet had any
breakfast, and——'

'If I had thought that you would be so unsympathetic I
would never, never have sent for you!' declared Lydia in
tremulous accents.

'Well, it is very difficult to be sympathetic when a person will do nothing but wring her hands, and say the sort
of things there really is no answer to,' said Pen reasonably.
'Do start at the beginning!'

Miss Daubenay bowed her head. 'I am the most unhappy
creature alive!' she announced. 'I have the misfortune to
be secretly betrothed to one whom my father will not
tolerate.'

'Yes, I thought you were. I suppose you went to meet
him in the wood last night?'

'Alas, it is true! But do not judge me hastily! He is the most unexceptionable—the most——'

'If he is unexceptionable,' interrupted Pen, 'why won't your father tolerate him?'

'It is all wicked prejudice!' sighed Lydia. 'My father quarrelled with his father, and they don't speak.'

'Oh! What did they quarrel about?'

'About a piece of land,' said Lydia mournfully.

'It sounds very silly.'

'It is silly. Only *they* are perfectly serious about it, and they do not care a fig for *our* sufferings! We have been forced to this hateful expedient of meeting in secret. I should tell you that my betrothed is the *soul* of honour! Subterfuge is repugnant to him, but what can we do? We love each other!'

'Why don't you run away?' suggested Pen practically.

Startled eyes leapt to hers. 'Run where?'

'To Gretna Green, of course.'

'Oh, I could not! Only think of the scandal!'

'I do think you should try not to be so poor-spirited. However, I dare say you can't help it.'

'You are the rudest boy I ever met!' exclaimed Lydia, 'I declare I wish I had not sent for you!'

'So do I, because this seems to be a silly story, and not in the least my concern,' said Pen frankly. 'Oh, pray don't start to cry! There, I am sorry! I didn't mean to be unkind! But why *did* you send for me?'

'Because, though you are rude and horrid, you did not seem to me like other young men, and I thought you would understand, and not take advantage of me.'

Pen gave a sudden mischievous chuckle. 'I shan't do *that,* at all events! Oh dear, I am getting so hungry! Do tell me why you sent for me!'

Miss Daubenay dabbed her eyes with a wisp of a handkerchief. 'I was so distracted last night I scarce knew what I was doing! And when I reached home, the most dreadful thing happened! Papa saw me! Oh, sir, he accused me of having gone out to meet P—— to meet my betrothed, and said I should be packed off again to Bath this very day, to stay with my Great-Aunt Augusta. The horridest, most disagreeable old woman! Nothing but backgammon, and spy-

ing, and everything of the most hateful! Sir, I felt myself
to be in desperate case! Indeed, I said it before I had time
to recollect the consequencs!'

'Said what?' asked Pen, patient but bored.

Miss Daubenay bowed her head again. 'That it was not
—not *that* man I had gone to meet, but another, whom I
had met in Bath, when I was sent to Great-Aunt Augusta
to—to cure me of what Papa called my *infatuation!* I said
I had been in the habit of meeting this other man c-clan-
destinely, because I thought that would make Papa afraid
to send me back to Bath, and might perhaps even rec-
oncile him to the Real Man.'

'Oh!' said Pen doubtfully. 'And did it?'

'No! He said he did not believe me.'

'Well, I must say I'm not surprised at that.'

'Yes, but in the end he did, and now I wish I had never
said it. He said if there was Another Man, who was it?'

'You ought to have thought of that. He was bound to ask
that question, and you must have looked very silly when
you could not answer.'

'But I did answer!' whispered Miss Daubenay, apparently
overcome.

'But how could you, if there wasn't another man?'

'I said it was you!' said Miss Daubenay despairingly.

◦§ *Chapter X* §◦

THE effect of this confession upon Pen was not quite what
Miss Daubenay had expected. She gasped, choked, and
went off into a peal of laughter. Affronted, Miss Daubenay
said: 'I don't see what there is to laugh at!'

'No, I dare say you don't,' said Pen, mopping her eyes.
'But it is excessively amusing for all that. What made you
say anything so silly?'

'I couldn't think of anything else to say. And as for its
being *silly,* you may think me very ill-favoured, but I have
already had *several* suitors!'

'I think you are very pretty, but I am not going to be a suitor,' said Pen firmly.

'I don't want you to be! For one thing, I find you quite odiously rude, and for another you are much too young, which is why I chose you, because I thought I should be quite safe in so doing.'

'Well you are, but I never heard of anything so foolish in my life! Pray, what was the use of telling your father such fibs?'

'I told you,' said Lydia crossly. 'I scarcely knew what I was saying, and I thought—— But everything has gone awry!'

Pen looked at her with misgiving. 'What do you mean?'

'Papa is going to wait on your cousin this morning.'

'What!' exclaimed Pen.

Lydia nodded. 'Yes, and he is not angry at all. He is pleased!'

'Pleased? How can he be pleased at your holding clandestine meetings with a strange man?'

'To be sure, he did say that that was very wrong of me. But he asked me your name. Of course I don't know it, but your cousin told me his name was Wyndham, so I said yours was too.'

'But it isn't!'

'Well, how was I to know that?' demanded Lydia, aggrieved. 'I had to say something!'

'You are the most unprincipled girl in the world! Besides, why should he be pleased just because you said my name was Wyndham?'

'Apparently,' said Lydia gloomily, 'the Wyndhams are all fabulously wealthy.'

'You must tell him without any loss of time I am *not* a Wyndham, and that I haven't any money at all!'

'How can I tell him anything of the kind? I think you are being most unreasonable! Do but consider! If I said now that I had been mistaken in your name he would suppose you to have been trifling with me!'

'But you cannot expect me to pretend to be in love with you!' Pen said, aghast.

Lydia sniffed. 'Nothing could be more repulsive to me than such a notion. I am already sorry that I mentioned

you to Papa. Only I did, and now I don't know what to do.
He would be so angry if he knew that I had made it all up!'

'Well, I am very sorry, but it seems to me quite your
own fault, and I wash my hands of it,' said Pen.

She glanced at Miss Daubenay's flower-like countenance,
and made a discovery. Miss Daubenay's soft chin had
acquired a look of obstinacy; the fawn-like eyes stared
back at her with a mixture of appeal and determination.
'You can't wash your hands of it. I told you that Papa was
going to seek an interview with your cousin to-day.'

'You must stop him.'

'I can't. You don't know Papa!'

'No, and I don't want to know him,' Pen pointed out.

'If I told him it had all been lies, I do not know what he
might not do. I won't do it! I don't care what you may say:
I *won't!*'

'Well, I shall deny every word of your story.'

'Then,' said Lydia, not without triumph, 'Papa will do
something dreadful to you, because he will think it is you
who are telling lies!'

'It seems to me that unless he is a great fool he must
know you well enough by now to guess that it is *you* who
have told lies!' said Pen, with asperity.

'It's no use being disagreeable and rude,' said Lydia.
'Papa thinks you followed me to Queen Charlton.'

'You mean you told him so,' said Pen bitterly.

'Yes, I did. At least, he asked me, and I said yes before
I had had time to think.'

'Really, you are the most brainless creature! Do you
never think?' said Pen, quite exasperated. 'Just look what a
coil you've created! Either your Papa is coming to ask me
what my intentions are, or—which I think a great deal
more likely—to complain to Richard about my conduct!
Oh dear, whatever will Richard say to this fresh distur-
bance?'

It was plain that all this meant nothing to Miss Daubenay. For form's sake, she repeated that she was very sorry,
but added: 'I hoped you would be able to help me. But
you are a boy! You don't understand what it means to be
persecuted as I am!'

This remark could not but strike a chord of sympathy.

'As a matter of fact, I do know,' said Pen. 'Only, if helping you means offering for your hand, I won't do it. The more I think of it, the more ridiculous it seems to me that you should have dragged me into it. How could such an absurd tale possibly be of use?'

Lydia sighed. 'One does not think of those things in the heat of the moment. Besides, I didn't really mean to drag you in. It—it just happened.'

'I don't see how it could have happened if you didn't mean it.'

'One thing led to another,' Lydia explained vaguely. 'Almost before I knew it, the whole story had—had grown up. Of course I don't wish you to offer for my hand, but I do think you might pretend you want to, so that Papa shan't suspect me of telling lies.'

'No!' said Pen.

'I think you are very unkind,' whimpered Lydia. 'I shall be sent back to Bath, and Great-Aunt Augusta will spy on me, and I shall never see Piers again!'

'Who?' Pen's head was jerked around. 'Who will you never see again?'

'Oh, please do not ask me! I did not mean to mention his name!'

'Are you—' Pen stopped, rather white of face, and started again: 'Are you betrothed to Piers Luttell?'

'You know him!' Miss Daubenay clasped ecstatic hands.

'Yes,' said Pen, feeling as though the pit of her stomach had suddenly vanished. 'Yes, I know him.'

'Then you will help me!'

Miss Creed's clear blue eyes met Miss Daubenay's swimming brown ones. Miss Creed drew a long breath. 'Is—is Piers indeed in love with you?' she asked incredulously.

Miss Daubenay bridled. 'You need not sound so surprised! We have been plighted for a whole year! Why do you look so oddly?'

'I beg your pardon,' apologized Pen. 'But how he must have changed! It is very awkward!'

'Why?' asked Lydia, staring.

'Well, it—it—you wouldn't understand. Has he been meeting you in woods for a whole year?'

'No, because Papa sent me to Bath, and Sir Jasper forbade him to see me any more, and even Lady Luttrell said we were too young. But we love each other!'

'It seems extraordinary,' said Pen, shaking her head. 'You know, I find it very hard to believe!'

'You are the horridest boy! It is perfectly true, and if you know Piers you may ask him for yourself! I wish I had never clapped eyes on you!'

'So do I,' replied Pen frankly.

Miss Daubenay burst into tears. Pen surveyed her with interest, and asked presently in the voice of one probing mysteries: 'Do you always cry as much as this? Do you—do you cry at Piers?'

'I don't cry *at* people!' sobbed Miss Daubenay. 'And if Piers knew how horrid you have been to me he would very likely knock you down!'

Pen gave a hiccup of laughter. This incensed Lydia so much that she stopped crying, and dramatically commanded Pen to leave the orchard immediately. However, when she discovered that Pen was only too ready to take her at her word, she ran after her, and clasped her by the arm. 'No, no, you cannot go until we have decided what is to be done. You won't——oh, you *can't* be cruel enough to deny my story to Papa!'

Pen considered this. 'Well, provided you won't expect me to offer for you——'

'No, no, I promise I won't!'

Pen frowned. 'Yes, but it's of no use. There is only one thing for it: you will have to run away.'

'But——'

'Now, don't begin to talk about the scandal, and spoiling your dress!' begged Pen. 'For one thing, it is odiously miss-ish, and for another Piers will never be able to bear it.'

'Piers,' said Miss Daubenay, with swelling bosom, 'thinks me Perfect!'

'I haven't seen Piers for a long time, but he *can't* have grown up as stupid as that!' Pen pointed out.

'Yes, he—oh, I hate you, I hate you!' cried Lydia, stamping her foot. 'Besides, how can I run away?'

'Oh, Piers will have to arrange it! If Richard doesn't object, I daresay I may help him,' Pen assured her. 'You will have to escape at dead of night, of course, which puts me in mind of a very important thing: you will need a rope-ladder.'

'I haven't a rope-ladder,' objected Lydia.

'Well, Piers must make one for you. If he throws it up to your window, you could attach it securely, could you not, and climb down it?'

'I would rather escape by the door,' said Lydia, gazing helplessly up at her.

'Oh, very well, but it seems rather tame! However, it is quite your own affair. Piers will be waiting for you with a post-chaise-and-four. You will leap into it, and the horses will spring forward, and you will fly for the Border! I can see it all!' declared Pen, her eyes sparkling.

Lydia seemed to catch a little of her enthusiasm. 'To be sure, it does sound romantic,' she admitted. 'Only it is a great way to the Border, and everyone would be so cross with us!'

'Once you were married that wouldn't signify.'

'No. No, it wouldn't, would it? But I don't think Piers has any money.'

'Oh!' Pen's face fell. 'That certainly makes it rather awkward. But I daresay we shall contrive something.'

Lydia said: 'Well, if you don't mind, I would prefer *not* to go to Gretna, because although it would be romantic I can't help thinking it would be very uncomfortable. Besides, I couldn't have any attendants, or a wedding-dress, or a lace veil, or anything.'

'Don't chatter!' said Pen. 'I am thinking.'

Lydia was obediently silent.

'We must soften your father's heart!' declared Pen at length.

Lydia looked doubtful. 'Yes, I should like that of all things, but how?'

'Why, by making him grateful to Piers, of course!'

'But why should he be grateful to Piers? He says Piers is a young cub.'

'Piers,' said Pen, 'must rescue you from deadly peril.'

'Oh no, please!' faltered Lydia, shrinking. 'I should be frightened! And just think how dreadful it would be if he didn't rescue me!'

'What a little goose you are!' said Pen scornfully. 'There won't be any real danger!'

'But if there is no danger, how can Piers——'

'Piers shall rescue you from me!' said Pen.

Lydia blinked at her. 'I don't understand. How can Piers——'

'Do stop saying "How can Piers"!' Pen begged. 'We must make your father believe that I am a penniless young man without any prospects at all, and then we will run away together!'

'But I don't want to run away with you!'

'No, stupid, and I don't want to run away with you! It will just be a Plot. Piers must ride after us, and catch us, and restore you to your Papa. And he will be so pleased that he will let you marry Piers after all! Because Piers has very good prospects, you know.'

'Yes, but you are forgetting Sir Jasper,' argued Lydia.

'We can't possibly be plagued by Sir Jasper,' said Pen impatiently. 'Besides he is away. Now, don't make any more objections! I must go back to the George, and warn Richard. And I will consult with Piers as well, and I daresay we shall have it all arranged in a trice. I will meet you in the spinney this evening, to tell you what you must do.'

'Oh no, no, no!' shuddered Lydia. 'Not the spinney! I shall never set foot there again!'

'Well, here, then, since you are so squeamish. By the way, did you tell your Papa the whole? I mean, how you saw Captain Trimble kill the stammering-man?'

'Yes, of course I did, and he says I must tell it to Mr Philips! It is so dreadful for me! To think that my troubles had put it out of my head!'

'What a tiresome girl you are!' exclaimed Pen. 'You should not have said a word about it! Ten to one, we shall get into a tangle now, because Richard has already told Mr Philips *his* story, and I have told him mine, and now you are bound to say something quite different. Did you mention Richard to your Papa?'

'No,' confessed Lydia, hanging her head. 'I just said that I ran away.'

'Oh well, in that case perhaps there will be no harm

done!' said Pen optimistically. 'I am going now. I will meet you here again after dinner.'

'But what if they watch me, and I cannot slip away?' cried Lydia, trying to detain her.

Pen had climbed on to the wall, and now prepared to jump down into the road. 'You must think of something,' she said sternly, and vanished from Miss Daubenay's sight.

When Pen reached the George Sir Richard had not only finished his breakfast, but was on the point of sallying forth in search of his errant charge. She came into the parlour, flushed and rather breathless, and said impetuously: 'Oh, Richard, such an adventure! I have such a deal to tell you! All our plans must be changed!'

'This is very sudden!' said Sir Richard. 'May I ask where you have been?'

'Yes, of course,' said Pen, seating herself at the table, and spreading butter lavishly on a slice of bread. 'I have been with that stupid girl. You would not believe that anyone could be so silly, sir!'

'I expect I should. What has she been doing, and why did you go to see her?'

'Well, it's a long story, and *most* confused!'

'In that case,' said Sir Richard, 'perhaps I shall unravel it more easily if you do not tell it to me with your mouth full.'

Her eyes lit with laughter. She swallowed the bread-and-butter, and said: 'Oh, I'm sorry! I am so hungry, you see.'

'Have an apple,' he suggested.

She twinkled responsively. 'No, thank you, I will have some of that ham. Dear sir, what in the world do you suppose that wretched girl did?'

'I have no idea,' said Sir Richard, carving several slices of the ham.

'Why, she told her Papa that she had gone into the spinney last night to meet me!'

Sir Richard laid down the knife and fork. 'Good God, why?'

'Oh, for such an idiotic reason that it is not worth recounting! But the thing is, sir, that her Papa is coming to

see you about it this morning. She hoped, you see, that if
she said she had been in the habit of meeting me clandestinely in Bath——'

'In Bath?' interrupted Sir Richard in a faint voice.

'Yes, she said we had been meeting for ever in Bath, on
account of her Great-Aunt Augusta, and not wishing to be
sent there again. I quite understand *that*, but——'

'Then your understanding is very much better than
mine,' said Sir Richard. 'So far I have not been privileged
to understand one word of this story. What has her Great-
Aunt Augusta to do with it?'

'Oh, they sent Lydia to stay with her, you see, and she
did not like it! She said it was all backgammon and spy-
ing. I could not but feel for her over that, for I know
exactly what she means.'

'I am glad,' said Sir Richard, with emphasis.

'The thing is, that she thought if she told her Papa that
she had met me clandestinely in Bath, he would not send
her there again.'

'This sounds to me remarkably like mania in an acute
form.'

'Yes, so it did to me. But there is worse to come. She
says that instead of being angry, her Papa is inclined to be
pleased!'

'The madness seems to be inherited.'

'That is what I thought, but it appears that Lydia told
her Papa that my name was Wyndham, and now he thinks
that perhaps she is on the brink of making a Good Match!'

'Good God!'

'I knew you would be surprised. And there is another
circumstance too, which turns everything topsy-turvy.' She
glanced up fleetingly from her plate, and said with a little
difficulty: 'I discovered something which—which quite took
me aback. She told me whom she went to meet in the
wood last night.'

'I see,' said Sir Richard.

She flushed. 'Did you—did you know, sir?'

'I guessed, Pen.'

She nodded. 'It was stupid of me not to suspect. To tell
you the truth, I thought—— However, it doesn't signify. I
expect you did not like to tell me.'

'Do you mind very much?' he asked abruptly.

'Well, I—it—— You see, I had it fixed in my mind that Piers—and I—— So I daresay it will take me just a little while to grow accustomed to it, besides having all my plans overset. But never mind that! We have now to consider what is to be done to help Piers and Lydia.'

'We?' interpolated Sir Richard.

'Yes, because I quite depend on you to persuade Lydia's Papa that I am not an eligible suitor. That is most important!'

'Do you mean to tell me that this insane person is coming here to obtain my consent to your marriage with his daughter?'

'I think he is coming to discover how much money I have, and whether my intentions are honourable,' said Pen, pouring herself out a cup of coffee. 'But I daresay Lydia mistook the whole matter, for she is amazingly stupid, you know, and perhaps he is coming to complain to you about my shocking conduct in meeting Lydia in secret.'

'I foresee a pleasing morning,' said Sir Richard dryly.

'Well, I must say I think it will be very amusing,' Pen admitted. 'Because—why, what is the matter, sir?'

Sir Richard had covered his eyes with one hand. 'You think it will be very amusing! Good God!'

'Oh, now you are laughing at me again!'

'Laughing! I am recalling my comfortable home, my ordered life, my hitherto stainless reputation, and wondering what I can ever have done to deserve being pitchforked into this shameless imbroglio! Apparently, I am to go down to history as one who not only possessed a cousin who was a monster of precocious depravity, but who actually aided and abetted him in attempting to seduce a respectable young female.'

'No, no!' said Pen earnestly. 'Nothing of the kind, I assure you! I have it all arranged in the best possible way, and *your* part will be everything of the most proper!'

'Oh, well, in *that* case——!' said Sir Richard, lowering his hand.

'Now I know you are laughing at me! I am going to be the only son of a widow.'

'The unfortunate woman has all my sympathy.'

'Yes, because I am very wild, and she can do nothing with me. That is why you are here, of course. I cannot but see that I don't look quite old enough to be an eligible suitor. Do you think I do, sir?'

'No, I don't. In fact, I should not be surprised if Lydia's parent were to arrive with a birch-rod.'

'Good gracious, how dreadful! I never thought of that! Well, I shall depend upon you.'

'You may confidently depend upon me to tell Major Daubenay that his daughter's story is a farrago of lies.'

Pen shook her head. 'No, we can't do that. I said just the same myself, but you must see how difficult it would be to persuade Major Daubenay that we are speaking the truth. Consider, sir! She told him that I had followed her here, and I must admit it looks very black; because I *was* in the spinney last night, and you know we cannot possibly explain the real story. No, we must make the best of it. Besides, I quite feel that we ought to help Piers, if he does indeed wish to marry such a foolish creature.'

'I have not the slightest desire to help Piers, who seems to me to be behaving in a most reprehensible fashion.'

'Oh no, indeed he cannot help it! I see that I had better tell you their whole story.'

Without giving Sir Richard time to protest, she launched into a rapid and colourful account of the young lovers' tribulations. The account, being freely embellished with her own comments, was considerably involved, and Sir Richard several times interrupted it to crave enlightenment on some obscure point. At the end of it, he remarked without any noticeable display of enthusiasm: 'A most affecting history. For myself, I find the theme of Montague and Capulet hopelessly outmoded, however.'

'Well, I have made up my mind to it that there is only one thing for them to do. They must elope.'

Sir Richard, who had been playing with his quizzing-glass, let it fall, and spoke with startling severity. 'Enough of this! Now, understand me, brat, I will engage to fob off the irate father, but there it must end! This extremely tedious pair of lovers may elope to-morrow for anything

I care, but I will have no hand in it, and I will not permit you to have a hand in it either. Do you see?'

Pen looked speculatively at him. There was no smile visible in his eyes, which indeed looked much sterner than she had ever believed they could. Plainly, he would not lend any support to her scheme of eloping with Miss Daubenay herself. It would be better, decided Pen, to tell him nothing about this. But she was not one to let a challenge rest unanswered, and she replied with spirit: 'You may do as you choose, but you have *no* right to tell me what I must or must not do! It is not in the least your affair.'

'It is going to be very much my affair,' replied Sir Richard.

'I don't understand what you can possibly mean by saying anything so silly!'

'I daresay you don't, but you will.'

'Well, we won't dispute about that,' said Pen pacifically. He laughed suddenly. 'Indeed, I hope we shan't!'

'And you won't tell Major Daubenay that Lydia's story was false?'

'What do you want me to tell him?' he asked, succumbing to the coaxing note in her voice, and the pleading look in her candid eyes.

'Why, that I have been with my tutor in Bath, but that I was so troublesome that my Mama——'

'The widow?'

'Yes, and *now* you will understand why she is a widow!'

'If you are supposed to favour your mythical father, I do understand. He perished on the gallows.'

'That is what Jimmy Yarde calls the Nubbing Cheat.'

'I daresay it is, but I beg you won't.'

'Oh, very well! Where was I?'

'With your tutor.'

'To be sure. Well, I was so troublesome that my Mama sent you to bring me home. I expect you are a trustee, or something of that nature. And you may say all the horridest things about me to Major Daubenay that you like. In fact, you had better tell him that I am *very* bad, besides being quite a pauper.'

'Have no fear! I will draw such a picture of you as must

make him thankful that his daughter has escaped becoming betrothed to such a monster.'

'Yes, do!' said Pen cordially 'And then I must see Piers.'

'And then?' asked Sir Richard.

She sighed. 'I haven't thought of that yet. Really, we have so much on our hands that I cannot be teased with thinking of any more plans just now!'

'Will you let me suggest a plan to you, Pen?'

'Yes, certainly, if you can think of one. But first I should like to see Piers, because I still cannot quite believe that he truly wishes to marry Lydia. Why, she does nothing but cry, Richard!'

Sir Richard looked down at her enigmatically. 'Yes,' he said. 'Perhaps it would be better if you saw Piers first. People—especially young men—change a great deal in five years, brat.'

'True,' she said, in a melancholy tone. 'But *I* didn't change!'

'I think perhaps you did,' he said gently.

She seemed unconvinced, and he did not press the point. The waiter came in to clear away the covers, and hardly had he left the parlour than Major Daubenay's card was brought to Sir Richard.

Pen, changing colour, exclaimed: 'Oh dear, now I wish I weren't here! I suppose I can't escape now, can I?'

'Hardly. You would undoubtedly walk straight into the Major's arms. But I won't let him beat you.'

'Well, I hope you won't!' said Pen fervently. 'Tell me quickly, how does a person look depraved? *Do* I look depraved?'

'Not in the least. The best you can hope for is to look sulky.'

She retired to a chair in the corner, and sprawled in it, trying to scowl. 'Like this?'

'Excellent!' approved Sir Richard.

A minute later, Major Daubenay was ushered into the parlour. He was a harassed-looking man, with a high colour, and upon finding himself confronted by the tall, immaculate figure of a Corinthian, he exclaimed: 'Good Gad! You *are* Sir Richard Wyndham!'

Pen, glowering in the corner, could only admire the perfection of Sir Richard's bow. The Major's slightly protuberant eyes discovered her. 'And *this* is the young dog who has been trifling with my daughter!'

'*Again?*' said Sir Richard wearily.

The Major's eyes stared at him. 'Upon my soul, sir! Do you tell me that this—this young scoundrel is in the habit of seducing innocent females?'

'Dear me, is it as bad as that?' asked Sir Richard.

'No, sir, it is not!' fumed the Major. 'But when I tell you that my daughter has confessed that she went out last night to meet him clandestinely in a wood, and has met him many times before in Bath——'

Up came Sir Richard's quizzing-glass. 'I condole with you,' he said. 'Your daughter would appear to be a young lady of enterprise.'

'My daughter,' declared the Major, 'is a silly little miss! I do not know what young people are coming to! This young man—dear me, he looks no more than a lad!—is, I understand, a relative of yours?'

'My cousin,' said Sir Richard. 'I am—er—his mother's trustee. She is a widow.'

'I see that I have come to the proper person!' said the Major.

Sir Richard raised one languid hand. 'I beg you will acquit me of all responsibility, sir. My part is merely to remove my cousin from the care of a tutor who has proved himself wholly incapable of controlling his—er—activities, and to convey him to his mother's home.'

'But what are you doing in Queen Charlton, then?' demanded the Major.

It was plain that Sir Richard considered the question an impertinence. 'I have acquaintances in the neighbourhood, sir. I scarcely think I need trouble you with the reasons which led me to break a journey which cannot be other than—er—excessively distasteful to me. Pen, make your bow!'

'Pen?' repeated the Major, glaring at her.

'He was named after the great Quaker,' explained Sir Richard.

'Indeed! Then I would have you know, sir, that his behaviour scarcely befits his name!'

'You are perfectly right,' agreed Sir Richard. 'I regret to say that he has been a constant source of anxiety to his widowed parent.'

'He seems very young,' said the Major, scanning Pen critically.

'But, alas, old in sin!'

The Major was slightly taken aback. 'Oh, come, come, sir! I daresay it is not as bad as that! One must make allowances for young people. To be sure, it is very reprehensible, and I do not by any means exonerate my daughter from blame, but the springtime of life, you know, sir! Young people take such romantic notions into their heads —not but what I am excessively shocked to learn of clandestine meetings! But when two young persons fall in love, I believe——'

'In love!' interpolated Sir Richard, apparently thunderstruck.

'Well, well, I daresay you are surprised! One is apt to fancy the birds always too young to leave the nest, eh? But——'

'Pen!' said Sir Richard, turning awfully upon his supposed cousin. 'Is it possible that you can have made serious advances towards Miss Daubenay?'

'I never offered *marriage*,' said Pen, hanging her head.

The Major seemed to be in danger of suffering an apoplexy. Before he could recover the power of speech, Sir Richard had intervened. Upon the Major's bemused ears fell a description of Pen's shameless precocity that caused the object of it to turn away hastily to hide her laughter. According to Sir Richard's malicious tongue, Bath was strewn with her innocent victims. When Sir Richard let fall the information that this youthful moral leper was without means or expectations, the Major found enough breath to declare that the whelp ought to be horsewhipped.

'Precisely my own view,' bowed Sir Richard.

'Upon my word, I had not dreamed of such a thing! Penniless, you say?'

'Little better than a pauper,' said Sir Richard.

'Good Gad, what an escape!' gasped the Major. 'I do not know what to say! I am aghast!'

'Alas!' said Sir Richard, 'his father was just such another!

The same disarming air of innocence hid a wolfish heart.'

'You appall me!' declared the Major. 'Yet he looks a mere boy!'

Pen, feeling that it was time she bore a part in the scene, said with an air of innocence which horrified the Major: 'But if Lydia says I offered marriage, it is not true. It was all mere trifling. I do not wish to be married.'

This pronouncement once more bereft the Major of speech. Sir Richard's forefinger banished Pen to her corner, and by the time the outraged parent ceased gobbling, he had once more taken charge of the situation. He agreed that the whole affair must at all costs be hushed up, promised to deal faithfully with Pen, and finally escorted the Major out of the parlour, with assurances that such depravity should not go unpunished.

Pen, who had been struggling with an overwhelming desire to laugh, went off into a peal of mirth as soon as the Major was out of earshot, and had, in fact, to grasp a chairback to support herself. In this posture she was discovered by Mr Luttrell, who, as soon as Sir Richard and the Major had passed through the entrance-parlour, oblivious of his presence there, bounced in upon Pen, and said through shut teeth: 'So! You think it damned amusing, do you, you little cur? Well, I do *not!*'

Pen raised her head, and through brimming eyes saw the face of her old playmate swim before her.

Mr Luttrell, stuttering with rage, said menacingly: 'I heard you! I could not help but hear you! So you didn't intend marriage, eh? You—you *boast* of having t—trifled with an innocent female! And you think you c-can get off scot-free, do you! *I'll* teach you a lesson!'

Pen discovered to her horror that Mr Luttrell was advancing upon her with his fists clenched. She dodged behind the table, and shrieked: 'Piers! Don't you *know* me? Piers, look at me! I'm *Pen!*'

Mr Luttrell dropped his fists, and stood gaping. 'Pen?' he managed to utter. *'Pen?'*

·§ *Chapter XI* §·

THEY stood staring at one another. The gentleman found his voice first, but only to repeat in accents of still deeper amazement: *Pen?* Pen Creed!'

'Yes, indeed I am!' Pen assured him, keeping the table between them.

His fists unclenched. 'But—but what are you doing here? And in those clothes? I don't understand!'

'Well, it's rather a long story,' Pen said.

He seemed slightly dazed. He ran his hand through his hair, in a gesture she knew well, and said: 'But Major Daubenay—Sir Richard Wyndham——'

'They are both part of the story,' replied Pen. She had been looking keenly at him, and thinking that he had not greatly changed, and she added: 'I should have known you anywhere! Have I altered so much?'

'Yes. At least, I don't know. It's your hair, I suppose, cut short like that, and—and those clothes!'

He sounded shocked, which made her think that perhaps he had changed a little. 'Well, I truly am Pen Creed,' she said.

'Yes, I see that you are, now that I have had time to look at you. But I cannot understand it! I could not help hearing some of what was said, though I tried not to— until I heard Miss Daubenay's name!'

'Please, Piers, don't fly into a rage again!' Pen said rather nervously, for she distinctly heard his teeth grind together. 'I can explain everything!'

'I do not know whether I am on my head or my heels!' he complained. 'You have been imposing on her! How could you do such a thing? *Why* did you?'

'I haven't!' said Pen. 'And I must say, I do think you might be a little more glad to see me!'

'Of course I am glad! But to come here masquerading as a boy, and playing pranks on a defenceless—— *That* was why she failed last night!'

150

'No, it wasn't! She saw the stammering-man killed, and ran away, you stupid creature!'

'How do you know?' he asked suspiciously.

'I was there, of course.'

'With her?'

'Yes, but——'

'You *have* been imposing on her!'

'I tell you it's no such thing! I met her by the merest chance.'

'Tell me this!' commanded Piers. 'Does she know that you are a girl?'

'No, but——'

'I knew it!' he declared. 'And I distinctly heard the Major say that she had met you in Bath! I don't know why you did it, but it is the most damnable trick in the world! And Lydia—deceiving me—encouraging your advances—oh, my eyes are open now!'

'If you say another word, I shall box your ears!' said Pen indignantly. 'I would not have believed you could have grown into such a stupid, tiresome creature! I never met Lydia Daubenay in my life until last night, and if you don't believe me you may go and ask her!'

He looked rather taken aback, and said in an uncertain tone: 'But if you did not know her, how came you to be with her in the wood last night?'

'That was chance. The silly little thing swooned, and I——'

'She is not a silly little thing!' interrupted Piers, firing up.

'Yes, she is, very silly. For what must she do, upon reaching home, but tell her Papa that it was not you she had gone to meet, but me!'

This announcement surprised him. His bewildered grey eyes sought enlightenment in Pen's face; he said with a rueful grin: 'Oh Pen, do sit down and explain! You never could tell a story so that one could make head or tail of it!'

She came away from the table, and sat down on the window-seat. After a pained glance at her attire, Piers seated himself beside her. Each took critical stock of the other, but whereas Pen looked Piers frankly over, he sur-

veyed her rather shyly, and showed a tendency to avert
his gaze when it encountered hers.

He was a well-favoured young man, not precisely handsome, but with a pleasant face, a good pair of shoulders,
and easy, open manners. Since he was four years her senior,
he had always seemed to her, in the old days, very large,
far more experienced than herself, and quite worthy of
being looked up to. She was conscious, as she sat beside
him on the window-seat, of a faint feeling of disappointment. He seemed to her little more than a boy, and instead of assuming his old mastery in his dealings with her,
he was obviously shy, and unable to think of anything to
say. Their initial encounter had of course been unfortunate,
but Pen thought that he might, upon discovering her identity, have exhibited more pleasure at meeting her again.
She felt forlorn all at once, as though a door had been
shut in her face. A vague suspicion that what was behind
the shut door was not what she had imagined only made
her the more melancholy. To hide it, she said brightly:
'It is such an age since I saw you, and there is so much
to say! I don't know where to begin!'

He smiled, but there was a pucker between his brows.
'Yes, indeed, but it seems so strange! Why did she say she
had gone out to meet you, I wonder?'

It was apparent to Pen that Miss Daubenay possessed
his thoughts to the exclusion of everyone else. Repressing
a strong desire to favour him with her opinion of that
young lady, she recounted as briefly as she could what had
passed between her and Lydia in the orchard. Any expectation she might have had of his viewing his betrothed's
conduct in the same light as she did was banished by his
exclaiming rapturously: 'She is such an innocent little thing!
It is just like her to have said that! I see it all now!'

This was too much for Pen. 'Well, I think it was a ridiculous thing to have said.'

'You see, she knows nothing of the world, Pen,' he said
earnestly. 'Then, too, she is impulsive! Do you know, she
always makes me think of a bird?'

'A goose, I suppose,' said Pen somewhat tartly.

'I meant a wild bird,' he replied, with dignity. 'A fluttering, timid, little——'

'She didn't seem to me very timid,' Pen interrupted. 'In fact, I thought she was extremely bold to ask a perfectly strange young man to pretend to be in love with her.'

'You don't understand her. She is so trusting! She needs someone to take care of her. We have loved one another ever since our first meeting. We should have been married by now if my father had not picked a foolish quarrel with the Major. Pen, you cannot think what our sufferings have been! There seems to be no end to them! We shall never induce our fathers to consent to our marriage, never!'

He sank his head in his hands with a groan, but Pen said briskly: 'Well, you will have to marry without their consent. Only you both of you seem to be so poor-spirited that you will do nothing but moan, and meet in woods! Why don't you elope?'

'Elope! You don't know what you are saying, Pen! How could I ask that fragile little thing to do anything of the sort! The impropriety, too! I am persuaded she would shrink from the very thought of it!'

'Yes, she did,' agreed Pen. 'She said she would not be able to have attendants, or a lace veil.'

'You see, she has been very strictly reared—has led the most sheltered life! Besides, why should she not have a lace veil, and—and those things which females set store by?'

'For my part,' Pen said, 'I would not care a fig for such fripperies if I loved a man!'

'Oh, you are different!' said Piers. 'You were always more like a boy than a girl. Just look at you now! Why are you masquerading as a boy? It seems to me most peculiar, and not quite the thing, you know.'

'There were circumstances which—which made it necessary,' said Pen rather stiffly. 'I had to escape from my aunt's house.'

'Well, I still don't see why——'

'Because I was forced to climb out of a window!' snapped Pen. 'Moreover, I could not travel all by myself as a female, could I?'

'No, I suppose you could not. Only you should not be travelling by yourself at all. What a madcap you are!' A thought occurred to him; he glanced down at Pen with a sudden frown. 'But you were with Sir Richard Wyndham

when I came in, and you seemed to be on mighty close
terms with him, too! For heaven's sake, Pen, what are you
about? How do you come to be in his company?'

The interview with her old playmate seemed to be
fraught not only with disappointment, but with unforeseen
difficulties as well. Pen could not but realize that Mr Luttrell was not in sympathy with her. 'Oh, that—that is too
long a story to tell!' she replied evasively. 'There were reasons why I wished to come home again, and—and Sir
Richard would not permit me to go alone.'

'But, Pen!' He sounded horrified. 'You are surely not
travelling with him?'

His tone swept away adventure, and invested her exploit
instead with the stigma of impropriety. She coloured hotly,
and was searching her mind for an explanation that would
satisfy Piers when the door opened, and Sir Richard came
into the room.

One glance at Mr Luttrell's rigidly disapproving countenance; one glimpse of Pen's scarlet cheeks and over-bright
eyes, were enough to give Sir Richard a very fair notion
of what had been taking place in the parlour. He closed
the door, saying in his pleasant drawl: 'Ah, good-morning,
Mr Luttrell! I trust the—er—surprising events of last night
did not rob you of sleep?'

A sigh of relief escaped Pen. With Sir Richard's entrance the reeling world seemed, miraculously, to have
righted itself. She left the window-seat, and went instinctively towards him. 'Sir, Piers says—Piers thinks——' She
stopped, and raised a hand to her burning cheek.

Sir Richard looked at Piers with slightly raised brows.
'Well?' he said gently. 'What does Piers say and think?'

Mr Luttrell got up. Under that ironical, tolerant gaze,
he too began to blush. 'I only said—I only wondered how
Pen comes to be travelling in your company!'

Sir Richard unfobbed his snuff-box, and took a pinch.
'And does no explanation offer itself to you?' he enquired.

'Well, sir, I must say it seems to me—I mean——'

'Perhaps I should have told you,' said Sir Richard drawing Pen's hand through his arm, and holding it rather
firmly, 'that you are addressing the future Lady Wyndham.'

The hand twitched in Sir Richard's, but in obedience to the warning pressure of his fingers Miss Creed remained silent.

'Oh, I see!' said Piers, his brow clearing. 'I beg pardon! It is famous news indeed! I wish you very happy! But— but why must she wear those clothes, and what are you doing here? It still seems very odd to me! I suppose since you are betrothed it may be argued that—— But it is most eccentric, sir, and I do not know what people may say!'

'As we have been at considerable pains to admit no one but yourself into the secret of Pen's identity, I hardly think that people will say anything at all,' replied Sir Richard calmly. 'If the secret were to leak out—why, the answer is that we are a very eccentric couple!'

'It will never leak out through me!' Piers assured him. 'It is no concern of mine, naturally, but I can't help wondering what should have brought you here, and why Pen had to get out of a window. However, I don't mean to be inquisitive, sir. It was only that—having known Pen all my life, you see!'

It was Miss Creed's turn now to give Sir Richard's hand a warning pinch. In fact, so convulsive was her grip that he glanced down at her with a reassuring little smile.

'I am afraid I cannot tell you our reasons for coming here,' he said. 'Certain circumstances arose which made the journey necessary. Pen's attire, however, is easily explained. Neither of us wished to burden ourselves with a duenna upon a mission of—er—extreme delicacy; and the world, my dear Luttrell, being a censorious place, it was judged expedient for Pen to pretend to be, instead of my affianced wife, my young cousin.'

'To be sure, yes! of course!' said Piers, mystified, but overborne by the Corinthian's air of assurance.

'By now,' said Sir Richard, 'we should be on our way back to London, had it not been for two unfortunate circumstances. For one of these, you, I must regretfully point out to you, are responsible.'

'I?' gasped Piers.

'You,' said Sir Richard, releasing Pen's hand. 'The lady to whom you, I apprehend, are secretly betrothed, has, in a

somewhat misguided attempt to avert suspicion from the
truth informed her parent that Pen is the man with whom
she had an assignation in the spinney last night.'

'Yes, Pen told me that. Indeed, I wish she had not done
it, sir, but she is so impulsive, you know!'

'So I have been led to infer,' said Sir Richard. 'Unhappily, since I am for the present compelled to remain in
Queen Charlton, her impulsiveness has rendered our situation a trifle awkward.'

'Yes, I see that,' owned Piers. 'I am very sorry for it,
sir. But must you remain here?'

'Yes,' replied Sir Richard. 'No doubt it has escaped your
memory, but a murder was committed in the spinney last
night. It was I who discovered Brandon's body, and conveyed the news to the proper quarter.'

Piers looked troubled at this, and said: 'I know, sir, and
I do not like it above half! For, in point of fact, I first
found Beverley, only you told me not to say so!'

'I hope you did not?'

'No, because it is so excessively awkward, on account of
Miss Daubenay's presence in the spinney! But if she has
said that she went there to meet Pen——'

'You had better continue to preserve a discreet silence,
my dear boy. The knowledge that you also were in the spinney would merely confuse poor Mr Philips. You see, I
have the advantage of knowing who killed Brandon.'

'I think,' said Pen judicially, 'we ought to tell Piers about
the diamond necklace, sir.'

'By all means,' agreed Sir Richard.

The history of the diamond necklace, as recounted by
Miss Creed, made Mr Luttrell forget for a few moments his
graver preoccupations. He seemed very much more the
Piers of her childhood when he exclaimed: 'What an adventure!' and by the time he had described to her his surprise at receiving a visit from Beverley, whom he had
known but slightly up at Oxford; and had exchanged im-
pressions of Captain Horace Trimble, they were once more
upon very good terms. Sir Richard, who thought that his
own interests would best be served by allowing Pen unin-
terrupted intercourse with Mr Luttrell, soon left them to
themselves; and after Piers had once more felicitated Pen

on her choice of a husband—felicitations which she received in embarrassed silence—the talk soon returned to his own difficulties.

She listened to his enraptured description of Miss Daubenay with as much patience as she could muster, but when he begged her not to divulge her sex to the lady for fear lest her nice sense of propriety must suffer too great a shock, she was so much incensed that she was betrayed into giving him her opinion of Miss Daubenay's morals and manners. A pretty squabble at once flared up, and might have ended in Piers' stalking out of Pen's life for ever had she not remembered, just as he reached the door, that he had engaged herself to further his pretensions to Lydia's hand.

It took a few moments' coaxing to persuade him to relax his air of outraged dignity, but when it was borne in upon him that Lydia had summoned Pen to her side that morning, he did seem to feel that such forward conduct called for an explanation. Pen waved his excuses aside, however. 'I don't mind that, if only she would not cry so much!' she said.

Mr Luttrell said that his Lydia was all sensibility, and deprecated, with obvious sincerity, a suggestion that a wife suffering from an excess of sensibility might prove to be a tiresome acquisition. As he seemed to feel that the support of Lydia was his life's work, Pen abandoned all thought of trying to wean him from his attachment to the lady, and announced her plans for his speedy marriage.

These palpably took Mr Luttrell aback. Lydia's refusal to elope with him he regarded as natural rather than craven, and when Pen's false-abduction scheme was enthusiastically described to him he said that she must be mad to think of such a thing.

'I declare I have a good mind to wash my hands of the whole affair!' said Pen. 'Neither of you has the courage to make the least push in the matter! The end of it will be that your precious Lydia will be married to someone else, and then you will be sorry!'

'Oh, don't suggest such a thing!' he begged. 'If only my father would be a little conciliating! He used to like the Major well enough before they quarrelled.'

'You must soften the Major's heart.'

'Yes, but how?' he asked. 'Now, don't, pray, suggest any more foolish abduction schemes, Pen! I daresay you think them very fine, but if you would but consider the difficulties! No one would ever believe we had not planned it all, because if she eloped with you she would not then wish to marry me, now, would she?'

'No, but we could say that I had forcibly abducted her. Then you could rescue her from me.'

'How should I know that you had abducted her?' objected Piers. 'And just think what a pucker everyone would be in! No, really, Pen, it won't answer! Good God, I should have to fight a duel with you, or something of that nature! I mean, how odd it would look if all I did was to take Lydia home!'

'Well, so we could!' said Pen, her eyes brightening, as new horizons swam into her ken. 'I could have my arm in a sling, and say that you had wounded me! Oh, do let us, Piers! It would be such a famous adventure!'

'You don't seem to me to have changed in the least!' said Piers, in anything but a complimentary tone. 'You are the most complete hand indeed! I cannot conceive how you came to be betrothed to a man of fashion like Wyndham! You know, you will have to mend your ways! In fact, I cannot conceive of your being married at all! You are a mere child.'

Another quarrel might at this point have sprung up between them, had not Sir Richard come back into the room just then, with Mr Philips in his wake. He was looking faintly amused, and the instant expression of extreme trepidation which transformed the countenances of the youthful couple by the window made his lips twitch involuntarily. However, he spoke without a tremor in his voice. 'Ah, Pen! Would you explain, if you please, your—er—owl-story, to Mr. Philips?'

'Oh!' said Pen, blushing furiously.

The magistrate looked severely across at her. 'From the information I have since received, young man, I am forced to the conclusion that your story was false.'

Pen glanced towards Sir Richard. Instead of coming to

her rescue, he smiled maliciously, and said: 'Stand up, my boy, stand up, when Mr Philips addresses you!'

'Oh yes, of course!' said Pen, rising in a hurry. 'I beg pardon! My owl-story! Well, you see, I did not know what to say when you asked why I had not been with my cousin last night.'

'Did not know what to say! You had only one thing to say, and that was the truth!' said Mr Philips austerely.

'I could not,' replied Pen. 'A lady's reputation was at stake!'

'So I am informed. Well, I do not say that I do not sympathize with your motive, but I must warn you, sir, that any further prevarication on your part may lead to serious trouble. Serious trouble! I say nothing of your conduct in meeting Miss Daubenay in a manner I can only describe as clandestine. It is no concern of mine, no concern at all, but if you were a son of mine—— However, that is neither here nor there! Fortunately——' He cast a reproachful glance at Sir Richard—'fortunately, I repeat, Miss Daubenay's evidence corroborates the information that this shocking crime was perpetrated by a person corresponding with the description furnished me of the man Trimble. Were it not for this circumstance—for I will not conceal from you that I am far from being satisfied! Very far indeed! You must permit me to say, Sir Richard, that your presence in the spinney last night points to your having positively aided and abetted your cousin in his reprehensible—— But I am aware that *that* is Major Daubenay's concern!'

'No, no, you have it wrong!' Pen assured him. 'My cousin was searching for me! In fact, he was very angry with me for going to the spinney, were you not, Richard?'

'I was,' admitted Sir Richard. 'Very.'

'Well, the whole affair seems to me very strange!' said Philips. 'I will say no more than that *yet!*'

'You behold me—er—stricken with remorse,' said Sir Richard.

The magistrate snorted, jerked a bow, and took himself off.

'My reputation! oh, my reputation!' mourned Sir Richard. 'Horrible and unprincipled brat, *why* the owl?'

'Well, I had to say something!' Pen pointed out.

'I am afraid,' said Piers, conscience-stricken, 'that it is a *little* Lydia's fault. But indeed, sir, she meant no harm!'

'I know,' said Sir Richard. 'She is so impulsive! I feel a hundred years old.'

He went out on the words, and Pen at once rounded on Mr Luttrell, saying in accusing accents: 'There! You see now what your precious Lydia has done!'

'She is no worse than you are! In fact, not as bad!' retorted Piers. '*She* would not masquerade about the country as a boy! I do not wonder at Sir Richard's feeling a hundred years old. If I were betrothed to you, I should feel the same!'

Miss Creed's eyes flashed. 'Well, I will tell you something, Piers Luttrell! I have got a cousin with a face like a fish, and *he* wants to marry me, which is why I escaped out a window. *But*—do you hear me?—I would a great deal rather marry him than you. If I had to marry you, I would drown myself! You are stupid, and rude, and spiritless!'

'Merely because I have a little common sense,' began Piers, very stiff, and rather flushed.

He was interrupted. A waiter came in with the news that a Young Person desired instant speech with Mr Wyndham.

Correctly divining this mythical being to be herself, Pen said: 'What can that nonsensical girl want now? I wish I had never come to Queen Charlton! Oh, very well! Show the young person in!'

'Good God, can it be Lydia?' exclaimed Piers, when the waiter had withdrawn.

The young person was not Miss Daubenay, but her personal maid, a rosy damsel, who appeared to be strongly imbued with her mistress's romantic ideals. She came in heavily veiled, and presented Pen with a sealed letter. While Pen tore it open, and read its agitated message, Piers besieged the girl with urgent questions, to which, however, she only replied with evasive answers, punctuated by giggles.

'Good gracious!' exclaimed Pen, deciphering Miss Daubenay's scrawl. 'Matters are now desperate! She says she will elope with you.'

'What?' Piers abandoned the servant, and strode to Pen's side. 'Here, give it to me!'

Pen warded him off. 'She says they are going to send her to the Wilds of Lincolnshire.'

'Yes, yes, that is where her grandmother lives! When does she go?'

'I can't read it—oh yes, I see! To-morrow morning, with her Papa. She says I am to tell you to arrange for the elopement this evening, without fail.'

'Good God!' Piers snatched the letter from her, and read it for himself. 'Yes, you are right: she does say to-morrow morning! Pen, if she goes, it will be the end of everything! I never meant to do anything so improper as to elope with her, but I have now no choice! It is not as though her parents disapprove of me, or—or that I am not eligible. If *that* were so, it would be different. But until they quarrelled—however, talking is to no purpose!' He turned to the maidservant, who had by this time put back her veil, and was listening to him with her mouth open. 'Are you in your mistress's confidence?' he demanded.

'Oh yes, sir!' she assured him, adding with another giggle: 'Though the master would tear me limb from limb if he knew I was taking letters to you, sir.'

Piers ignored this somewhat exaggerated statement. 'Tell me, is your mistress indeed resolved upon this course?'

'Oh!' said the damsel, clasping her plump hands together, 'she was never more resolved in her life, sir! "I must Fly!" she says to me, clean distracted. "Lucy," she says, "I am Utterly Undone, for All is Discovered!" So I popped on my bonnet, sir, and slipped out when Cook's back was turned, "for," says my poor young mistress, with tears standing in her eyes fit to break anyone's heart, "if I am whisked off to Lincolnshire, I shall die!" And so she will sir, no question!'

Pen sat down again, hugging her knees. 'Nothing could be better!' she declared. 'I always liked the notion of your eloping to Gretna Green. In fact, it was my suggestion. Only, Lydia told me that you have no money, Piers. Shall we make Richard pay for the post-chaise?'

'Certainly not!' he replied. 'Of course I have enough money for *that!*'

'I think you ought to have four horses,' she warned him. 'Posting charges are very high, you know.'

'Good God, Pen, I'm not penniless! Lydia meant only that I am dependent upon my father. If he refuses to forgive us, I shall be obliged to find some genteel occupation, but I am persuaded that once the deed is done he will very soon come round. Oh, Pen! is she not an angel? I am quite overcome! Is it not affecting that she should trust me so implicitly?'

Pen opened her eyes at this. 'Why shouldn't she?' she asked, surprised.

'Why shouldn't she? Really, Pen, you don't understand in the least! Think of her placing her life, honour, all, in my care!'

'I don't see anything wonderful in that,' replied Pen contemptuously. 'I think it would be a great deal more extraordinary if she didn't trust you.'

'I remember now that you never had much sensibility,' said Piers. 'You are such a child!' He turned again to the interested abigail. 'Now, Lucy, attend to me! You must take a letter back to your mistress, and assure her besides that I shall not fail. Are you prepared to accompany us to Scotland?'

She gaped at him for a moment, but however strange the idea might have been to her it apparently pleased her, for she nodded vehemently, and said: 'Oh yes, sir, thank you, sir!'

'Who ever heard of taking a maid on an elopement?' demanded Pen.

'I will not ask Lydia to fly with me without some female to go with her!' declared Piers nobly.

'Dear me, I should think she would wish the girl at Jericho!'

'Lydia is quite unused to waiting upon herself,' said Piers. 'Moreover, the presence of her maid must lend respectability to our flight.'

'Has she a little lap-dog she would like to take with her too?' asked Pen innocently.

Piers cast her a quelling look, and stalked across the

room to a small writing-table near the window. After testing the pen that lay on it, mending it, and dipping it in the standish, he then sat while the ink dried on it, frowning over what he should write to his betrothed. Finally, he dipped the pen in the standish once more, and began to write, punctuating his labour with reminders to Lucy to see that her mistress had a warm cloak, and did not bring too many bandboxes with her.

'Or the parrot,' interpolated Pen.

'Lor', sir, Miss Lydia hasn't got any parrot!'

'If you don't hold your tongue, Pen——!'

'No little lap-dog either?' Pen asked incredulously.

'No, sir, 'deed, no! There's only her love-birds, the pretty things, and her doves!'

'Well, you will not have room in the chaise for a dovecot, but you should certainly bring the love-birds,' said Pen, with an irrepressible chuckle.

Piers flung down his pen. 'Another word from you, and I'll put you out of the room!'

'No, you won't, because this is a private parlour, and you are nothing but a guest in it.'

'But will I tell Miss to bring the love-birds?' asked Lucy, puzzled.

'No!' said Piers. 'Oh, do stop, Pen! You are driving me distracted! Listen, I have told Lydia that I will have a chaise waiting in the lane behind the house at midnight. Do you think that is too early? Will her parents go to her room as late as that?'

'No, sir, that they won't!' said Lucy. 'The Major does be such a one for retiring early! He'll be in bed and asleep by eleven, take my word for it, sir!'

'Fortunately, it is moonlight,' Piers said, shaking sand over his letter. 'Listen, Lucy! I depend upon you to see that your mistress goes early to bed; she must get what sleep she can! And you must wake her at the proper time, do you understand? Can I trust you to pack for her, and to bring her safely to me?'

'Oh, yes, sir!' replied Lucy, bobbing a curtsey. 'For I wouldn't be left to face the Major, not for ever so!'

'You had best go back to the house with all possible speed,' Piers said, applying a wafer to the folded letter, and handing it to her. 'Mind, now! that letter must not fall into the wrong hands!'

'If anyone tries to take it from you, you must swallow it,' put in Pen.

'Swallow it, sir?'

'Pay no heed to my friend!' said Piers hastily. 'There! Be off with you, and remember that I depend upon your fidelity!'

Lucy curtseyed herself out of the room. Piers looked at Pen, still hugging her knees on the window-seat, and said severely: 'I suppose you flatter yourself you have been helpful!'

Impish lights danced in her eyes. 'Oh, I have! Only think if you had had to turn back to fetch the love-birds, which very likely you would have had to do if I had not reminded the abigail about them!'

He could not help grinning. 'Pen, if she does bring them, I'll—I'll turn back just to wring your neck! Now I must go to arrange for the hire of a chaise, and four fast horses.'

'Where will you find them?' she asked.

'There is a posting-house at Keynsham where they keep very tolerable cattle. I shall drive over there immediately.'

'Famous! Go where you are known, and let the news of your wanting a chaise for midnight spread all over the countryside within three hours!'

He checked. 'I had not thought of that! The devil! This means I must go into Bristol, and I can ill spare the time, with so much to attend to.'

'Nothing of the sort!' said Pen, jumping up. 'Now I will be helpful indeed! I will drive to Keynsham with you, and *I* will order the chaise.'

His brow cleared. 'Oh Pen, will you? But Sir Richard! Will he not object, do you think? Of course, I would take every care of you, but——'

'No, no, he will not object, I assure you! I shall not tell him anything about it,' said Pen ingenuously.

'But that would not be right! And I should not wish to do anything——'

'I will leave a message for him with the landlord,' promised Pen. 'Did you walk into the village, or have you a carriage here?'

'Oh, I drove in! The gig is in the yard now. I confess, if you feel it would not be wrong of you to go with me, I should be glad of your help.'

'Only wait while I get my hat!' Pen said, and darted off in search of it.

◄§ *Chapter XII* §►

MISS CREED and Mr Luttrell, partaking of midday refreshment in Keynsham's best inn, and exhaustively discussing the details of the elopement, were neither of them troubled by doubts of the wisdom of the gentleman's whisking his betrothed off to Scotland at a moment when that lady had become entangled in a case of murder. Indeed, Mr Luttrell, a single-minded young man, was in a fair way to forgetting that he had ever had Beverley Brandon to stay with him. He had left his mother trying to write a suitable letter to Lady Saar, and if he thought about the unfortunate affair at all it was to reflect comfortably that Lady Luttrell would do everything that was proper. His conversation was confined almost exclusively to his own immediate problems, but he digressed several times animadvert on Pen's unconventional exploits.

'Of course,' he conceded, 'it is not so shocking now that you are betrothed to Wyndham, but I own it does surprise me that he—a man of the world!—should have countenanced such a prank. But these Corinthians delight in oddities, I believe! I dare say no one will wonder at it very much. If you were not betrothed it would be different, naturally!'

Pen's clear gaze met his steadily. 'I think you make a great bustle about nothing,' she said.

'My dear Pen!' He gave a little laugh. 'You are such a child! I believe you haven't the smallest notion of the ways of the world!'

She was obliged to admit that this was true. It occurred to her that since Piers seemed to be well-informed on this subject she might with advantage learn a little from him. 'If I were not going to marry Richard, would it be very dreadful?' she asked.

'Pen! What things you do say!' he exclaimed. 'Only think of your situation, travelling all the way from London in Wyndham's company, without even your maid to go with you! Why, you *must* marry him now!'

She tilted her chin. 'I don't see that I must at all.'

'Depend upon it, if you do not, he does. I must say, I think it excessively strange that a man of his years and—and *milieu*—should have wished to marry you, Pen.' He realized his speech was scarcely complimentary, and hastened to add: 'I don't mean *that* precisely, only you are so much younger than he is, and such a little innocent!'

She pounced on this. 'Well, that is one very good reason why I need not marry him!' she said. 'He is so much older than I am that I dare say no one would think it in the smallest degree odd that we should have taken this journey together.'

'Good Gad, Pen, he is not as old as that! What a strange girl you are! Don't you wish to marry him?'

She stared at him with puckered brows. She thought of Sir Richard, of the adventures she had encountered in his company, and of the laughter in his eyes, and of the teasing note in his voice. Suddenly she flushed rosily, and the tears started to her own eyes. 'Yes. Oh, yes, I do!' she said.

'Well! But what is there to cry over?' demanded Piers. 'For a moment I quite thought—— Now, don't be silly, Pen!'

She blew her nose defiantly, and said in somewhat watery accents: 'I'm not crying!'

'Indeed, I can't conceive why you should. I think Wyndham a very good sort of man—a famous fellow! I suppose you will become very fashionable, Pen, and cut the deuce of a dash in town!'

Pen, who could see no future beyond a life spent within the walls of her aunt's respectable house, agreed to this, and made haste to direct the conversation into less painful channels.

Although Keynsham was situated only a few miles dis-

tant from Queen Charlton, it was close on the dinner-hour
when Piers set Pen down at the George Inn again. By this
time, a post-chaise had been hired, and four good horses
chosen to draw it, the whole being appointed to arrive at a
rendezvous outside the gates of Crome Hall at half-past
eleven that evening. Beyond a certain degree of anxiety
concerning the extent of the baggage his betrothed would
wish to bring with her, and some fears that her flight might
be intercepted at the outset, Mr Luttrell had nothing
further to worry about, as his guide and mentor frequently
assured him.

Pen would have liked to have been present at the fatal
hour, but this offer Piers declined. They bade each other
farewell, therefore, at the door of the George Inn, neither
suffering the smallest pang at the notion that each was
about to be joined in wedlock to another.

Having waved a last good-bye to her old playmate, Pen
went into the inn, and was met by Sir Richard, who looked
her up and down, and said: 'Abominable brat, you had
better make a clean breast of the whole! Where have you
been, and what mischief have you done?'

'Oh, but I left a message for you!' Pen protested. 'Did
they not give it to you, sir?'

'They did. But the intelligence that you had gone off
with young Luttrell merely filled me with misgiving. Confess!'

She twinkled up at him. 'Well, perhaps you will not be
quite pleased, but indeed I did it all for the best, Richard!'

'This becomes more and more ominous. I am persuaded
you have committed some devilry.'

She passed into the parlour, and went to the mirror
above the fireplace to pat her crisp, dishevelled curls into
order. 'Not *devilry,* precisely,' she demurred.

Sir Richard who had been observing her in some amusement, said: 'I am relieved. Yes, I think the sooner you put
on your petticoats again the better, Pen. That is a very
feminine trick, let me tell you.'

She coloured, laughed, and turned away from the mirror. 'I forgot. Well, it doesn't signify, after all, for it seems
to me that I have reached the end of my adventure.'

'Not quite,' he replied.

'Yes, I have. You do not know!'

'You look extremely wicked. Out with it!'

'Piers and Lydia are going to elope to-night!'

The laugh died out of his eyes. 'Pen, is this your doing?'

'Oh no, indeed it is not, sir! In fact, I had quite a different plan, only I dared not tell you, and, as a matter of fact, Piers did not think well of it. I wanted to abduct Lydia, so that Piers could rescue her from me, and so soften her Papa's heart. However, I dare say you would not have approved of that.'

'I should not,' said Sir Richard emphatically.

'No, that's why I said nothing to you about it. In the end Lydia decided to elope.'

'You mean that you bullied the wretched girl——'

'I did not! You are most unjust, sir! On my honour, I did not! I don't say that I didn't perhaps put the notion into her head, but it was all the Major's doing. He threatened to take her to Lincolnshire to-morrow morning, and of course she could not support life there! Oh, here comes the waiter! I will tell you the whole story presently.'

She retired to her favourite seat in the window while the covers were laid, and Sir Richard, standing with his back to the mighty fireplace, watched her. The waiter took his time over the preparations for dinner, and during one of his brief absences from the parlour, Pen said abruptly: 'You were quite right: he has changed, sir. Only you were wrong about one thing: he does not think I have changed at all.'

'I did not suspect him to be capable of paying you so pretty a compliment,' said Sir Richard, raising his brows.

'Well, I don't think he meant it to be a compliment,' said Pen doubtfully.

He smiled but said nothing. The waiter came back into the room with a laden tray, and began to set various dishes on the table. When he had withdrawn, Sir Richard pulled a chair out for Pen, and said: 'You are served, brat. Hungry?'

'Not very,' she replied, sitting down.

He moved to his own place. 'Why, how is this?'

'Well, I don't know. Piers is going to elope with Lydia at midnight.'

'I trust that circumstance has not taken away your appetite?'

'Oh no! I think they will deal famously together, for they are both very silly.'

'True. What had you to do with their elopement?'

'Oh, very little, I assure you, sir! Lydia made up her mind to do it without any urging from me. All I did was to hire the post-chaise for Piers, on account of his being well-known in Keynsham.'

'I suppose that means that we shall be obliged to sustain another visit from Major Daubenay. I seem to be plunging deeper and deeper into a life of crime.'

She looked up enquiringly. 'Why, sir? You have done nothing!'

'I am aware. But I undoubtedly should do something.'

'Oh no, it is all arranged! There is truly nothing left to do.'

'You don't think that I—as one having reached years of discretion—might perhaps be expected to nip this shocking affair in the bud?'

'Tell the Major, do you mean?' Pen cried. 'Oh, Richard, you would not do such a cruel thing? I am persuaded you could not!'

He refilled his glass. 'I could, very easily, but I won't. I am not, to tell you the truth, much interested in the affairs of a pair of lovers whom I have found, from the outset, extremely tiresome. Shall we discuss instead our own affairs?'

'Yes, I think we ought to,' she agreed. 'I have been so busy to-day I had almost forgot the stammering-man. I do trust, Richard, we shall not be arrested!'

'Indeed, so do I!' he said, laughing.

'It's very well to laugh, but I could see that Mr Phillips did not like us at all.'

'I fear that your activities disarranged his mind. Fortunately, news has reached him that a man whom I suspect of being none other than the egregious Captain Trimble has been taken up by the authorities in Bath.'

'Good gracious, I never thought he would be caught! Pray, had he the necklace?'

'That, I am as yet unable to tell you. It is to be hoped

that Luttrell and his bride will not prolong their honeymoon, since I fancy Lydia will be wanted to identify the prisoner.'

'If she knew that, I dare say she would never come back at all,' said Pen.

'A public-spirited female,' commented Sir Richard.

She giggled. 'She has no spirit at all. I *told* you so, sir! Will the—the authorities wish to see me?'

'I hardly think so. In any event, they are not going to see you.'

'No, I must say I feel it might be excessively awkward if I were forced to appear,' remarked Pen. 'In fact, sir, I think—I think I had better go home, don't you?'

He looked at her. 'To your Aunt Almeria, brat?'

'Yes, of course. There is nowhere else for me to go.'

'And Cousin Fred?'

'Well, I hope that after all the adventures I have gone through he will not want to marry me any more,' said Pen optimistically. 'He is very easily shocked, you know.'

'Such a man would not be at all the husband for you,' he said, shaking his head. 'You must undoubtedly choose some one who is not at all easily shocked.'

'Perhaps I had better mend my ways,' said Pen, with a swift unhappy smile.

'That would be a pity, for your ways are delightful. I have a better plan than yours, Pen.'

She got up quickly from the table. 'No, no! Please no, sir!' she said in a choking voice.

He too rose, and held out his hand. 'Why do you say that? I want you to marry me, Pen.'

'Oh Richard, I wish you would not!' she begged, retreating to the window. 'Indeed, I don't want you to offer for me. It is extremely obliging of you, but I could not!'

'Obliging of me! What nonsense is this?'

'Yes, yes, I know why you have said it!' she said distressfully. 'You feel that you have compromised me, but indeed you haven't, for no one will ever know the truth!'

'I detect the fell hand of Mr Luttrell,' said Sir Richard rather grimly. 'What pernicious rubbish has he been putting into your head, my little one?'

This term of endearment made Pen wink away a sudden tear. 'Oh no! Only I was stupid not to think of it before. Really, I have no more sense than Lydia! But you are so much older than I am that it truly did not occur to me— until Piers came, and that you told him, to save my face, that we were betrothed! *Then* I saw what a little fool I had been! But it does not signify, sir, for Piers will never breathe a word, even to Lydia, and Aunt Almeria need not know that I have been with you all the time.'

'Pen, will you stop talking nonsense? I am not in the least chivalrous, my dear: you may ask my sister, and she will tell you that I am the most selfish creature alive. I never do anything to please anyone but myself.'

'That I know to be untrue!' Pen said. 'If your sister thinks it, she doesn't know you. And I am not talking nonsense. Piers was shocked to find me with you, and you *did* think he had reason, or you would not have said what you did.'

'Oh yes!' he responded. 'I am well aware of what the world would think of this escapade, but, believe me, my little love, I don't offer marriage from motives of chivalry. To be plain with you, I started on this adventure because I was drunk, and because I was bored, and because I thought I had to do something which was distasteful to me. I stayed in it because I found myself enjoying it as I have not enjoyed anything for years.'

'You did not enjoy the stage-coach,' she reminded him.

'No, but we need not make a practice of travelling by the stage-coach, need we?' he said, smiling down at her. 'Briefly, Pen, when I met you I was about to contract a marriage of convenience. Within twelve hours of making your acquaintance, I knew that no matter what might happen, I would not contract *that* marriage. Within twenty-four hours, my dear, I knew that I had found what I had come to believe did not exist.'

'What was that?' she asked shyly.

His smile was a little twisted. 'A woman—no, a chit of a girl! An impertinent, atrocious, audacious brat—whom I am very sure I cannot live without.'

'Oh!' said Pen, blushing furiously. 'How *kind* of you to

say that to me! I know just why you do, and indeed I am very grateful to you for putting it so prettily!'

'And you don't believe a word of it!'

'No, for I am very sure you would not have thought of marrying me if Piers had not been in love with Lydia Daubenay,' she said simply. 'You are sorry for me, because of that, and so——'

'Not in the least.'

'I think you are a little, Richard. And I quite see that to a person like you—for it is no use to pretend to me that you are selfish, because I know that you are nothing of the sort—to a person like you, it must seem that you are bound in honour to marry me. Now, confess! That is true, is it not? Don't—*please* don't tell me polite lies!'

'Very well,' he replied. 'It is true that having embroiled you in this situation I ought in honour to offer you the protection of my name. But I am offering you my heart, Pen.'

She searched feverishly for her handkerchief, and mopped her brimming eyes with it. 'Oh, I *do* thank you!' she said in a muffled voice. 'You have such beautiful manners, sir!'

'Pen, you impossible child!' he exclaimed. 'I am trying to tell you that I love you, and all you will say is that I have beautiful manners!'

'You cannot fall in love with a person in three days!' she objected.

He had taken a step towards her, but he checked himself at that. 'I see.'

She gave her eyes a final wipe, and said apologetically: 'I beg your pardon! I didn't mean to cry, only I think I am a little tired, besides having had a shock on account of Piers, you know.'

Sir Richard, who had been intimately acquainted with many woman, thought that he did know. 'I was afraid of that,' he said. 'Did you care so much, Pen?'

'No, but I thought I did, and it is all very lowering, if you understand what I mean, sir.'

'I suppose I do. I am too old for you, am I not?'

'I am too young for you,' said Pen unsteadily. 'I dare

say you think I am amusing—in fact, I know you do, for
you are for ever laughing at me—but you would very
soon grow tired of laughing, and—and perhaps be sorry
that you had married me.'

'I am never tired of laughing.'

'Please do not say any more!' she implored. 'It has been
such a splendid adventure until Piers came, and forced
you to say what you did! I—I would rather that you didn't
say any more, Richard, if you please!'

He perceived that his careful strategy in allowing her to
meet her old playfellow before declaring himself had been
mistaken. There did not seem to be any way of explaining
this. No doubt, he thought, she had from the outset regarded him in an avuncular light. He wondered how
deeply her affections had been rooted in the dream-figure
of Piers Luttrell, and, misreading her tears, feared that her
heart had indeed suffered a severe wound. He wanted very
much to catch her up in his arms, overbearing her resis-
tance and her scruples, but her very trust in him set up a
barrier between them. He said, with a shadow of a smile:
'I have given myself a hard task, have I not?'

She did not understand him, and so said nothing. Not
until Piers had shown her a shocked face, and Sir Richard
had claimed her as his prospective wife, had she questioned her own heart. Sir Richard had been merely her delightful travelling companion, an immensely superior personage on whom one could place one's dependence. The
object of her journey had obsessed her thoughts to such a
degree that she had never paused to ask herself whether
the entrance into her life of a Corinthian had not altered
the whole complexion of her adventure. But it had; and
when she had encountered Piers, it had been suddenly
borne in upon her that she did not care two pins for him.
The Corinthian had ousted him from her mind and heart.
Then Piers had turned the adventure into a faintly sordid
intrigue, and Sir Richard had made his declaration, not because he had wanted to (for if he had, why should he have
held his tongue till then?) but because honour had forced
the words out of him. It was absurd to think that a man
of fashion, nearing his thirtieth year, could have fallen

head-over-ears in love with a miss scarcely out of the schoolroom, however easily the miss might have tumbled into love with him.

'Very well, Miss Creed,' said Sir Richard. 'I will woo you in form, and according to all the dictates of convention.'

The ubiquitous waiter chose this moment to come into the parlour to clear the table. Turning to gaze out of the window, Miss Creed reflected that in a more perfect world no servant would intrude upon his legitimate business at unreasonable moments. While the waiter, who seemed from his intermittent sniffs to be suffering from a cold in the head, shuffled about the room, clattering plates and dishes together on a tray, she resolutely winked away another tear, and fixed her attention on a mongrel dog, scratching for fleas in the middle of the street. But this object of interest was presently sent scuttling to cover by the approach of a smart curricle drawn by a pair of fine bays, and driven by a young blood in a coat of white drab cloth, with as many as fifteen capes, and two tiers of pockets. A Belcher handkerchief protruded from an inner pocket, and the coat was flung open to display an astonishing view of a kerseymere waistcoat, woven in stripes of blue and yellow, and a cravat of white muslin spotted with black. A bouquet was stuck in a button-hole of the driving-coat, and a tall hat with a conical crown and an Allen brim was set at a rakish angle on the head of this exquisite.

The equipage drew up outside the George, and a small Tiger jumped down from the back of the curricle, and ran to the horses' heads. The exquisite cast aside the rug that covered his legs, and alighted, permitting Miss Creed a glimpse of white corduroy breeches, and short boots with very long tops. He passed into the inn while she was still blinking at such a vision, and set up a shout for the landlord.

'Good gracious, sir, such an odd creature has arrived! I wish you could have seen him!' Pen exclaimed. 'Only fancy! He has a blue-and-yellow striped waistcoat, and a spotted tie!'

'I wear them myself sometimes,' murmured Sir Richard apologetically.

She turned, determined to keep the conversation to such

unexceptionable subjects. 'You, sir? I cannot believe such
a thing to be possible!'

'It sounds remarkably like the insignia of the Four-
Horse Club,' he said. 'But what in the name of all that's
wonderful should one of our members be doing in Queen
Charlton?'

A confused sound of conversation reached them from
the entrance-parlour. Above it the landlord's voice, which
was rather high-pitched, said clearly: 'My best parlour is
bespoke by Sir Richard Wyndham, sir, but if your honour
would condescend——'

'*What?*'

There was no difficulty at all in hearing the monosyl-
lable, for it was positively shouted.

'Oh, my God!' said Sir Richard, and turned to run a quick
eye over Miss Creed. 'Careful now, brat! I fancy I know
this traveller. What in the world have you done to that
cravat? Come here!'

He had barely time to straighten Miss Creed's crumpled
tie when the same penetrating voice uttered: 'Where? In
there? Don't be a fool, man! I know him well!' and hasty
footsteps were heard crossing the entrance-parlour.

The door was flung open; the gentleman in the fifteen-
caped driving-coat strode in, and, upon setting eyes on Sir
Richard, cast his hat and gloves from him, and started forward, exclaiming: '*Ricky!* Ricky, you dog, what are you
doing here?'

Pen, effacing herself by the window, watched the tall
young man wring Sir Richard's hand, and wondered where
she could have seen him before. He seemed vaguely familiar to her, and the very timbre of his reckless voice
touched a cord of memory.

'Well, upon my soul!' he said. 'If this don't beat all! I
don't know what the deuce you're doing here, but you're
the very man I want to see. Ricky, does that offer of yours
hold good? Damme, if it does, I'm off to the Peninsula by
the first boat! There's the devil and all to pay in the family
this time!'

'I know it,' Sir Richard said. 'I take it you have heard
the news about Beverley?'

'My God, don't tell me *you've* heard it?'

'I found him,' Sir Richard said.

The Honourable Cedric clapped a hand to his head. 'Found him? What, *you* weren't looking for him, Ricky, were you? How many more people know about it? Where's that damned necklace?'

'Unless the law-officers have now got it, I fancy it is in one Captain Trimble's pocket. It was once in my possession, but I handed it over to Beverley, to—er—restore to your father. When he was murdered——'

Cedric recoiled, his jaw dropping. 'What's that? Murdered? Ricky, not Bev?'

'Ah!' said Sir Richard, 'so you *didn't* know?'

'Good God!' Cedric said. His roving eye alighted on the decanter and the glasses which the waiter had left upon the table. He poured himself out a glass, and tossed it off. 'That's better. So Bev's been murdered, has he? Well, I came here with a little notion of murdering him myself. Who did it?'

'Trimble, I imagine,' Sir Richard replied.

Cedric paused in the act of refilling his glass, and looked up quickly. 'For the sake of the necklace?'

'Presumably.'

To Pen's astonishment, Cedric broke into a shout of laughter. 'Oh, by God, but that's rich!' he gasped. 'Oh, blister me, Ricky, that's hell's own jest!'

Sir Richard put up his eyeglass, surveying his young friend through it with faint surprise. 'I did not, of course, expect the news to prostrate you with grief, but I confess I was hardly prepared——'

'Paste, dear old boy! nothing but paste!' said Cedric, doubled up over a chair-back.

The eyeglass dropped. 'Dear me!' said Sir Richard. 'Yes, I ought to have thought of that. Saar?'

'Years ago!' Cedric said, wiping his streaming eyes with the Belcher handkerchief. 'Only came out when I—I, mark you, Ricky!—set the Bow Street Runners on to it! I thought m' father was devilish lukewarm over the affair. Never guessed, however! There was m' mother sending messenger upon messenger up to Brook Street, and the girls nagging at me, so off I went to Bow Street. Fact is, my head's never at its best in the morning. No sooner had I set

the bloodhounds on to the damned necklace than I began
to think the thing over. I told you Bev was a bad man,
Ricky. I'll lay you a monkey he stole the necklace.'

Sir Richard nodded. 'Quite true.'

'Damme, I call that going too far! M' mother had a secret hiding-place made for it in her chaise. M' father
knew. I knew. Bev knew. Dare say the girls knew. But no
one else, d'ye mark me? Thought it all out at White's. Nothing like brandy for clearing the head! Then I remembered
that Bev took himself off to Bath last week. Never could
imagine why! Thought I'd better look into things m'self.
Just made up my mind to take a little journey to Bath,
when in walked m' father in a deuce of a pucker. He'd
heard from Melissa that I'd been to Bow Street. Pounced
on me, looking as queer as Dick's hatband, and wanting
to know what the devil I meant by setting the Runners on
to it. Now, Ricky, dear boy, would you say I was a green
'un? Give you my word I never guessed what was coming!
Always thought m' father meant to stick to the diamonds!
He sold 'em three years ago when he had that run of bad
luck! Had 'em copied, so that no one was the wiser, not
even my mother! He was as mad as Bedlam with me, and
damme, I don't blame him, for if my Runner ran the necklace to earth there'd be the devil to pay, and no pitch hot!
So that's why I'm here. But what beats me is, what in
thunder brought *you* here?'

'You told me to run,' murmured Sir Richard.

'So I did, but to tell you the truth I never thought you
would, dear boy. But why here? Out with it, Ricky! You
never came here in search of Bev!'

'No, I didn't. I came upon purely—er—family affairs. I
fancy you have never met my young cousin, Pen Brown?'

'Never knew you had a cousin of that name. Who is he?'
said Cedric cheerfully.

Sir Richard made a slight movement, indicating Pen's
presence. The room was deeply shadowed, for the waiter
had not yet brought in the candles, and the twilight was
fading. Cedric turned his head, and stared with narrowed
eyes towards the window-seat, where Pen had been sitting,
half hidden by the curtains. 'Damme, I never saw you!' he
exclaimed. 'How d'ye do?'

'Mr Brandon, Pen,' Sir Richard explained.

She came forward to shake hands, just as the waiter entered with a couple of chandeliers. He set them down upon the table, and moved across the room to draw the curtains. The sudden glow of candlelight for a moment dazzled Cedric, but as he released Pen's hand his vision cleared, and became riveted on her guinea-gold curls. A portentous frown gathered on his brow, as he struggled with an erratic memory. 'Hey, wait a minute!' he said. 'I haven't seen you before, have I?'

'No, I don't think so,' replied Pen in a small voice.

'That's what I thought. But there's something about you —did you say he was a cousin of yours, Ricky?'

'A distant cousin,' amended Sir Richard.

'Name of Brown?'

Sir Richard sighed. 'Is it so marvellous?'

'Damme, dear boy, I've known you from m' cradle, but I never heard of any relative of yours called Brown! What's the game?'

'If I had guessed that you were so interested in the ramifications of my family, Cedric, I would have informed you of Pen's existence.'

The waiter, interested, but unable to prolong his labours in the parlour, slowly and sadly withdrew.

'Something devilish queer about this!' pronounced Cedric, with a shake of his head. 'Something at the back of my mind, too. Where's that burgundy?'

'Well, I thought at first that I had met you before,' offered Pen. 'But that was because of your likeness to the stam—to the other Mr Brandon.'

'Don't tell me you knew him!' exclaimed Cedric.

'Not very well. We happened to meet him here.'

'I'll tell you what, my lad: he was no fit company for a suckling like you,' said Cedric severely. He frowned upon her again, but apparently abandoned the effort to recall the errant memory, and turned back to Sir Richard. 'But your cousin don't explain your being here, Ricky. Damme, what *did* bring you to this place?'

'Chance,' replied Sir Richard. 'I was—er—constrained to escort my cousin to this neighbourhood, upon urgent family affairs. Upon the way, we encountered an individual who was being pursued by a Bow Street Runner—your Runner, Ceddie—and who slipped a certain necklace into my cousin's pocket.'

'You don't mean it! But did you know Bev was here?'

'By no means. That fact was only revealed to me when I overheard him exchanging somewhat unguarded recriminations with the man whom I suppose to have murdered him. To be brief with you, there were three of them mixed up in this lamentable affair, and one of the three had bubbled the other two. I restored the necklace to Beverley, on the understanding that it should go back to Saar.'

Cedric cocked an eyebrow. 'Steady now, Ricky, steady! I'm not cork-brained, dear old boy! Bev never consented to give the diamonds back—unless he was afraid you were going to mill his canister. Devilish lily-livered, Bev! Was that the way of it?'

'No,' said Sir Richard. 'That was not the way of it.'

'Ricky, you fool, don't tell me you bought him off!'

'I didn't.'

'Promised to, eh? I warned you! I warned you to have nothing to do with Bev! However, if he's dead there's no harm done! Go on!'

'There is really very little more to tell you. Beverley was found—by me—dead, in a spinney not far from here, last night. The necklace had vanished.'

'The devil it had! Y'know, Ricky, this is a damned ugly business! And, the more I think of it the less I understand why you left town in such a hurry, and without a word to anyone. Now, don't tell me you came on urgent family affairs, dear boy! You were disguised that night! Never seen you so foxed in my life! You said you were going to walk home, and by what the porter told George you had it fixed in your head your house was somewhere in the direction of Brook Street. Well, I'll lay anyone what odds they like you did not go to serenade Melissa! Damme, what did happen to you?'

'Oh, I went home!' said Sir Richard placidly.

'Yes, but where did this young sprig come into it?' demanded Cedric, casting a puzzled glance at Pen.

'On my doorstep. He had come to find me, you see.'

'No, damn it, Ricky, that won't do!' protested Cedric. 'Not at three in the morning, dear boy!'

'Of course not!' interposed Pen. 'I had been awaiting him—oh, for hours!'

'On the doorstep?' said Cedric incredulously.

'There were reasons why I did not wish the servants to know that I was in town,' explained Pen, with a false air of candour.

'Well, I never heard such a tale in my life!' said Cedric. 'It ain't like you, Ricky, it ain't like you! I called to see you myself next morning, and I found Louisa and George there, and the whole house in a pucker, with not a man-jack knowing where the devil you'd got to. Oh, by Jupiter, and George would have it you had drowned yourself!'

'Drowned myself! Good God, why?'

'Melissa, dear boy, Melissa!' chuckled Cedric. 'Bed not slept in—crumpled cravat in the grate—lock of—' He broke off, and jerked his head round to stare at Pen. 'By God, I have it! *Now* I know what was puzzling me! That hair! It was yours!'

'Oh, the devil!' said Sir Richard. 'So that was found, was it?'

'One golden curl under a shawl. George would have it it was a relic of your past. But hell and the devil confound it, it don't make sense! You never went to call on Ricky in the small hours to get your hair cut, boy!'

'No, but he said I wore my hair too long, and that he would not go about with me looking *so*,' said Pen desperately. 'And he didn't like my cravat either. He was drunk, you know.'

'He wasn't as drunk as that,' said Cedric. 'I don't know who you are, but you ain't Ricky's cousin. In fact, it's my belief you ain't even a boy! Damme, you're Ricky's past, that's what you are!'

'I am not!' said Pen indignantly. 'It is quite true that I'm not a boy, but I never saw Richard in my life until that night!'

'Never saw him until that night?' repeated Cedric, dazed.

'No! It was all chance, wasn't it, Richard?'

'It was,' agreed Sir Richard, who seemed to be amused. 'She dropped out of a window into my arms, Ceddie.'

'She dropped out of—give me some more burgundy!' said Cedric.

⋞ *Chapter XIII* ⋟

HAVING fortified himself from the decanter, Cedric sighed, and shook his head. 'No use, it still seems devilish odd to me. Females don't drop out of windows.'

'Well, I didn't drop out precisely. I climbed out, because I was escaping from my relations.'

'I've often wanted to escape from mine, but I never thought of climbing out of a window.'

'Of course not!' said Pen scornfully. 'You are a man!'

Cedric seemed dissatisfied. 'Only females escape out of windows? Something wrong there.'

'I think you are excessively stupid. I escaped out of the window because it was dangerous to go by the door. And Richard happened to be passing at the time, which was a very fortunate circumstance because the sheets were not long enough, and I had to jump.'

'Do you mean to tell me you climbed down the sheets?' demanded Cedric.

'Yes, of course. How else could I have got out, pray?'

'Well, if that don't beat all!' he exclaimed admiringly.

'Oh, that was nothing! Only when Sir Richard guessed that I was not a boy he thought it would not be proper for me to journey to this place alone, so he took me to his house, and cut my hair more neatly at the back, and tied my cravat for me, and—and *that* is why you found those things in his library!'

Cedric cocked an eye at Sir Richard. 'Damme, I knew you'd shot the cat, Ricky, but I never guessed you were as bosky as that!'

'Yes,' said Sir Richard reflectively, 'I fancy I must have been rather more up in the world than I suspected.'

'Up in the world! Dear old boy, you must have been clean raddled! And how the deuce did you get here? For I remember now that George said your horses were all in the stables. You never travelled in a hired chaise, Ricky!'

'Certainly not,' said Sir Richard. 'We travelled on the stage.'

'On the—on the——' Words failed Cedric.

'That was Pen's notion,' Sir Richard explained kindly. 'I must confess I was not much in favour of it, and I still consider the stage an abominable vehicle, but there is no denying we had a very adventurous journey. Really, to have gone post would have been sadly flat. We were overturned in a ditch; we became—er—intimately acquainted with a thief; we found ourselves in possession of stolen goods; assisted in an elopement and discovered a murderer. I had not dreamt life could hold so much excitement.'

Cedric, who had been gazing at him open-mouthed, began to laugh. 'Lord, I shall never get over this! *You,* Ricky! Oh Lord, and there was Louisa ready to swear you would never do anything unbefitting a man of fashion, and George thinking you at the bottom of the river, and Melissa standing to it that you had gone off to watch a mill! Gad, she'll be as mad as fire! Out-jockeyed, by Jupiter! Piqued, repiqued, slammed, and capotted!' He once more mopped his eyes with the Belcher handkerchief. 'You'll have to buy me that pair of colours, Ricky: damme, you owe it to me, for I told you to run, now, didn't I?'

'But he did not run!' Pen said anxiously. 'It was I who ran. Richard didn't.'

'Oh yes, I did!' said Sir Richard taking snuff.

'No, no, you know you only came to take care of me; you said I could not go alone!'

Cedric looked at her in a puzzled way. 'Y'know, I can't make this out at all! If you only met three nights ago, you can't be eloping!'

'Of course we're not eloping! I came here on—on a private matter, and Richard pretended to be my tutor. There is not a question of eloping!'

'Tutor? Lord! I thought you said he was your cousin?'

'My dear Cedric, do try not to be so hidebound!' begged

Sir Richard. 'I have figured as a tutor, an uncle, a trustee, *and* a cousin.'

'You seem to me to be a sad romp!' Cedric told Pen severely. 'How old are you?'

'I am seventeen, but I do not see that it is any concern of yours.'

'Seventeen!' Cedric cast a dismayed glance at Sir Richard. 'Ricky, you madman! You're in the basket now, the pair of you! And what your mother and Louisa will say, let alone that sour-faced sister of mine——! When is the wedding?'

'That,' said Sir Richard, 'is the point we were discussing when you walked in on us.'

'Better get married quietly somewhere where you ain't known. You know what people are!' Cedric said, wagging his head. 'Damme, if I won't be best man!'

'Well, you won't,' said Pen, flushing. 'We are not going to be married. It is quite absurd to think of such a thing.'

'I know it's absurd,' replied Cedric frankly. 'But you should have thought of that before you started jauntering about the country in this crazy fashion. There's nothing for it now: you'll have to be married!'

'I won't!' Pen declared. 'No one need ever know that I am not a boy, except you, and one other, who doesn't signify.'

'But my dear girl, it won't do! Take it from me, it won't do! If you don't know that, I'll be bound Ricky does. I daresay you don't fancy the notion, but he's a devilish fine catch, you know. Blister it, we were looking to him to bring our family fortunes about, so we were!' he added, with an irrepressible chuckle.

'I think you are vulgar and detestable!' said Pen. 'I have got a great deal of money of my own; in fact, I'm an heiress, and I have a very good mind not to marry anyone!'

'But only think what a waste!' protested Cedric. 'If you are an heiress, and you can't stomach the notion of marrying Ricky, for which I won't blame you, for the Lord knows he's no lady's man!—a hardened case, m'dear: never looked seriously at a female in his life!—I suppose you wouldn't make shift with your humble servant?'

'Your conversation, my dear Cedric, is always edifying,' said Sir Richard icily.

But Pen, instead of being offended, giggled. 'No, thank you. I shouldn't like to marry you at all.'

'I was afraid you wouldn't. You'll have to take Ricky, then: nothing else for it! But you're too young for him: no getting away from that! Damme, if I know what maggot got into your heads to set you off on this crazy adventure!'

'You are labouring under a misapprehension, Cedric,' said Sir Richard. 'There is nothing I desire more than to marry Pen.'

'Well, of all things!' gasped Cedric. 'And here was I thinking you a hopeless case!'

'I am going to bed,' stated Pen.

Sir Richard moved across the door to open it for her. 'Yes my child: go to bed. But pray do not let Cedric's art-less chatter prejudice you! For addle-pated folly I have never met his equal.' He possessed himself of her hand, as he spoke, and lifted it to his lips. 'Pleasant dreams, brat,' he said softly.

She felt a lump rise in her throat, achieved a tremulous smile, and fled, but not before she had heard Cedric ex-claim in tones of the liveliest surprise: 'Ricky, you ain't really in love with that chit, are you?'

'I think,' said Sir Richard, closing the door, 'that we shall be more usefully employed in discussing the circum-stances which brought you here, Cedric.'

'Oh, by all means!' Cedric said hastily. 'Beg pardon! No intention of prying into your affairs, dear boy; not the least in the world! Now, don't get into a miff! You know how it is with me! Never could keep a discreet tongue in my head!'

'That is what I am afraid of,' Sir Richard said dryly.

'Mum as an oyster!' Cedric assured him. 'But that you of all men, Ricky——! That's what beats me! However, no concern of mine! What's all this you were telling me about Bev?'

'He's dead. That seems to be the most important thing.'

'Well, it's no good expecting me to pull a long face over it. He was a bad man, take my word for it! What was he doing in this spinney you talk of?'

'As a matter of fact, he went there to meet me,' said Sir Richard.

Cedric frowned at him. 'More in this than meets the eye. Why, Ricky?'

'To be plain with you, he had hit upon the notion of extorting money from me by threatening to make known the fact that my supposed cousin was a girl in disguise.'

'Yes, that's Bev all over,' nodded Cedric, quite unsurprised. 'Offered to pay his debts, didn't you?'

'Oh, I had offered that earlier in the day! Unfortunately Captain Trimble learned of my appointment with Beverley in the spinney, and went there before me. I fancy he had nothing more than robbery in mind. There was a witness to the meeting, who described how a quarrel sprang up, and how Trimble struck Beverley down, searched his pockets, and made off. Possibly he thought he had merely stunned him. When I found him his neck was broken.'

'Jupiter!' said Cedric, giving a whistle of consternation. 'It's worse than I thought, then! The devil! There will be no hushing this up. They don't suspect you of having a hand in it, do they, Ricky?'

'I am fast acquiring a most unsavoury reputation in this neighbourhood, but so far I have not been arrested for murder. What precise object had you in coming here?'

'Why, to choke the truth out of Bev, of course! Couldn't get it out of my head he was at the bottom of that robbery. He was badly dipped, y'know. M' father wants my bloodhound called off, too, but I'm damned if I can come up with any trace of him. If you met the fellow on the Bristol road, that would account for my missing him. I went to Bath. Last I heard of Bev was that he was there, with Freddie Fotheringham. Freddie told me Bev had gone off to stay with some people called Luttrell, living at a place near here. So I saw m' mother, got the full story of the robbery out of her, and came on here. *Now* what's to do?'

'You had better make the acquaintance of the local magistrate. A man who might well be Trimble was taken up in Bath to-day, but whether the necklace was on him I know not.'

'Must lay my hands on that plaguey necklace!' frowned

Cedric. 'Won't do if the truth about that were to come out. But what are you going to do, Ricky? It seems to me you're in the deuce of a coil too.'

'I shall no doubt be able to answer that question when I have talked the matter over with Pen to-morrow,' Sir Richard replied.

But Sir Richard was not destined to have the opportunity of talking over any matter with Miss Creed upon the morrow. Miss Creed, going dejectedly up to bed, sat for a long time at the open window of her room, and gazed blindly out upon the moonlit scene. She had spent, she decided, quite the most miserable day of her life, and the sudden incursion of Cedric Brandon had done nothing to alleviate her heaviness of heart. It was apparent that Cedric considered her adventure only one degree less fantastic than the notion that she was to marry Sir Richard. According to his own words, he had known Sir Richard from the cradle, so that it was fair to assume that he was very well acquainted with him. He gave it as his opionion that she must marry Sir Richard, which was tantamount to saying, she reflected, that she had put Sir Richard into the uncomfortable position of being obliged to offer for her. It was most unjust, Pen thought, for Sir Richard had not been sober when he had insisted on accompanying her into Somerset, and he had, moreover, done it out of sheer solicitude for her safety. It had not occurred to her that a gentleman so many years her senior could be supposed to compromise her, or to engage his own honour so disastrously. She had liked him from the moment of setting eyes on him; she had plunged into terms of intimacy with him in the shortest possible time; and had, indeed, felt as though she had known him all her life. She thought herself more stupid even than Lydia Daubenay not to have realized before ever they had reached Queen Charlton, that she had tumbled headlong in love with him. She had refused to look beyond her meeting with Piers, yet she could not but admit to herself now that she had been by no means anxious to summon Piers to her side when she had arrived at the George. By the time she did come face to face with him, he would have had to have been a paragon indeed to have won her from Sir Richard.

His conduct had been anything rather than that of a paragon. He had spoiled everything, Pen thought. He had accused her of impropriety, and had forced Sir Richard into making a declaration he had surely not wanted to make.

'Because I don't suppose he loves me at all,' Pen argued to herself. 'He never said so until Piers was so odious: in fact, he treated me just as if he really was a trustee, or an uncle, or somebody years and years older than I am, which I dare say was what made it all seem quite proper to me, and not in the least scandalous. Only then we fell into so many adventures, and he was obliged to fob off Aunt Almeria, and then the stammering-man guessed I was a girl, and Piers was disagreeable, and I got into a scrape through Lydia's folly, and the Major came, and now this other Mr Brandon knows about me, and the end of it is I have placed poor Richard in the horridest situation imaginable! There is only one thing for it: I shall have to run away.'

This decision, however, made her feel so melancholy that several large tears brimmed over her eyelids and rolled down her cheeks. She wiped them away, telling herself it was stupid to cry. 'Because if he doesn't want to marry me, I don't want to marry him—much; and if he does, I dare say he will come to visit me at Aunt's house. No, he won't. He'll forget all about me, or very likely be glad that he is rid of a badly behaved, tiresome ch-charge! Oh dear!'

So sunk in these dismal reflections did she become that it was a long time before she could rouse herself sufficiently to prepare for bed. She even forgot the elopement she had helped to arrange, and heard the church-clock strike midnight without so much as recalling that Lydia should now be stepping up into the hired post-chaise, with or without a cage of love-birds.

She spent a miserable night, disturbed by unquiet dreams, and tossing from side to side in a way that soon untucked all the sheets and blankets, and made the bed so uncomfortable that by six in the morning, when she finally awoke to find the room full of sunlight, she was very glad to leave it.

A considerable portion of her waking hours had been spent in considering how she could run away without Sir Richard's knowing anything about it. A carrier was used to go into Bristol on certain days, she remembered, and she made up her mind either to buy a seat on his wagon, or, if it was not one of his days, to walk to Bristol, and there book a seat on the London stage-coach. Bristol was not more than six or seven miles distant from Queen Charlton, and there was, moreover, a reasonable hope of being offered a lift in some conveyance bound for the town.

She dressed herself, and very nearly started to cry again when she struggled with the folds of the starched muslin cravat, because it was one of Sir Richard's. Once dressed, she packed her few belongings in the cloak-bag he had lent her, and tiptoed downstairs to the parlour.

The servants, though she could hear them moving about in the coffee-room, and the kitchen, had not yet come into the parlour to draw back the blinds, and to set the room to rights. In its untidy, overnight state it looked dispiriting. Pen pulled the blinds apart, and sat down at the writing-table to compose a letter of farewell to Sir Richard.

It was a very difficult letter to write, and seemed to entail much nose-blowing, and many watery sniffs. When she had at last finished it, Pen read it through rather dubiously, and tried to erase a blot. It was not a satisfactory letter, but there was no time to write another, so she folded, and sealed it, wrote Sir Richard's name on it and propped it up on the mantelpiece.

In the entrance-parlour she encountered the pessimistic waiter who had served them on the previous evening. His eyes seemed even duller than usual, and beyond staring in a ruminative fashion at her cloak-bag, he evinced no interest in Pen's early rising.

She explained to him glibly that she was obliged to go into Bristol, and asked if the carrier would be passing the George. The waiter said that he would not be passing, because Friday was not his day. 'If you had wanted him yesterday, it would have been different,' he added reproachfully.

She sighed. 'Then I shall be obliged to walk.'

The waiter accepted this without interest, but just as she reached the door he bethought him of something, and said in a voice of unabated gloom: 'The missus is going to Bristol in the trap.'

'Do you think she would take me with her?'

The waiter declined to offer an opinion, but he volunteered to go and ask the missus. However, Pen decided to go herself, and, penetrating to the yard at the back of the inn, found the landlord's wife packing a basket into the trap, and preparing to mount into it herself.

She was surprised at Pen's request, and eyed the cloakbag with suspicion, but she was a stout, good-natured woman, and upon Pen's assuring her mendaciously that Sir Richard was well-aware of her projected expedition, she allowed her to get into the trap, and to stow the cloakbag under the seat. Her son, a phlegmatic young man, who chewed a straw throughout the journey, took the reins, and in a few minutes the whole party was proceeding up the village street at a sober but steady pace.

'Well, I only hopes, sir, as I'm not doing wrong,' said Mrs Hopkins, as soon as she had recovered from the exertion of hoisting her bulk into the trap. 'I'm sure I was never one to pry into other folks' business, but if you *was* running away from the gentleman which has you in charge, I should get into trouble, that's what.'

'Oh no, indeed you won't!' Pen assured her. 'You see, we have not our own carriage with us, or—or I should not have been obliged to trouble you in this way.'

Mrs Hopkins said that she was not one to grudge trouble, and added that she was glad of company. When she discovered. Pen had had no breakfast, she was very much shocked, and after much tugging and wheezing, pulled out the basket from under the seat, and produced out of it a large packet of sandwiches, a pie wrapped in a napkin, and a bottle of cold tea. Pen accepted a sandwich, but refused the pie, a circumstance which made Mrs Hopkins say that although the young gentleman would have been welcome to it, it was, in point of fact, a gift for her aunt, who lived in Bristol. She further disclosed that she was bound for the town to meet her sister's second girl, who was coming down on the London stage to work as a chambermaid at the George. The ball of conversation having been set rolling in this easy fashion, the journey passed pleasantly enough, Mrs Hopkins furnishing Pen with so exhaustive an account of the various trials and vicissitudes which had befallen every member of her family, that by the time the trap drew up at an inn in the centre of Bristol, Pen felt that there could be little she did not know about the good lady's relatives.

The stage was not due to arrive in Bristol until nine o'clock, at which hour the coach setting out for London would leave the inn. Mrs Hopkins set off to visit her aunt, and Pen, having booked a seat on the stage, and deposited the cloak-bag at the inn, sallied forth to lay out her last remaining coins on provisions to sustain her during the journey.

The streets were rather empty at such an early hour, and some of the shops had not yet taken down their shutters, but after walking for a few minutes and observing with interest the changes which, in five years, had taken place in the town, Pen found a cook-shop that was open. The smell of freshly baked pies made her feel hungry, and she went into the shop, and made a careful selection of the viands offered for sale.

When she came out of the shop, there was still half-an-hour to while away before the coach was due to start, and she wandered into the market-place. Here there were quite a number of people already busy about the day's business. Pen caught sight of Mrs Hopkins bargaining with a salesman over the price of a length of calico, but since she did not feel that she wanted to learn any more details about the Hopkins family, she avoided her, and pretended to be interested in a clockmaker's shop. So intent was she on avoiding Mrs Hopkins's motherly eye, that she was blissfully unaware that she herself was being closely scrutinized by a thickset man in a duffle coat, and a wide-brimmed hat, who, after gazing fixedly at her for some moments, stepped up to her, and laying a heavy hand on her shoulder, said deeply: 'Got you!'

Pen jumped guiltily, and looked round in sudden alarm. The voice sounded familiar; to her dismay she found herself staring up into the face of the Bow Street Runner who had overtaken Jimmy Yarde at the inn near Wroxhall.

'Oh!' she said faintly. 'Oh! Are you not the—the man I met—the other day? Good—good-morning! A fine day, isn't—isn't it?'

'That's so, young sir,' said the Runner, in a grim tone. 'And a werry complete hand you be, and no mistake! I've been wanting another touch at you. Ah, and when Nat Gudgeon wants a touch at a cove, he gets it, and no mistake about that neither! You come along with me!'

'But I haven't done anything wrong! Indeed I haven't!' said Pen.

'If you haven't, then there's no call for you to be scared of me,' said Mr Gudgeon, with what seemed to her a fiendish leer. 'But what I been thinking, young sir, is, that you and that fine gentleman what was with you loped off mighty quick from that there inn. Why, anyone might have thought, so they might, as how you had took an unaccountable dislike to me!'

'No, no, we didn't! But there was nothing to stay for, and we were already much delayed.'

'Well,' said Mr Gudgeon, shifting his elbow to her arm, and grasping this firmly above the elbow, 'I've got a fancy to question you more particular, young sir. Now, don't you make the werry great mistake of trying to struggle with me, because it won't do you no good. Maybe you ain't never heard tell on a cove by the name o' Yarde: likewise you wouldn't reckernize a set o' sparklers if you was to see one. Lor'! If I had a brace of meggs for every green-looking young chub like you which I've took up—ah, and shut up in the Whit just as snug as you please!—I'd be a werry rich man, so I would. You come along of me, and stop trying to gammon me, because I've got a werry strong notion you know a deal more about a certain set o' sparklers nor what you're wishful I should get wind of.'

By this time, the attention of several persons had been attracted, and a small crowd was beginning to gather. Pen cast a hunted look around. She saw the aghast face of Mrs Hopkins, but no means of escape, and gave herself up for lost. Mr Gudgeon evidently meant to march her off to the gaol, or at any rate to some place of safe-keeping, where her sex, she suspected, would soon be discovered. Meanwhile, the crowd was swelling, several members of it loudly demanding to know what the young gentleman had done, and one knowledgeable individual explaining to his neighbours that that was one of the Bow Street Runners from London, that was. Nothing would serve her, Pen decided, but a certain measure of frankness. Accordingly, she made no attempt to break away from the Runner's hold, but said in as calm a tone as she was able to assume: 'Indeed, I do not mind going with you at all. In fact, I know just what you want, and I dare say I can furnish you with some very valuable information.'

Mr Gudgeon, who was not accustomed to be met with any appearance of sang-froid, was not in the least softened by this speech. He said in a shocked voice: 'There's a sauce! Ay, you're a rare gager, young as you be! Why, you young varmint, and you with your mother's milk not dry on your lips! You come along, and no bamming, now!'

A section of the crowd showed a disposition to accompany them, but Mr Gudgeon addressed these gentry in such fierce accents that they dispersed in a hurry, and left him to escort his captive out of the market-place in lonely state.

'You are making a great mistake,' Pen told the Runner. 'You are searching for the Brandon diamonds, are you not? Well, I know all about them, and, as a matter of fact, Mr Brandon wishes you to stop searching for them.'

'Ho!' said Mr Gudgeon, with deep meaning. 'He does, does he? Dang me, if ever I see the equal of you for sauce!'

'I wish you will listen to me! I know who has the diamonds, and, what is more, he murdered the other Mr Brandon to get them!'

Mr Gudgeon shook his head in speechless wonder.

'He *did,* I tell you!' Pen said desperately. 'His name is Trimble, and he was in a plot with Jimmy Yarde to steal the necklace! Only it went awry, and the necklace was restored to Mr Beverley Brandon, and then Captain Trimble killed him, and made off with the diamonds. And Mr Cedric Brandon is searching for you high and low, and if you will only go to Queen Charlton you will find him there, and he will tell you that what I say is true!'

'I never heard the like!' gasped Mr Gudgeon, affronted.

'A werry thorough-going young rascal you be, and no mistake about that! And how might you come to know such a powerful deal about these sparklers, might I take the liberty of asking?'

'I know Mr Brandon well,' answered Pen. '*Both* Mr Brandons! And I was in Queen Charlton when the murder was committed. Mr Philips, the magistrate, knows all about me, I assure you!'

Mr Gudgeon was a little shaken by this announcement, and said more mildly: 'I don't say as I disbelieve you, nor I don't say as I believe you neither; but it's an unaccountable queer story you're telling me, young sir, and that's a fact.'

'Yes, I dare say it may seem so to you,' Pen agreed. She felt his grip slacken on her arm, and decided to press home her advantage. 'You had better come with me to Queen Charlton at once, because Mr Brandon wants to see you, and I expect Mr Philips will be very glad of your help in finding Captain Trimble.'

Mr Gudgeon looked at her sideways. 'Either I've been mistook,' he said slowly, 'or you're the most precious young warmint I ever did see. Maybe I will go to this place you talks about, and maybe while I'm gone you'll sit waiting for me where you won't do no harm.'

They had turned into a broad thoroughfare with streets leading off from it on either side. Pen, who had no intention of returning to Queen Charlton, or of being locked up in Bristol gaol, made up her mind, now that Mr Gudgeon's grasp on her arm had become little more than perfunctory, to try the chances of escape. She said airily: 'Just as you please, only I warn you, Mr Brandon will be excessively angry if he hears that you have molested me. Naturally, I do not wish to—— Oh, look, look! Quick!'

They were abreast of one of the side streets by this time, and Pen's admirable start brought the Runner to a dead halt. She clasped his arm with her free hand, and exclaimed: 'Over there, just turning into that road! It was he! Captain Trimble! He must have seen me, for he set off running at once! oh, do be quick!'

'Where?' demanded Mr Gudgeon, taken off his guard, and looking round wildly.

'*There!*' panted Pen, and tore herself free from his hold, and ran like a deer down the side-street.

She heard a shout behind her, but wasted no time in looking back. A woman engaged in scrubbing her front doorstep set up a cry of Stop, thief! and an errand boy with a large basket on his arm, gave a shrill cat-call. Pen reached the end of the street with the sound of the hue and cry behind her, turned the corner, saw an alley leading to a huddle of mean dwellings, and sped down it.

It led her into a labyrinth of narrow streets, with dirty gutters, and crazy cottages, and backyards noisome with the refuse left to rot in them. She had never penetrated into this part of the town before, and was soon quite lost. This circumstance did not trouble her much, however, for the noise of the chase had died away in the rear. She did not think that anyone had seen her dive into the alley so that she was able to entertain a reasonable hope of shaking off the pursuit. She stopped running, and began to walk, rather breathlessly, in what she trusted was an easterly direction. After traversing a number of unknown streets, she came at last to a more respectable part of the town, and ventured to enquire the way to the inn where she had left her cloak-bag. She discovered that she had overshot it, and, further, that the time was now a few minutes after nine. She looked so dismayed that her informant, a stout man in corduroys and a frieze coat, who was just preparing to climb into a gig, asked her whether she wanted the London stage-coach. Upon her admitting that she did, he said philosophically: 'Well, you've missed it.'

'Oh dear, what shall I do?' said Pen, foreseeing a day spent in skulking about the town to escape discovery by Mr Gudgeon.

The farmer, who had been looking her over in a ruminative fashion, said: 'Be you in a hurry?'

'Yes, yes! That is, I have paid for my seat, you see.'

'Well, I'm going to Kingswood myself,' said the farmer. 'You can get up alongside me in the gig, if you like. You'll likely catch up with the stage there.'

She accepted this offer gratefully, for she thought that even if she did not succeed in overtaking the stage she would be safer from Mr Gudgeon at Kingswood than in

Bristol. Happily, however, the farmer was driving a fast-trotting young horse, and they reached the main London road before the heavy stage had drawn out of the town. The farmer set Pen down in Kingswood, at the door of the inn, and having ascertained that the coach had not yet called there, bade her a cheerful farewell, and drove off.

Feeling that she had escaped disaster by no more than a hair's breadth, Pen sat down upon the bench outside the inn to await the arrival of the stage. It was late in coming, and the guard, when Pen handed him her ticket, seemed to take it as a personal affront that she had not boarded it in Bristol. He told her, with malign satisfaction, that her cloak-bag had been left behind at the 'Talbot' Inn, but after a good deal of grumbling he admitted that she had a right to a seat in the coach, and let down the steps for her to mount into it. She squeezed herself into a place between a fat man, and a woman nursing a peevish infant; the door was shut, the steps let up again, and the vehicle resumed its ponderous journey to London.

⋖§ *Chapter XIV* §⋗

SIR RICHARD WYNDHAM was not an early riser, but he was roused from sleep at an unconscionably early hour upon the morning of Pen's flight by the boots, who came into his room with a small pile of linen, which had been laundered in the inn, and his top-boots, and told him diffidently that he was wanted belowstairs.

Sir Richard groaned, and enquired what time it was. With even greater diffidence, the boots said that it was not quite eight o'clock.

'What the devil?' exclaimed Sir Richard, bending a pained glance upon him.

'Yes, sir,' agreed the boots feelingly, 'but it's that Major Daubenay, sir, in such a pucker as you never did see!'

'Oh!' said Sir Richard. 'It is, is it? The devil fly away with Major Daubenay!'

The boots grinned, but awaited more precise instructions. Sir Richard groaned again, and sat up. 'You think I ought to get up, do you? Bring me my shaving water, then.'

'Yessir!'

'Oh, ah! Present my compliments to the Major, and inform him that I shall be with him shortly!'

The boots went off to execute these commands, and Sir Richard, surveying the beauty of the morning with a jaundiced eye, got out of bed.

When the boots came back with a jug of hot water, he found Sir Richard in his shirt and breeches, and reported that the Major was pacing up and down the parlour more like a wild beast in a circus than a Christian gentleman.

'You appall me,' said Sir Richard unemotionally. 'Just hand me my boots, will you? Alas! Biddle, I never realized your worth until I was bereft of you!'

'Beg pardon, sir?'

'Nothing,' said Sir Richard, inserting his foot into one of the boots, and pulling hard.

Half an hour later he entered the parlour to find his matutinal guest fuming up and down the floor with a large watch in his hand. The Major, whose cheeks were unbecomingly flushed, and whose eyes started quite alarmingly, stabbed at this timepiece with one quivering finger, and said in a suppressed roar: 'Forty minutes, sir! Forty minutes since I entered this room!'

'Yes, I have even surprised myself,' said Sir Richard, with maddening nonchalance. 'Time was when I could not have achieved this result under an hour, but practice, my dear sir, practice, you know, is everything!'

'An hour!' gobbled the Major. 'Practice! Bah, I say! Do you hear me, sir?'

'Yes,' said Sir Richard, flicking a speck of dust from his sleeve. 'And I imagine I am not the only one privileged to hear you.'

'You are a dandy!' uttered the Major, with loathing. 'A dandy, sir! That's what you are!'

'Well, I am glad that the haste with which I dressed has not obscured that fact,' replied Sir Richard amiably. 'But the correct term is Corinthian.'

'I don't care a fig what the correct term may be!' roared the Major, striking the table with his fist. 'It's all the same to me: dandy, Corinthian, or pure popinjay!'

'If I lose my temper with you, which, however, I should be loth to do—at all events, at this hour of the morning —you will discover that you are mistaken,' said Sir Richard. 'Meanwhile, I presume that you did not bring me out of my bed to exchange compliments with me. What, sir, do you want?'

'Don't take that high and mighty tone with me, sir!' said the Major. 'That whelp of yours has made off with my daughter!'

'Nonsense!' said Sir Richard calmly.

'Nonsense, is it? Then let me tell you that she has gone, sir! Gone, do you hear me? And her maid with her!'

'Accept my condolences,' said Sir Richard.

'Your condolences! I don't want your damned condolences, sir! I want to know what you mean to do!'

'Nothing at all,' replied Sir Richard.

The Major's eyes positively bulged, and a vein stood out on his heated brow. 'You stand there, and say that you mean to do nothing, when your scoundrel of a cousin has eloped with my daughter?'

'Not at all. I mean to do nothing because my cousin has not eloped with your daughter. You must forgive me if I point out to you that I am getting a little weary of your parental difficulties.'

'How dare you, sir? how dare you?' gasped the Major. 'Your cousin meets my daughter by stealth in Bath, lures her out at dead of night here, deceives her with false promises, and now—*now,* to crown all, makes off with her, and you say—*you* say that you are weary of *my* difficulties!'

'Very weary of them. If your daughter has left your roof —and who shall blame her?—I advise you not to waste your time and my patience here, but to enquire at Crome Hall whether Mr Piers Luttrell is at home, or whether he also is missing.'

'Young Luttrell! By God, if it were so I should be glad of it! Ay, glad of it, and glad that any man rather than that vicious, scoundrelly whelp of yours, had eloped with Lydia!'

'Well, that is a fortunate circumstance,' said Sir Richard.

'It is nothing of the kind! You know very well it is not young Luttrell! She herself confessed that she had been in the habit of meeting your cousin, and the young dog said in this very room—in this very room, mark you, with you standing by——'

'My good sir, your daughter and my cousin talked a great deal of nonsense, but I assure you they have not eloped together.'

'Very well, sir, very well! Where then is your cousin at this moment?'

'In his bed, I imagine.'

'Then send for him!' barked the Major.

'As you please,' Sir Richard said, and strolled over to the bell, and pulled it.

He had scarcely released it when the door opened, and the Honourable Cedric walked in, magnificently arrayed in brocade dressing-gown of vivid and startling design. 'What the deuce is the matter?' he asked plaintively. 'Never heard such an ungodly racket in my life! Ricky, dear old boy, you ain't *dressed?*'

'Yes,' sighed Sir Richard. 'It is a great bore, however.'

'But, my dear fellow, it ain't nine o'clock!' said Cedric in horrified tones. 'Damme if I know what has come over you! You can't start the day at this hour: it ain't decent!'

'I know, Ceddie, but when in Rome, one—er—is obliged to cultivate the habits of the Romans. Ah, allow me to present Major Daubenay—Mr Brandon!'

'Servant, sir!' snapped the Major, with the stiffest of bows.

'Oh, how d'ye do?' said Cedric vaguely. 'Deuced queer hours you keep in the country!'

'I am not here upon a visit of courtesy!' said the Major.

'Now, don't tell me you've been quarrelling, Ricky!' begged Cedric. 'It sounded devilish like it to me. Really, dear boy, you might have remembered I was sleeping above you. Never at my best before noon, y'know. Besides, it ain't like you!'

He lounged, yawning, across the room to an armchair by the fireplace, and dropped into it, stretching his long legs out before him. The Major glared at him, and said pointedly that he had come to see Sir Richard upon a private matter.

This hint passed over Cedric's head. 'What we want is some coffee—strong coffee!' he said.

A maid-servant in a mobbed cap came in just then, and seemed astonished to find the room occupied. 'Oh, I beg pardon, sir! I thought the bell rang!'

'It did,' said Sir Richard. 'Have the goodness to tap on Mr Brown's door, and to request him to step downstairs as soon as he shall have dressed. Major Daubenay wishes to speak to him.'

'Hey, wait a minute!' commanded Cedric. 'Bring some coffee first, there's a good girl!'

'Yes, sir,' said the maid, looking flustered.

'Coffee!' exploded Major Daubenay.

Cedric cocked an intelligent eyebrow. 'Don't like the notion? What shall it be? Myself, I think it's too early for brandy, but if you fancy a can of ale, say the word!'

'I want nothing, sir! Sir Richard, while we waste time in such idle fripperies as these, that young dog is abducting my daughter!'

'Fetch Mr Brown,' Sir Richard told the servant.

'Abduction, by Jupiter!' said Cedric. 'What young dog?'

'Major Daubenay,' said Sir Richard, 'is labouring under the delusion that my cousin eloped last night with his daughter.'

'Eh?' Cedric blinked. An unholy gleam stole into his eyes as he glanced from Sir Richard to the Major; he said unsteadily: 'No, by Jove, you don't mean it? You ought to keep him in better order, Ricky!'

'Yes!' said the Major. 'He ought indeed! But instead of that he has—— I will not say *abetted* the young scoundrel —but adopted an attitude which I can only describe as callous, sir, and supine!'

Cedric shook his head. 'That's Ricky all over.' His gravity broke down. 'Oh lord, what the deuce put it into your head your daughter had gone off with his cousin? I'll tell you what, it's the richest jest I've heard in months! Ricky, if I don't roast you for this for years to come!'

'You are going to the Peninsula, Ceddie,' Sir Richard said with a lurking smile.

'You are amused, sir!' the Major said, bristling.

'Lord, yes, and so would you be if you knew as much about Wyndham's cousin as I do!'

The maid-servant came back into the room. 'Oh, if you please, sir! Mr Brown's not in his room,' she said, dropping a curtsey.

The effect of this pronouncement was startling. The Major gave a roar like that of a baffled bull; Cedric's laughter was cut short; and Sir Richard let his eyeglass fall.

'I knew it! Oh, I knew it!' raged the Major. 'Now, sir!'

Sir Richard recovered himself swiftly. 'Pray do not be absurd, sir!' he said, with more asperity than Cedric ever remembered to have heard in his voice before. 'My cousin has in all probability stepped out to enjoy the air. He is an early riser.'

'If you please, sir, the young gentleman has taken his cloak-bag with him.'

The Major seemed to be having considerable difficulty in holding his fury within bounds. Cedric, observing his gobblings with a sapient eye, begged him to be careful. 'I knew a man once who got into just such a taking. He burst a blood-vessel. True as I sit here!'

The maid-servant, upon whom the Honourable Cedric's charm of manner had not fallen unappreciated, smothered a giggle, and twisted one corner of her apron into a screw. 'There was a letter for your honour upon the mantelshelf when I did the room out,' she volunteered.

Sir Richard swung round on his heel, and went to the fireplace. Pen's note, which she had propped up against the clock, had fallen down, and so missed his eye. He picked it up, a little pale of countenance, and retired with it to the window.

'My dear Richard,' Pen had written. *'This is to say good-bye to you, and to thank you very much for all your kindness. I have made up my mind to return to Aunt Almeria, for the notion of our being obliged to marry is preposterous. I shall tell her some tale that will satisfy her. Dear*

*sir, it was truly a splendid adventure. Your very obliged
servant, Penelope Creed.*
'*P.S. I will send back your cravats and the cloak-bag, and
indeed I thank you, dear Richard.*'

Cedric, watching his friend's rigid face, dragged himself
out of his chair, and lounged across to lay a hand on Sir
Richard's shoulder. 'Ricky, dear boy! Now, what is it?'

'I demand to see that letter!' barked the Major.

Sir Richard folded the sheet, and slipped it into his inner
pocket. 'Be content, sir: my cousin has not eloped with
your daughter.'

'I don't believe you!'

'If you mean to give me the lie——' Sir Richard checked
himself, and turned to the abigail. 'When did Mr Brown
leave this place?'

'I don't know, sir. But Parks was downstairs—the waiter,
sir.'

'Fetch him.'

'If your cousin has not gone off with my daughter, show
me that letter!' demanded the Major.

The Honourable Cedric let his hand fall from Sir Richard's shoulder, and strolled into the middle of the room,
an expression of disdain upon his aristocratic countenance.
'You sir—Daubenay, or whatever your name may be—I
don't know what maggot's got into your head, but damme,
I'm tired of it! For the lord's sake, go away!'

'I shall not stir from this room until I know the truth!'
declared the Major. 'I should not be surprised if I found
that you were both in league with that young whipper-
snapper!'

'Damme, there's something devilish queer about the air
of this place!' said Cedric. 'It's my belief you're all mad!'

At this moment the gloomy waiter came into the room.
His disclosure that Pen had gone to Bristol with Mrs Hopkins made Sir Richard's face assume a more masklike expression than ever, but they could not fail to assuage one
at least of the Major's alarms. He mopped his brow, and
said gruffly that he saw that he had made a mistake.

'That's what we've been telling you,' Cedric pointed out.

'I'll tell you another thing, sir: I want my breakfast, and I'll be damned if I'll sit down to it with you dancing about the room, and shouting in my ear. It ain't restful!'

'But I don't understand!' complained the Major in a milder tone. 'She said she went out to meet your cousin, sir!'

'I have already told you, sir, that your daughter and my cousin both talked a deal of nonsense,' said Sir Richard, over his shoulder.

'You mean she said it to make me believe—to throw dust in my eyes? Upon my soul!'

'Now, don't start that again!' begged Cedric.

'She has gone off with young Luttrell!' exploded the Major. 'By God, I'll break every bone in his body!'

'Well, we don't mind that,' said Cedric. 'You go and do it, sir! Don't waste a moment! Waiter, the door!'

'Good God, this is terrible!' exclaimed the Major, sinking into a chair, and clapping a hand to his brow. 'Depend upon it, they are half-way to the Scottish border by now! As though that were not enough! But there is Philips wanting me to take that wretched girl to Bath this morning, to see whether she can recognize some fellow they have caught there! What am I to say to him? The scandal! My poor wife! I left her prostrate!'

'Run back to her at once!' urged Cedric. 'You have not a moment to spare! Tell me, though, had this fellow the diamonds upon him?'

The Major made a gesture as of one brushing aside a gnat. 'What should I care for that? It is my misguided child I am thinking about!'

'I dare say you don't care, but I do. The man who was murdered was my brother, and those diamonds belong to my family!'

'Your brother? Good Gad, sir, I am astonished!' said the Major, glaring at him. 'No one—no one, believe me!—would credit you with having sustained such a loss! Your levity, your——'

'Never mind my levity, old gentleman! Has that damned necklace been found?'

'Yes, sir, I understand that the prisoner had a necklace

in his possession. And if that is your only concern in this appalling affair——'

'Ricky, I must get my hands on that necklace. I hate to leave you, dear boy, but there's nothing for it! Where the devil's that coffee? Can't go without my breakfast!' He caught sight of the waiter, who had reappeared in the doorway. 'You there! What the devil do you mean by standing gaping? Breakfast, you gaby!'

'Yes, sir,' said the waiter, sniffing. 'And what will I tell the lady, sir, *if* you please?'

'Tell her we ain't receiving!—— What lady?'

The waiter proffered a tray with a visiting card upon it. 'For Sir Richard Wyndham,' he said lugubriously. 'She would be obleeged by the favour of a word with him.'

Cedric picked up the card, and read aloud: 'Lady Luttrell. Who the deuce is Lady Luttrell, Ricky?'

'Lady Luttrell!' said the Major, starting up. 'Here? Ha, is this some dastardly plot?'

Sir Richard turned, a look of surprise in his face. 'Show the lady in!' he said.

'Well, I always knew country life would never do for me,' remarked Cedric, 'but damme, I never realized one half of it till now! Not nine o'clock, and the better part of the county paying morning calls! Horrible, Ricky, horrible!'

Sir Richard had turned away from the window, and was watching the door, his brows slightly raised. The waiter ushered in a good-looking woman of between forty and fifty years of age, with brown hair flecked with grey, shrewd humorous eyes, and a somewhat masterful mouth and chin. Sir Richard moved to meet her, but before he could say anything the Major had burst into speech.

'So, ma'am! So!' he shot out. 'You wish to see Sir Richard Wyndham, do you? You did not expect to meet me here, I dare say!'

'No,' agreed the lady composedly. 'I did not. However, since we shall be obliged, I understand, to meet one another in future with an appearance at least of complaisance, we may as well make a start. How do you do, Major?'

'Upon my word, you are might cool, ma'am! Pray, are you aware that your son has eloped with my daughter?'

'Yes,' replied Lady Luttrell. 'My son left a letter behind to inform me of this circumstance.'

Her calm seemed to throw the Major out of his stride. He said rather lamely: 'But what are we to do?'

She smiled. 'We have nothing to do but to accept the event with as good a grace as we can. You do not like the match, and nor do I, but to pursue the young couple, or to show the world our disapproval, will only serve to make us both ridiculous.' She looked him over with a rather mocking light in her eyes, but he seemed so much taken aback, that she relented, and held out her hand to him. 'Come, Major! We may as well bury the hatchet. I cannot be estranged from my only son; you, I am persuaded, would be equally loth to disown your daughter.'

He shook hands with her, not very graciously. 'I do not know what to say! I am utterly confounded! They have behaved very ill towards us, very ill indeed!'

'Oh yes!' she sighed. 'But did we perhaps behave ill towards them?'

This was plainly going too far for the Major, whose eyes began to bulge again. Cedric intervened hastily: 'Don't set him off again, ma'am, for lord's sake!'

'Hold your tongue, sir!' snapped the Major. 'But you came here to see Sir Richard Wyndham, ma'am! How is this?'

'I came to see Sir Richard Wyndham upon quite another matter,' she replied. Her glance dwelled for an instant on Cedric, and travelled past him to Sir Richard. 'And you, I think, must be Sir Richard Wyndham,' she said.

He bowed. 'I am at your service, ma'am. Permit me to present Mr Brandon to you!'

She looked quickly towards Cedric. 'Ah, I thought your face familiar! Sir, I hardly know what to say to you, except that I am more deeply distressed than I am well able to express to you.'

Cedric looked startled. 'Nothing to be distressed about on my account, ma'am, nothing in the world! Must beg your ladyship to excuse my appearance! The fact is, these early hours, you know, put a man out!'

'Lady Luttrell refers, I apprehend, to Beverley's death,' said Sir Richard dryly.

'Bev? Oh, of course, yes! Shocking affair! Never was more surprised in my life!'

'It is a source of profound dismay to me that such a thing should have happened while your brother was a guest in my house,' said Lady Luttrell.

'Don't give it a thought, ma'am!' begged Cedric. 'Not your fault—always thought he would come to a bad end —might have happened anywhere!'

'Your callousness, sir, is disgusting!' proclaimed the Major, picking up his hat. 'I will not remain another instant to be revolted by such a display of heartless unconcern!'

'Well, damme, who wants you to?' demanded Cedric. 'Haven't I been trying to get you to go away this past half-hour? Never met such a thick-skinned fellow in my life!'

'Escort Major Daubenay to the door, Ceddie,' Sir Richard said. 'I understand that Lady Luttrell wishes to see me upon a private matter.'

'Private as you please, dear boy! Ma'am, your very obedient! *After* you, Major!' He bowed the Major out with a flourish, winked at Sir Richard, and went out himself.

'What an engaging scapegrace!' remarked Lady Luttrell, moving forward into the middle of the parlour. 'I confess, I much disliked his brother.'

'Your dislike was shared by most of his acquaintance, ma'am. Will you not be seated?'

She took the chair he offered, and looked him over rather penetratingly. 'Well, Sir Richard,' she said, perfectly mistress of the situation, 'you are wondering, I dare say, why I have come to call upon you.'

'I think I know,' he replied.

'Then I need not beat about the bush. You are travelling with a young gentleman who is said to be your cousin, I understand. A young gentleman who, if my mind is to be believed, answers to the somewhat unusual name of Pen.'

'Yes,' said Sir Richard. 'We should have changed that.'

'Pen Creed, Sir Richard?'

'Yes, ma'am! Pen Creed.'

Her gaze did not waver from his impassive countenance. 'A trifle odd, sir, is it not?'

'The word, ma'am, should have been fantastic. May I know how you came by your information?'

'Certainly you may. I have lately supported a visit from Mrs Griffin and her son, who seemed to expect to find Pen with me. They told me that she had left their roof in her cousin's second-best suit of clothes, by way of the window. That sounded very like Pen Creed to me. But she was not with me, Sir Richard. It was not until this morning that my maid told me of a golden-haired boy who was putting up with his cousin—yourself, Sir Richard—at this inn. That is why I came. I am sure that you will appreciate that I felt a certain degree of anxiety.'

'Perfectly,' he said. 'But Pen is no longer with me. She left for Bristol this morning, and is now, I must suppose, a passenger on the London stage-coach.'

She raised her brows. 'Still more surprising! I hope that you mean to satisfy my curiosity, sir?'

'Obviously I must do so,' he said, and in a cool, expressionless voice, recounted to her all that had happened since Pen had dropped from her rope of sheets into his arms.

She heard him in attentive silence, and all the time watched him. When he had done, she did not say anything for a moment, but looked thoughtfully at him. After a pause, she said: 'Was Pen very much distressed to find my son head over ears in love with Lydia Daubenay?'

'I did not think so.'

'Oh! And my son, I think you said, showed himself to be shocked at the seeming impropriety of her situation?'

'Not unnaturally, though I could have wished that he had not shown his disapproval quite so plainly. She is very young, you see. It had not occurred to her that there was anything amiss.'

'Piers had never the least tact,' she said. 'I expect he told her that you were in honour bound to marry her.'

'He did, and he spoke no less than the truth.'

'Forgive me, Sir Richard, but did you offer for Pen because you felt your honour to be involved?'

'No, I asked her to marry me because I loved her, ma'am.'

'Did you tell her so, Sir Richard?'

'Yes. But she did not believe me.'

'Perhaps,' suggested Lady Luttrell, 'you had not previously given her reason to suppose that you had fallen in love with her?'

'Madam,' said Sir Richard, with a touch of impatience, 'she was in my care, in a situation of the utmost delicacy! Would you have expected me to abuse her confidence by making love to her?'

'No,' she said, smiling. 'From the little I have seen of you, I should have expected you to have treated her just as I imagine you did: as though you were indeed her uncle.'

'With the result,' he said bitterly, 'that that is how she regards me.'

'Is it indeed?' she said tartly. 'Let me tell you, Sir Richard, that men of twenty-nine, with your air, countenance, and address, are not commonly regarded by young females in the light of uncles!'

He flushed, and smiled a little wryly. 'Thank you! But Pen is not like other young females.'

'Pen,' said Lady Luttrell, 'must be a very odd sort of a female if she spent all this while in your company and not succumbed to a charm of manner which you must be so well aware that you possess that I do not scruple to mention it. I consider that your conduct in aiding the chit to escape was disgraceful, but since you were drunk at the time I suppose one must overlook that. I do not blame you for anything you have done since you found yourself in the stage-coach: indeed, you have behaved in a manner that would, if I were twenty years younger, make me envy Pen exceedingly. Finally, if she did not spend the better part of last night crying her eyes out, I know nothing about my own sex! Where is the letter she left for you? May I see it?'

He drew it from his pocket. 'Pray read it, if you wish. It contains nothing, alas, that may not be read by other eyes than mine.'

She took it from him, read it, and handed it back. 'Just as I thought! Breaking her heart, and determined you shall not know it! Sir Richard, for a man of experience, which I judge you to be, you are a great fool! You never kissed her!'

An unwilling laugh was dragged out of him at this unexpected accusation. 'How could I, situated as we were? She recoiled from the very thought of marriage!'

'Because she thought you had asked her to marry you out of pity! Of course she recoiled!'

'Lady Luttrell, are you serious? Do you indeed think—'

'Think, I know!' said her ladyship. 'Your scruples were very fine, I make no doubt, but how should a chit of Pen's age understand what you were about? She would not care a fig for your precious honour, and I dare say—indeed, I am sure!—that she thought your forbearance mere indifference. And the long and the short of it is that she has gone back to her aunt, and will very likely be bullied into marrying her cousin!'

'Oh no, she will not!' said Sir Richard, with a glance at the clock on the mantelshelf. 'I am desolated to be obliged to leave you, ma'am, but if I am to overtake that stage-coach this side of Chippenham, I must go.'

'Excellent!' she said, laughing. 'Do not waste a thought on me! But having caught the stage, what do you propose to do with Pen?'

'Marry her, ma'am! What else?'

'Dear me, I hope you do not mean to join my foolish son at Gretna Green! I think you had better bring Pen to Crome Hall.'

'Thank you, I will!' he said, with the smile which she privately thought irresistible. 'I am very much in your debt, ma'am.'

He raised her hand to his lips, and kissed it, and left the room, calling for Cedric.

Cedric, who had been partaking of breakfast in the coffee-room, lounged out into the entrance-parlour. 'The devil take you, Ricky, you're as restless as that plaguey friend of yours! What's the matter now?'

'Ceddie, were you driving your own horses yesterday?'

'Dear old boy, of course I was, but what has that to say to anything?'

'I want 'em,' said Sir Richard.

'But, Ricky, I've got to go back to Bath to get hold of that necklace before it's discovered to be made of paste!'

'Take the landlord's gig. I must have a fast pair immediately.'

'The landlord's gig!' gasped Cedric, reeling under the shock. 'Ricky, you *must* be mad!'

'I am not in the least mad. I am going after the London stage, to recover that brat of mine. Be a good fellow, now, and tell them to harness the horses at once!'

'Oh, very well!' Cedric said. 'If that's the way it is! But I'll be satisfied with nothing less than a cavalry regiment, mind!'

'You shall have anything you like!' promised Sir Richard, already half-way up the stairs.

'Mad, quite mad!' said Cedric despairingly, and set up a shout for an ostler.

Ten minutes later, the bays were harnessed to the curricle, and Sir Richard had stepped out into the yard, pulling on his gloves. 'Famous!' he said. 'I hoped you were driving your bays.'

'If you lame 'em——'

'Ceddie, are you—is it possible that you are going to tell me how to drive?' asked Sir Richard.

Cedric, who was still clad in his exotic dressing-gown, leaned against the door-post, and grinned. 'You'll spring 'em. *I* know you!'

'If I lame them, I will make you a present of my own greys!' said Sir Richard, gathering up the reins.

'Part with your greys?' exclaimed Cedric. 'No, no, you'd never bring yourself to do that, Ricky!'

'Don't disturb yourself: I shan't have to.'

Cedric made a derisive sound, and lingered to watch him mount on to the box-seat. A commotion behind him distracted his attention, and he turned in time to see Mrs Hopkins enter the inn through the front-door, closely followed by a thick-set man in a frieze coat, and a broad-brimmed hat. Mrs Hopkins was labouring under great agitation, and sank immediately into a chair, volubly explaining to the bewildered landlord that she had never had such a turn in her life, and did not expect to recover from her

palpitations for a twelvemonth. 'Took up by a Bow Street
Runner, Tom!' she panted. 'And him so innocent-seeming
as never was!'

'Who?' demanded her spouse.

'That poor young gentleman which is Sir Richard's
cousin! Under my very eyes, Tom, and me not dreaming
of such a thing! And then if he didn't break away, the
which I can't but be glad of, whatever any one may say,
Mr Gudgeon not excepted, for a nicer-spoken young gentleman I never did see, and I'm a mother myself, and I have
a heart, though others may not, naming no names, and
meaning no offence!'

'My God, here's a pretty coil!' exclaimed Cedric, grasping with remarkable swiftness the gist of her remarks. 'Hi,
Ricky, wait!'

The bays were dancing with impatience. 'Stand away
from their heads!' commanded Sir Richard.

'And here's Mr Gudgeon himself, wishful to see Sir
Richard and Mr Brandon very particular, which I was
obliged to take him up in the trap, though little I want Bow
Street Runners, or the like, in my house, as you well know,
Tom!'

'*Ricky!*' shouted Cedric, striding out into the yard.
'Wait, man! That bloodhound of mine is here, and there's
the devil to pay!'

'Fob him off, Ceddie, fob him off!' called Sir Richard
over his shoulder, and swept out of the yard into the street.

'Ricky, you madman, hold a minute!' roared Cedric.

But the curricle had bowled out of sight. The ostler enquired whether he should run after it.

'Run after my bays?' said Cedric scornfully. 'You'd need
wings, not legs, to catch them, my good fool!'

He turned back to the inn, encountering in the doorway
Lady Luttrell, who had come out to see what all the shouting was about.

'What is the matter, Mr Brandon?' she asked. 'You seem
very much put out.'

'Matter, ma'am! Why, here's Richard gone off after the
London Stage, and that crazy girl of his taken up by the
Bow Street Runner in Bristol!'

'Good God, this is horrible!' she exclaimed. 'Sir Richard must be recalled at all costs! The child must be rescued!'

'Well, by all accounts she seems to have rescued herself,' said Cedric. 'But where she may be now, the Lord only knows! However, I'm glad that Runner has arrived: I was getting deuced tired of hunting for him.'

'But is it impossible to stop Sir Richard?' she asked urgently.

'Lord, ma'am, he's half-way to the London road by now!' said Cedric.

This pronouncement was not strictly accurate. Sir Richard, driving out of Queen Charlton at very much the same time as Miss Creed was boarding the Accommodation coach at Kingswood, chose to take the road to Bath rather than that which led to Keynsham, and thence, due north through Oldland to join the Bristol road at Warmley. His experience of Accommodation coaches was not such as to induce him to place much confidence in their being likely to cover more than eight miles an hour, and he calculated that if the stage had left Bristol at nine o'clock, which seemed probable, it would not reach the junction of the Bath and Bristol roads until noon at the earliest. The Honourable Cedric's bays, drawing a light curricle, might be depended upon to arrive at Chippenham considerably in advance of that hour, and the Bath road had the advantage of being well known to Sir Richard.

The bays, which seemed to have been fed exclusively on oats, were in fine fettle, and the miles flashed by. They were not, perhaps, an easy pair to handle, but Sir Richard, a notable whip, had little trouble with them, and was so well satisfied with their pace and stamina that he began to toy seriously with the idea of making the Honourable Cedric a handsome offer for them. He was obliged to rein them in to a sedate pace whilst threading his way through the crowded streets of Bath, but once clear of the town he was able to give them their heads on the long stretch to Corsham, and arrived finally in Chippenham to learn that the Accommodation coach from Bristol was not due there for nearly another hour. Sir Richard repaired to the best posting-inn, superintended the disposal of the sweating bays, and ordered breakfast. When he had consumed a dish of ham-and-eggs, and drunk two cups of coffee, he had the bays put-to again, and drove westward along the Bristol road, at a leisurely pace, until he came to a fork, where a weather-beaten signpost pointed northward to Nettleton and Acton Turville, and westward to Wroxhall, Marshfield, and Bristol. Here he reined in, to await the approach of the stage.

It was not long in putting in an appearance. It rounded a bend in the deserted road ahead, a green-and-gold monstrosity, rocking and swaying top-heavily in the centre of the road, with half a dozen outside passengers on the roof, the boot piled high with baggage, and the guard sitting up behind with the yard of tin in his hand.

Sir Richard drew the curricle across the road, hitched up his reins, and jumped lightly down from the box-seat. The bays were quiet enough by this time, and except for some fidgeting, showed no immediate disposition to bolt.

Finding his way barred, the stage-coachman pulled up his team, and demanded aggrievedly what game Sir Richard thought he was playing.

'No game at all!' said Sir Richard. 'You have a fugitive aboard, and when I have taken him into custody, you are at liberty to proceed on your way.'

'Ho, I am, am I?' said the coachman, nonplussed, but by no means mollified. 'Fine doings on the King's Highway! Ah, and so you'll find afore you're much older!'

One of the inside passengers, a red-faced man with very bushy whiskers, poked his head out of the window to discover the reason for the unexpected halt; the guard climbed down from the roof to argue with Sir Richard; and Pen, squashed between a fat farmer, and a woman with a perpetual sniff, had a sudden fear that she had been overtaken by the Bow Street Runner. The sound of the guard's voice, saying: 'There, and if I didn't suspicion him from the werry moment I set eyes on him at Kingswood!' did nothing to allay her alarms. She turned a white, frightened face towards the door, just as it was pulled open, and the steps let down.

The next instant, Sir Richard's tall, immaculate person

filled the opening, and Pen, uttering an involuntary sound between a squeak and a whimper, turned first red, and then white, and managed to utter the one word: *'No!'*

'Ah!' said Sir Richard briskly. 'So there you are! Out you come, my young friend!'

'Well, I never did in all my life!' gasped the woman beside Pen. 'Whatever has he been and gone and done, sir?'

'Run away from school,' replied Sir Richard, without a moment's hesitation.

'I haven't! It isn't t-true!' stammered Pen. 'I won't go with you, I w-won't!'

Sir Richard, leaning into the coach, and grasping her hand, said: 'Oh, won't you, by Jove? Don't you dare to defy me, you—brat!'

'Here, guv'nor, steady!' expostulated a kindly man in the far corner. 'I don't know when I've taken more of a fancy to a lad, and there's no call for you to bully him, I'm sure! Dare say there's many of us have wanted to run away from school in our time, eh?'

'Ah,' said Sir Richard brazenly, 'but you do not know the half of it! You think he looks a young innocent, but I could tell you a tale of his depravity which would shock you.'

'Oh, how dare you?' said Pen indignantly. 'It isn't true! Indeed, it isn't!'

The occupants of the coach had by this time ranged themselves into two camps. Several persons said that they had suspected the young varmint of running away from the start, and Pen's supporters demanded to know who Sir Richard was, and what right he had to drag the poor young gentleman out of the coach.

'Every right!' responded Sir Richard. 'I am his guardian. In fact, he is my nephew.'

'I am not!' stated Pen.

His eyes looked down into hers, with so much laughter in them that she felt her heart turn over. 'Aren't you?' he said. 'Well, if you are not my nephew, brat, *what are you?'*

Aghast, she choked: 'Richard, you—you—*traitor!'*

Even the kindly man in the corner seemed to feel that Sir Richard's question called for an answer. Pen looked helplessly round, encountered nothing but glances either of disapproval, or of interrogation, and raised her wrathful eyes to Sir Richard's face.

'Well?' said Sir Richard inexorably. '*Are* you my nephew?'

'Yes—no! Oh, you are abominable! You wouldn't *dare!*'

'Yes, I would,' said Sir Richard. 'Are you going to get out, or are you not?'

A man in a plum-coloured coat recommended Sir Richard to dust the young rascal's jacket for him. Pen stared up at Sir Richard, read the determination behind the amusement in his face, and allowed herself to be pulled to her feet, and out of the stuffy coach.

'P'raps when you've quite finished, your honour, you'll be so werry obliging as to move that curricle of yourn!' said the coachman sardonically.

'Richard, I can't go back!' Pen said in a frantic undertone. 'That Runner caught me in Bristol, and I only just contrived to escape!'

'Ah, that must have been what Cedric was trying to tell me!' said Sir Richard, walking up to the bays, and backing them to the side of the road. 'So you were arrested, were you? What a splendid adventure for you, my little one!'

'And I have left your cloak-bag behind, and it's no use trying to drag me away with you, because I won't go! I won't, I won't!'

'Why won't you?' asked Sir Richard, turning to look down at her.

She found herself unable to speak. There was an expression in Sir Richard's eyes which brought the colour rushing into her cheeks again, and made her feel as though the world were whirling madly round her. Behind her, the guard, having let up the steps, and shut the door, climbed, grumbling, on to the roof again. The coach began to move ponderously forward. Pen paid no heed to it, though the wheels almost brushed her coat. 'Richard, you—you don't want me! You *can't* want me!' she said uncertainly.

'My darling!' he said. 'Oh, my precious, foolish little love!'

The coach lumbered on down the road; as it reached the next bend, the roof-passengers, looking back curiously to see the last of a very odd couple, experienced a shock that made one of them nearly lose his balance. The golden-haired stripling was locked in the Corinthian's arms, being ruthlessly kissed.

'Lawks a-mussy on us! whatever is the world a-coming to?' gasped the roof-passenger, recovering his seat. 'I never did in all my born days!'

'Richard, Richard, they can see us from the coach!' expostulated Pen, between tears and laughter.

'Let them see!' said the Corinthian.

THE LATEST BOOKS IN THE BANTAM BESTSELLING TRADITION

DON'T MISS
THESE CURRENT
Bantam Bestsellers

SPECIAL
MONEY SAVING
OFFER

Now you can have an up-to-date listing of Bantam's hundreds of titles plus take advantage of our unique and exciting bonus book offer. A special offer which gives you the opportunity to purchase a Bantam book for only 50¢. Here's how!

By ordering any five books at the regular price per order, you can also choose any other single book listed (up to a $4.95 value) for just 50¢. Some restrictions do apply, but for further details why not send for Bantam's listing of titles today!

Just send us your name and address plus 50¢ to defray the postage and handling costs.